# potter springs

# BRITTA COLEMAN

# potter springs

*a novel*

CENTER
STREET

*New York Boston Nashville*

Center Street

Time Warner Book Group
1271 Avenue of the Americas, New York, NY 10020

Visit our Web site at www.twbookmark.com

The Center Street name and logo are registered trademarks of the Time Warner Book Group.

Printed in the United States of America

First Center Street printing: June 2005

10  9  8  7  6  5  4  3  2  1

Library of Congress Cataloging-in-Publication Data

Coleman, Britta.
    Potter Springs / Britta Coleman. — 1st ed.
        p.  cm.
    ISBN 0-446-57778-2
    1. Clergy—Fiction.   2. Baptists—Fiction.   3. Married people—Fiction.
4. Panhandle (Tex.)—Fiction.   5. Spouses of clergy—Fiction.   6. Infants—
Death—Fiction.   I. Title.

    PS3603.O4325P67   2005
    813'.6—dc22                                            2004026738

*For Kern*

potter springs

# prologue

Mirages glistened on the steaming pavement of South Texas as Mark Reynolds gripped the steering wheel, fighting to keep his eyes from glazing over. The tires made a rhythmic *thump, thump, thump,* and mile signs waved like familiar friends.

Closer, they told him. You're getting closer.

Mr. Chesters' cries from the backseat subsided, sleep finally conquering the cat's frenzy.

Mark stretched his neck to either side, thankful for the silence. It had been a long ride, and they still had a ways to go.

Zooming by lonely pumpkin stands and a few skinny dogs, he turned up the radio and let his foot fall heavier on the pedal.

Time and distance passed while good old boys discussed farm subsidies and the price of oil.

A light flashed in his rearview mirror, bright as the sun on someone's chrome, but a quick glance told him otherwise.

The cops.

As he pulled over to the shoulder, the tires shot pebbles like angry hail. He checked his reflection in the rearview mirror. Ungodly November heat coated his skin with a fine sheen. A scratch drew a line across his cheek and his left eye ballooned in shades of black and blue.

The patrolman's boots crunched on the loose asphalt.

Mark rolled down the window and his palm slipped on the handle. "Yes? What's the problem?" He hadn't been pulled over since college, nearly a decade ago.

"See your license and insurance, sir." The policeman pulled out a notebook.

"Absolutely. Sorry about that." Mark dug in the glove compartment. Thank God he'd remembered the paperwork. He'd need it for the border crossing. "Was I speeding?"

Officer Martinez, according to the engraved bar, tipped his tan Stetson in answer. "Where you headed?"

"South."

"Not much south of here except Mexico," Martinez said. "Big storm headed that way. You crossing over?"

"Yes, sir."

"What for?"

"Looking for someone." Mark stared straight ahead.

"Who's that?"

Fear and frustration burned in his throat as he uttered the truth. "My wife."

The officer's mouth twitched. "Stay put, and I'll be back in a minute."

More gravel crunched, and Martinez left Mark to himself.

Inside the car, a fly buzzed against the windshield. It made circles and struck the glass, relentless in its efforts to escape. Just an inch from freedom. Cupping his hand, Mark ushered the insect to the window, where it looped away, stunned and sluggish.

He wondered how it ever lasted through summer without getting squashed.

Martinez returned and passed the credentials through the window. "Potter Springs? That's the Panhandle, isn't it? You're a far way from home."

Mark nodded, his image a warped jester in Martinez's mirrored lenses.

"What do you do up there in Potter?"

"Minister."

Martinez removed the shades and squinted. Taking in Mark's muscular build, beat-up face and wrinkled clothes. A neon logo painted his T-shirt—SUN YOUR BUNS!—over a photo of four women in thong bathing suits. "You don't look like any preacher I've ever seen."

Mark didn't argue. The car idled in the heat.

"Well." Martinez thumped the metal roof. "I'll let you go with a warning this time. Do me a favor and slow it down."

"I plan to." He adjusted his seat belt. "Thanks."

"For what it's worth"—Martinez took a step back, holding Mark's gaze—"I hope you find her."

Merging into traffic, the officer's black-and-white faded into the distance.

*I hope you find her.*

The blessing stirred Mark's memories. To the time before the losing began. Before the whirlwind and the changes and the wide, open spaces.

# CHAPTER 1

# brown penny

*Months Earlier*

Mark watched the Houston traffic snake around his building like a lazy, lethal predator. Smog drifted outside the wall-to-wall window, the glass impenetrable and sterile.

Turning to the velvet box on his desk, he opened the lid and a marquise diamond flashed at him. The gem was small, but flawless. He'd paid high dollar to make sure no internal flaws, no yellowish hue, marked the stone.

Amanda deserved at least that much.

A discreet knock sounded at the door. Mark palmed the jewel box just as James Montclair poked his salt-and-pepper head inside the office.

"Show time," James announced. "Ready, buddy?"

"Sure thing." Mark gathered his jacket and slid the treasure into an inside pocket, tapping it once for security.

Downstairs, he greeted a thousand faces. Perfumes and colognes and mothballs stained the air. The fine whir of silk and wool defined movements. Sit, rise, stand and sing.

Lights dimmed and the pews filled like a Broadway theater, anticipation broken by muffled coughs. Ten-thousand-dollar screens lowered to highlight PowerPoint images and cue the congregants to the next hymnal page.

Mark approached the stage with grace. He strode toward the podium and adjusted his tie microphone. "Good morning, everyone. Welcome. I'm Mark Reynolds, associate pastor here at Pleasant Valley Baptist Church and your host for today's services."

Morning worship ran smoothly, a well-oiled machine orchestrated to perfection. James Montclair, senior pastor, spoke from the pulpit like a middle-aged Billy Graham. Poised, beautiful even. His sermon on grace, punctuated with a guest testimonial from a former drug addict, jerked plenty of tears.

"Well done," attendees praised afterward, shaking James's hand as they withdrew in elegant fashion.

"Excellent devotion this morning," one matron complimented Mark. "You'll be taking over before long, I imagine."

"That's the plan." James chucked Mark on the shoulder. "I'll have to retire someday. We've got a fine runner-up here."

The praise flushed Mark's cheeks and made him feel even taller. To be James's successor, to helm this kind of megachurch, the biggest and fastest growing in Houston, had been his heart's desire since the day he entered seminary.

To actually work with a man like James Montclair, multipublished and nationally known, had been more than he could have hoped for.

When the last convert from the altar call slipped away, still sniffling into wadded tissues, James and Mark headed for the elevator to the executive-level offices.

"I meant that, you know," James said. "About you taking over. With the last book doing so well, they've mentioned more speaking engagements. Makes it tough to be here Sundays."

Emotion clogged Mark's vocal cords. "When?"

"It's all conjecture right now, and we're still a couple years out. But I thought I'd give you a heads-up. Course the board will have to approve."

"Of course," Mark said.

"But between you and me"—James grinned—"you're the man. Providing that you want it."

"You know I do."

"All right, then." The elevator shot upward, lit numbers dinging a faint rhythm. Muzak piped in through the speakers, instrumentals of the latest Christian pop.

Mark dreamed of future Sundays. He would helm the pulpit, and fill James's shoes to capacity. Maybe even better. The congregation would love him. The board would adore him. And his wife, his future wife, Amanda, would stand beside him.

He felt the ring in his pocket. His future started today.

"Where's Amanda?" James asked, as if reading Mark's thoughts. "Didn't see her this morning."

"Not sure," Mark said. Though Amanda made it a point to attend Pleasant Valley, her Presbyterian upbringing gave her full freedom to play hooky every now and then, guilt free. He almost envied that in her. "We're supposed to have lunch."

"Want to go with us? Sarah should have the kids wrestled into the van by now." Watching his reflection, James loosened his tie and unbuttoned the top of his dress shirt.

"No, but thanks. I better check on Amanda."

Back in his office, he autodialed her phone number. No answer.

Not at church, not home at her apartment, sick. Where?

The park. Watching people from her bench in Memorial Park, scribbling in that journal of hers. On a day like today, sunny and still cool for spring, she probably hadn't been able to resist the temptation of a morning outdoors.

He'd have to find her. He couldn't wait one more day. Not one more hour.

He'd waited too long already.

At the park, Mark slung his jacket over his shoulder and surveyed the grounds. Streams of sweaty joggers clogged the trails. Going against the flow, his size worked to his advantage, unpadded shoulders slicing through their disgruntled waves.

Then he saw her. In her favorite spot, away from the path next to a lush, landscaped area. He slowed, enjoying the chance to catch her unaware. Her copper hair shielded her face. Sunlight echoed off the waves in amber sparks. Legs tucked underneath her, she wrote furiously in the black book on her lap.

Amanda Thompson had the worst handwriting in the world. Mark often teased her that she had the laugh of a child, the lips of a goddess and the penmanship of a serial killer.

He inched through the grass, oxfords glinting in the dew. How close could he get before she noticed? "Mandy."

Startled, she slashed her pen stroke, running over the scrawls. "Oh. Mark." She sat straight, pushing her feet into the gravel. Pink polish sparkled against green flip-flops.

His girlfriend never wore socks, but kept an impeccable pedicure in five-dollar sandals.

"Hey, you." He brushed the concrete next to her and sat

down. Her head still only reached his shoulder. "Where you been?"

"Here." She shifted, touching knees to his and pulled the hair away from her face.

Freckles winked up at him from her nose. He'd memorized their pattern, spread out over her cheekbones, frail and high. He traced them now, the sweetness of the curve.

Her eyes fluttered closed, dark lashes against her cheeks, letting his hands love her this way.

"Missed you this morning," he whispered.

"Sorry." Her blue eyes shone like hot glass. The corner of her lips tugged up for a half second, then disappeared. "I'm glad you came." She squeezed his hands. "I figured you would find me."

Such strength, in those little hands. He loved the passion within her. How she laughed loud and cried hard and joked with him. She'd never hurt him, and her pure kindness wrapped around him until everything about her sang in his veins and made him alive and whole.

Belonging. She made him belong.

Two 10-speeds clicked by on the path. A car backfired on the busy road just over the bridge and a siren sounded in the distance.

Not exactly the piano serenade he'd planned in the upscale restaurant. But this spot was her oasis. The place she ran to. She'd read him a poem here one afternoon, from one of her ever-present books. Clear honey, her voice poured over him. Because he loved her, he hid his hatred of poetry and simply watched her as she read. Craving her nearness while he casually discarded the words.

Yet, one day, from a skinny volume of Yeats, the lines surprised him. They took life and crept inside his apathy, inscribed themselves into his heart.

*I whispered, "I am too young,"*
*And then, "I am old enough";*
*Wherefore I threw a penny*
*To find out if I might love.*
*"Go and love, go and love, young man,*
*If the lady be young and fair."*
*Ah, penny, brown penny, brown penny,*
*I am looped in the loops of her hair.*

She finished the last part theatrically, twirling her curls at him. Then she'd tossed the book aside, slapped her hands together and dug in the picnic basket. "What's for lunch?"

While his heart, invisible, lay twisted at her feet.

Now the rightness of it clicked inside him. *Her oasis,* he thought. *Brown Penny.* This was the right spot. The perfect spot. He should have trusted she would lead him to it.

"I've got something I want to ask you." He closed his hand around the box in his pocket. The box he'd hidden in his sock drawer for months. Bought and paid for. Ready.

Fear had kept him from giving it to her. Fear had kept him waiting for the right moment. Fear had paralyzed him. That she might say no. That she didn't love him enough to marry him, not enough to step down from her rich family to be a preacher's wife.

But today was the day. He knew it in his soul. *I am too young.* He pushed the whispers aside. *I am old enough.* He grasped her hand and felt no fear. *To find out if I might love.*

"Mandy." He set his face, his game face from a thousand football fields, and tossed the penny like he tossed the ball, far and sure and spiraling. "Will you . . ."

His hope shot forward with all the power he possessed,

swirling high and perfect. The sun crisp on his shoulders, the roar in his ears the roar of the crowds. Confidence surged through him, he'd timed it just right and she'd catch his heart and make him whole. . . .

She put a hand on his arm. "I'm pregnant."

# test

"*What?*"

Amanda saw the panic register on Mark's face before the word shot out of his mouth.

"Are you sure?" He ran a hand through his blond hair, making it stand on end. A Mad Hatter effect atop a heart-stopping face. Her Goldenboy.

"I took a test." Amanda spoke slowly, to let it sink in. She'd had a week to mull it over and still found the truth unbelievable. Like an exotic rock, she'd pull it out from time to time, feeling the ragged edges. Wondering at its depths, its crevices, before tucking it away again, to share later. Show-and-tell.

"A test? What kind of a test? Did you go to the doctor? Without me?" The questions rolled out of Mark at a lowered pitch as oblivious joggers crunched past them. The sun shone. The birds sang. They sat, two pretty people, the truth an invisible boulder between them.

"Blue lines. One if you're not, two if you are. We got two." She held up a peace sign to show him, as if it were some kind of victory. Allowing herself to smile.

He didn't smile back. "It could be wrong."

"It's not. I did more than one. To be sure." The tests only confirmed what she had already known from her swollen breasts, the calendar days not adding up.

Still, she had stared at those pieces of plastic long enough to know. Read the directions over and over, looking for a loophole, some miscalculation to put the tests in error.

At first, leaning against the tiled white of her bathroom counter, she willed that second line to disappear. Shook the test, blew on it, held it upside down to see if it would go away.

It didn't.

"I'm pregnant," she informed her reflection in the mirror, and saw the disbelief there. She lay down on the bathroom floor, fear pouring out in sobs and gasps.

The bathmat tickled her nose as she cried, yellow acrylic gathered in her fingers. Mr. Chesters, a silent witness to despair, brushed against her.

Amanda flipped to her back and grabbed toilet tissue from the roll above her head. She considered the ceiling and the heavens above.

Why?

No answer, only the pounding of her heart and the gurgles from her clogged sinuses.

The toughest part would be telling him. Harder than skulking in the drugstore with her illicit home pregnancy tests, like a beer-buying teenager. Worse than squatting over her potty, trying to hit the miniscule square on the wand.

Scarier even than owning up to what they'd done. Telling friends. Family. Church.

Though it terrified her, deep down she wanted this child. Without question. A secret exhilaration grew as the possibilities raced through her. A baby. Mark's baby. They'd be together, and have a family. A real one, not like either of the homes they'd come from.

She knew, with Mark by her side, the rest didn't matter. If only he'd stay by her side.

Now, on the stone bench that felt like quicksand, she prayed for strength. "I'm going to the doctor tomorrow. For blood tests—to find out how far along I am. You can come with me if you want."

"I just can't believe it." Mark shook his head, as if he hadn't heard her. Still cycling on the curve she'd thrown him. "You can't be pregnant. How is that possible? How did this happen?"

"Mark." She smoothed his hair. "I think we both know how this happened."

He flushed, that athletic color, high and red as if he'd been running sprints. Her heart stretched thin that she could love him even more, now.

She had first realized she loved him, oddly enough, on her initial visit to his church. He'd invited her after one of their early dates. A sense of curiosity, more than obligation, prompted her to go. Confirmed along with the rest of the sixth graders in her parents' church, Amanda had helped warm the family pew her entire childhood.

Still, church attendance as an adult had been spotty at best. Since college graduation three years ago, she'd landed the job at the communications firm and gotten caught up in life as a single girl in Houston. But something about Mark, his sincerity, his earnestness, fanned the flame of faith that still burned, quiet and long untended, within her.

She got up early, dressed in a fluttery jersey skirt and a yellow sweater. Mark would sing, not preach that morning. She was anxious to see him at work, to meet his friends and his boss, to watch him in his home base.

The glossy building held no intimidation for her, but the crowds of strangers did. She chose a seat a few rows back from the stage, wanting a good view but not the spotlight. She hoped no one would notice her, but other attendees greeted her anyway. They shook her hand at the "Welcome Friends" portion of the service.

With the stubby pencil from the pew in front, she discreetly checked off her bulletin. Choir, check. Opening anthem, check. Communion, check. She doodled in the margins, flowers and stars, waiting for the best part.

Special music.

Up front, Mark stood alone with his guitar. He strummed the strings with a practiced hand, cleared his throat at the side of the microphone, and started singing.

His song—she couldn't think of the words now, but the tune stayed with her. The notes soared from him, unworldly and rare. The guitar played itself, matching his voice seamlessly. Perfect.

The music pierced her, picked her out among all those suits and panty hose, to cut to her very soul.

His song tied her to him, fused like wings to an angel. Bound by his precious heart. He caught her stare, just once, at the end.

*See?* his face asked. *Do you see?*

*Yes.*

The rest of the service blurred as she stood and sat and prayed like a normal person. A person whose heart hadn't been revealed and broken and healed by a song. Changed.

How do you tell someone, *I'm bound to you for an eternity because I heard you sing and I saw your heart and wherever you go I will follow and now I believe in your dream because you were living it and it was beautiful*?

Afterward, he strode directly to her side. Claiming her.

She had gone willingly, and never looked back. Now, she must be gentle, and help him understand what she already knew. That, regardless of timing, together, they were home. Scooting forward, she brushed his hair away from his face and kissed him on the forehead. "Are you asking, literally, how did this happen? The time, you mean?"

"No, I don't mean that." He ran his hands down his slacks, the sharp crease wilted from the humidity. "What I wonder is, what are we going to do?" Bewilderment softened his face, made him look younger.

"I know what I'm going to do." She pressed her face to his neck. "How about you?"

He pushed her away. For a moment, her worst fears bloomed into reality.

But then his hand disappeared inside his coat pocket. An instant later, he was on his knees, on his knees in the dusty gravel in his very best suit. A tiny pop and a stone, brilliant bright, flashed up at her and he said the words. The words her ears had grown tired of straining to hear. The words her heart had been weary of waiting for him to say.

"Will you marry me?"

Pebbles ground her shins as she knelt too, her toes gritty, not caring, as she pulled those broad shoulders to her. "Yes, yes, yes, oh yes!"

He slid the ring on her finger and she pulled away to admire it.

"I love it," she announced. A marquise from her Mark. "When did you . . ." She raised her gaze, expecting his joy to mirror her own.

Instead, sadness swept his features. A look of resignation. Still on his knees, he no longer seemed heroic, but defeated.

Her question died in her throat and fell, the words drifted like leaves to the ground. Unspoken, they rustled, whispering in her heart. Not when, but why?

Had he asked her for honor? Or for love?

# progression

On Tuesday, after spending his day off making plans, practicing speeches, Mark waited outside James Montclair's office. The sun barely tipped the edges of the morning traffic, but it looked like James had been hitting it hard already.

A phone dangled from his ear and a pile of paperwork cluttered the streamlined desk. Still busy with the call, James motioned for Mark to enter. He rolled up starched white sleeves as he spoke. "Yes, Mrs. Timsley. I'll let the committee know. Thanks for your prayers, Lord knows we need them." He rolled his eyes at Mark and said his good-byes.

"What do you need?" James checked his Omega watch.

"To talk."

"Sure. Just a sec." A thought line divided his brows as he clicked more keys.

Mark took the time to admire James's office. Leatherbound books on the shelves, ivy dangling from spare corners, a hand-painted oil of the baptism of Jesus. The painting depicted a white dove descending on the Master's shoulders with John clad in camel hair and shadows in the background.

"Okay, I'm all yours." James leaned back. "What's up?"

"I don't know how to say this." Practicing in front of the mirror this morning only made Mark see the unnatural color of his face. He felt green even now.

"Just shoot."

"It's about Amanda. And me." Mark's legs seemed overlong for the visitor's chair, even though he'd sat there many times.

A slow grin spread on James's features. "Are congratulations in order? Did you finally do it? Ask her to marry you?"

"Um. Yes. In a sense."

"That's fantastic!" James rose from the desk and grasped Mark's hand in a vigorous shake. "She'll fit in perfect here. Sarah loves her to pieces. It'll be great to have another minister's wife. They can run the women's retreats and the luncheons—"

"She's pregnant."

Confusion dulled James's face and the handshake stopped. "No, after the last one, Sarah had her tubes—" He stopped, catching himself. "Oh," he said stupidly. "You mean Amanda."

Disappointment filled the room, like a silent, unwelcome guest.

"I'm sorry. I'm so sorry." Mark pulled away, rubbing his temples. Not able to look his mentor in the eye.

"How did this happen?" James's voice echoed Mark's earlier bewilderment.

"That's what I said."

"How long have you two been . . ." Ever the genteel ambassador, James let the question trail as he collapsed into his chair.

"Months," Mark admitted. "It's not like we meant to, it was just an accident."

"It's never an accident." Anger tinged the declaration.

Mark snapped his head up.

"You don't just trip and suddenly you're having sex. There's a progression."

"Okay. It wasn't an accident." Mark couldn't help the anger, the defensiveness. "We're getting married."

"Do you love her?"

"With everything I am."

"Then why didn't you wait?"

Regret twisted in Mark as James voiced the question he'd asked himself in the mirror. The one his conscience asked him. The one he ignored even as his flesh melted into hers. "I don't know." He did know, but couldn't say. *Wouldn't* say in this room where he'd prayed and planned sermons. "I should have. But we didn't. Now what? How do we handle this?"

"*We,* as in you and Amanda?"

"No, we're clear," Mark said. "She's excited about the baby, the wedding. We still have to tell our parents."

"Your mother." James sighed, familiar with Marianne Reynolds.

"I know," Mark agreed.

They pondered that particular coming collision in silence.

"I may wait until after the wedding, just so she doesn't make some kind of a scene." Although Mark knew that where his mother was concerned, *some* kind of a scene was a guarantee. "What I mean is *we,* as in you and me. The church. How do we deal with this?"

"Well, to be honest, I'm a little thrown, Mark." His voice held an instructor's tone.

"Yeah, me too."

"It's not what I expected of you. At all." The anger rose in degrees.

Mark took it like a tackle, impassive.

"I'll have to talk to the board." James flipped open his calendar.

"Would you?" Hope descended like the dove in the painting, breaking through the clouds of gray with specks of holy light. Mark spoke in a rush. "I'll go before them, tell them what happened, and that we're getting married. Before the church if I have to, like a testimony, tell them how even people in leadership, in the church, can make mistakes and that we're not perfect, just forgiven—"

"Mark," James said, gentle and sad. "It's over."

"Over?" The specks disappeared, the shadows covered the flight, as if it never happened. Turning what had been hope to an overwhelming gray.

"We have to let you go. Surely you can see that. Being on staff here—doing what you've been doing—we can't keep you on."

"Wait. Sure, the timing's off—that was a mistake. But we're in *love.* We're getting *married.* It's not like this is a totally awful thing."

"All that will help you, and I'm glad for it. No, it's not totally awful, but it doesn't fit with your purposes, our plans for you here. I'll call the board chairman, we'll work something out. To help with the wedding. And the baby." James picked up the phone, the sad smile lingering still.

"James, it's not like I'm the only one. Half the congregation, more than half, I bet—"

"You'd have made a fine pastor, Mark. Maybe somewhere down the line, you still will. But it won't be here."

*     *     *

*PROGRESSION.* STOPPED IN traffic on the way home, Mark thought about progression.

He'd met Amanda at some forgettable social. A single's mixer in downtown Houston, a friend of a friend. She teased him, called him a preacher boy. Flirting. Her head tilted up to his—her figure, full-blown curves on a petite frame. Completely unself-conscious and confident, the room dazzled where she saw fit to land, circling with this group and then that. A woman amidst silly girls. He couldn't keep his eyes off her.

*I'll catch you if I can,* he thought. She awakened the wolf in him, and he decided to chase.

*Progression.* He took her dancing on their second date. To a run-down bar on Houston's east side, where no Pleasant Valley Baptists would ever go. Because he wanted to hold her tight, too tight for propriety. They slid across sawdust floors, denim rubbed friction as he spun her fast, then slow, feeling the heat between their bellies while Patsy Cline poured her silken croons around them.

He'd kissed her full on the mouth for the first time, tasting beer and salt and her own sweet flavor, and it tasted so good he went back again and again.

*Progression.* After months of the chase, she invited him to her family's lake house for a weekend with Ben and Katy Thompson, her parents. He put on his shiny face. Ready to make the important introductions. To meet great expectations and surpass them. Except her parents didn't show because Katy had a "thing" to go to and Ben wanted to tinker in his garage.

"You don't mind, do you?" Amanda had asked, innocent. "Want to stay the weekend anyway?"

His conscience whispered no, but he ignored it and chose the path. Enjoyed the ramble down the highway where love and lust tangled so firmly, he couldn't see the light of day for the fire all around.

The two of them, alone with the waves and the water. He'd kissed her, her arms around him and the crickets singing. Love and lust, ancient and stronger than his own will reared like a warrior and laid him down. Lying down with her on a blanket, the moon high and round and the crickets screaming. He dipped into her, sweet and slow, and was damned by it in his own heart. But he didn't stop. He entered his lust and broke his trust, dying down with her. Painted himself a hypocrite while he lost himself in her. Tossing his future and his calling like a cheap brown penny. *I am looped in the loops of her hair.*

Then morning sunlight streamed on what he'd done. On him, sick with regret for not honoring her. For not holding the wolf in check.

But she'd smiled so sweet and hugged him tight, no furrow of fury or regret on her brow, but crazily, unexpectedly—love. She didn't say she was sorry, and when he did, she hushed him and handed him coffee.

The words *I love you, let's get married* died on his lips and he drank it, bitter, down his throat. Warming him as the sin-sickness slid from his gut.

The serpent whispered *Later* and Mark listened.

*Progression.* They'd danced again and again, not bothering with the sawdust floors, his conscience held at bay. He separated the white from the black and fed the darkness in himself with the power of their passion and dressed in glorious white each Sunday morning. The shadow eclipsed by the halo, coating his insides with shame while it tied him, tighter and tighter, until he couldn't speak.

The wolf caught in the net of his own weaving. He'd screamed for help too late. He'd broken the silence and spoke the truth, yet there he lay. Wounded by his choices, his purpose and his plans, gone.

*Progression.*

Still, he wouldn't be alone. Somehow, in spite of his stumblings and failures, he'd won the desire of his eyes and the love of his heart. He'd obtained a pearl of great price, Amanda as his bride.

Yet by heeding the wrong voice—*Later,* it had whispered—the cost was higher than he'd ever imagined.

You'd have made a fine pastor, James had said.

*Would have.*

CHAPTER 4

rotisserie

The drizzly morning matched Amanda's mood as she battled for a parking spot near the upscale restaurant. She punched the pedal of her red Toyota hatchback, sped past a Starbucks and a Talbots to nab an empty space from a retreating SUV.

Wheeling in to a squeaky halt, she bared her teeth to the rearview mirror to check for lipstick smudges. She snapped off the radio and grabbed the leather handbag Mother bought her for Christmas in college: *It's a classic, honey. You'll carry it for the rest of your life.*

She hadn't cared for the light shade of the purse, but it was no use arguing with Mother. Besides, she was usually right.

Usually, but not always. This time, Mother was wrong.

Leaping over pothole puddles, Amanda gave herself a pep talk.

She would not argue. She would state her case, pass on the information, then leave. Mother could take the news however she wanted, Amanda's only job was to tell the truth.

Then she'd treat herself to an afternoon of watching movies with Mark. Maybe she could cheer him up with the Three Stooges or *Blazing Saddles*. Something silly, to make him laugh.

News of the meeting with James had sent Amanda into a tailspin, yet Mark seemed determined to finish out his tenure as best he could.

It was almost as if the firing hadn't taken place. They never really talked about it, and Amanda hadn't seen Mark get angry, or sad, or even call James ugly names like she did in her heated moments.

He didn't seem to fear what would happen next, where they would go or what they would do. He simply went to work each day like nothing had ever happened. When she pushed him, he'd say, "It'll all work out. Give it time, and everything will be okay."

Amanda didn't see how, but she believed him anyway.

Inside the overcrowded French café, fresh-baked quiches lay behind sparkling glass and rotisserie chickens spun like headless dancers on steel rods. Amanda spotted Katy Thompson seated at a corner table, cozied up to the riverstone fireplace, partially secluded by a palm. Mother insisted on the best tables. She'd been known to move three times in one dining experience.

"Morning." Essence of rose swept over Amanda as she kissed her mother's cheek. The familiar smell she'd known forever. The scent of perfection.

One she'd never quite been able to mimic. As a girl, she'd doused herself from the heavy bottle on Katy's vanity, but it wasn't the same. On Amanda, the fragrance had become loud and clumsy and she'd taken a steamy bath with deodorant soap to hide the embarrassment.

If Mother noticed her daughter's theft, she never said so. But a week later, Amanda found a pretty gift set on her own bathroom counter, full of beautiful soaps and a small vial of fresh scent. When Amanda tried it, it suited her.

She still had one of the soaps tucked in a drawer somewhere, knowing even as a child not to waste it all.

At the brunch, Katy dressed in fabulous shades of taupe and burgundy red, which offset her golden highlights. An unobtainable high-end form of panty hose, known only to Junior League presidents and sometimes favorite underlings, encased her slim ankles.

"Amanda." After air-kissing her daughter's cheek, Katy Thompson gave her a cool once-over, then sat down and stirred coffee. Not cappuccino, but the blackest roast with the heaviest cream.

A dark-haired waiter, wearing an oxford shirt under a white apron, brought a breadbasket with muffins and biscuits. He took their order and gave Amanda a warm look, more personal than customer service required.

*I'm pregnant and the waiter's flirting with me. He's ogling a mommy, and doesn't even know it.*

She smiled impersonally into his Tabasco-print tie and grabbed the biggest muffin. She was starving, and the dense carbs might help settle her stomach.

While they waited for their food, Katy released a slender cigarette from a metallic case. "So, how's your preacher friend? Mark, isn't it?"

*Preacher friend.* Somehow the woman spoke condescendingly of both Mark's chosen profession and his relationship with her daughter in two callous words. Highly irritating.

Amanda forced a smile, marveling how her mother could smoke a cigarette and look like a 1940s silver-screen diva. Her own attempts at the habit in high school, practiced in front of a mirror, had made her look more like trailer trash.

"Mark's great. And you know his name." Amanda spun the slim ring on her finger, left hand hidden under the heavy table-cloth. She nibbled her muffin and watched her mother smoke.

The silence seemed heavier in a room filled with chatterers. Katy's complacency reminded Amanda of an old Western, the proud and beautiful Indian chief high on a horse.

*An impasse,* she thought. *We are at an impasse.*

Careful not to let the stuck-together ice slap back in her face and soak her shirt, Amanda wet her mouth with the chilled water. "Actually, that's part of the reason I wanted to have break-fast this morning. To talk about Mark. And me," she clarified, clearing her throat. "Mark and me."

"And here I thought you wanted a pleasant brunch with your lonely, old mother sheerly for the sake of my company."

Amanda let that slip by. "He's really wonderful." She hated that she had to promote Mark, to soft sell him to anyone. Mark was better than wonderful—he was glorious, tender and brilliant. If Katy Thompson couldn't admit that, this might be the quickest brunch in history. "You just need to get to know him."

Katy blinked curled eyelashes, singly defined with jet-black mascara. No comment.

"We've been spending a lot of time together," Amanda added. "I want you to like him, Mother. I need you to accept him. For me." She fought the urge to plead, hating that sound in her voice. The mama-won't-you-approve-of-me whine that accompanied every boyfriend, every dress she ever picked out, every new job or life choice.

Amanda pressed on. "He's the one."

"The one?" Katy's brows shot up. "How could you possibly know if he's the one? You've been dating for less than a year." She ground out her cigarette for emphasis and removed another from the case, snapping the lid shut.

Chain-smoking. Not a good sign.

"Now, if you would date other men—it's not like I don't *care* for Mark—but more *professional* men like I've introduced you to, maybe you would have some frame of *reference*. Instead of limiting yourself." Katy shook her head at the pity of it all. "So exclusive."

"Is it the exclusivity that bothers you? Or the fact Mark doesn't take home six figures?"

"Don't use that tone with me."

"Mother, I don't need a frame of reference. I know. We love each other."

"Well, of course he loves you, Amanda. You are beautiful, gifted, smart and *young*. Far too young to tie yourself to a preacher who will never be able to support you in the way you are accustomed. Trust me." Katy took a deep drag, the thin burn line pulling halfway down the cigarette. The tower of ashes, a miniature Pisa, held on, leaning, before she flicked it in the marble ashtray. The tower didn't disintegrate but fell, broken in two, atop the other ashes.

"Mother." Amanda twisted the linen napkin in her lap, making a storkish-looking bird shape. "I love him," she repeated. She met her mother's gaze. "We're getting married."

Through the elegant swirls of smoke, Katy Thompson's deep blue eyes widened, then narrowed.

Amanda brought forward her hand to reveal the ring. The marquise tilted to the side and slid upside down. She balanced it so the diamond would show.

Katy squinted at the ring as if to assess the quality of the stone, then leaned back and brought the dying cigarette to her matte red mouth. "It doesn't fit."

"We have to take it in."

"He didn't know your size? Nice." Katy ran a buffed fingernail over her lips, examining her daughter.

Amanda felt like a one-celled microorganism under her stare, with no supporting skeletal structure.

"Are you pregnant?" Katy's voice broke the quiet. Almost a whisper, but piercing.

"Yes." Amanda hooded her eyes and fiddled with her fork.

"On purpose?"

"Mother!"

"I know how much you want to have a family. It's what you've always wanted since you were a little girl with your dolls."

*The ones you wouldn't let me play with, high on the shelf, too precious for my awkward hands.*

"No, not on purpose. But I'm not sorry." Amanda lifted her chin. "I'm ready for a family, with Mark. To make a life together, build a marriage." *Not like yours* went unsaid.

"I understand about the baby. It happens." Katy sniffed. "To the best of us."

The Thompsons' shotgun wedding still sent kicks through the family, aftershocks Amanda felt on nearly every birthday. Ben Thompson, a redneck pilot from nowhere, landed a society bird dripping in oil money. Opposites attracting, but not sticking. Loosely jointed for two and a half decades, always on the verge of collapse.

Amanda had asked her father once when he knew for certain he loved her mother. "Why, I guess when her daddy left her all that money," he drawled, then popped the tab on his beer. The worst part was she couldn't tell if he was joking or not. The idea of being locked in a marriage like her parents' kept Amanda awake some nights.

Which is why she knew Mark was perfect for her. She made him laugh and he loved her for it, flaws and all. He didn't hide out in the garage, like her father, but reveled in all the world had to offer. Effortlessly gliding through the social channels with the skill of a chameleon. Everyone loved him, so how could she not? Goldenboy.

Besides, Mark and Amanda had *it*. Whatever it was, that intangible thing, a gut-level connection. They didn't seem to struggle as much as other couples, but had an almost rhythmic, unspoken communication.

They faced their first real hurdle with this early pregnancy, and Amanda could admit, it was a doozy. Still, she thought they both handled it rather well.

Katy sighed, and sat silent for a moment. "So, it's a done deal then."

"Yes." Amanda refused to slump or cry under the weight of her mother's resignation. It blanketed her, but she would not wrestle against it, knowing it would only tangle her further.

She looked at her mother, and kept her expression clear. *I will not cry. I will not fall apart in this snooty uptown restaurant with unbelievably delicious quiche. I wonder if I could get another slice to go?*

"I never wanted you to repeat my mistakes." Katy's voice could barely be heard.

"It's not a mistake. I know what I'm doing." Amanda watched the headless chickens spin, oil shining on their flanks. Twirling. Imprisoned for the delight of the feasting diners.

"You don't have to go through with it." Katy leaned forward. "You know I'll help you . . . whatever it takes."

"I know." Amanda wiped a wayward tear. "But this is what I

want. I want Mark. I want this baby." She was off the silver spindle, ready to dance on her own, to break free and begin her own adventure. With Mark, her favorite person, at her side.

"You're sure?"

"No question." Perhaps she hadn't started in the right order, according to some, but she'd landed the man of her dreams. And a baby too. Not too shabby for a rich girl from Houston, destined to serve on volunteer committees in the best panty hose.

Katy nodded once. "Don't tell your father. I'll do it when the time is right." She stamped out the cigarette butt with a final tap, signaling an end to that strain of conversation.

She cradled Amanda's cheek with a tobacco-scented hand. "It's going to be okay, baby."

The tenderness in the endearment nearly slayed Amanda's bravado, but she nodded and accepted the gesture.

Katy Thompson shifted back and surveyed her daughter over an ivory coffee cup. "We've got a wedding to plan, little girl." And with that announcement, she bestowed her first genuine smile of the morning.

# click

The dim atmosphere of St. Paul's Presbyterian Church did nothing to quench the morning heat. Ancient air conditioners wheezed against Houston's early-summer temperatures while the sanctuary, with its stone walls and intricate stained glass, registered a whopping ten degrees cooler than the humid ninety-eight outside.

Mark stood at the front and smiled at the gathering assembly. He played host again today, but for an entirely different purpose. The warmth that radiated from his chest, under his arms and from his hairline didn't reach his fingertips, cold as ice. He flexed them, willing the blood to ease their chill. Amanda would need a warm grasp after the gauntlet they faced this morning.

The wedding. Hastily assembled by an undaunted Katy

Thompson, full-throttle *Southern Living* style in a matter of weeks. Amazing.

The house of worship was one of the oldest and most beautiful in Houston, with stone masonry, mahogany beams, glimmering chandeliers and commissioned artwork. Naturally, Amanda's parents were lifetime members. Mark couldn't imagine how Katy had wrangled a Saturday time spot in the middle of June. He didn't want to know.

Until yesterday, Mark had never stepped foot in a Presbyterian church and, judging from his mother's sniffs of disapproval, Marianne Reynolds hadn't either.

"Where's the baptismal?" she asked too loudly during the awkward rehearsal. Her question reverberated through the sanctuary.

"They sprinkle, Mom," he whispered to quiet her, wishing he'd never picked her up at the airport.

"Oh!" The look of shock she gave the entire Thompson family suggested they might all be in danger of hellfire, not having their sins properly washed by a full-body dunking.

Even now, the aisle marked the Red Sea division between the Baptists and the Presbyterians. Marianne sat in the front pew, encased in yellow, already dabbing her eyes. She liked to cry in church.

He knew, without searching the remaining rows, that James Montclair would not be in attendance this morning.

Shortly after Mark's confession in the corner office, his former boss made an emotional announcement from the pulpit of Pleasant Valley. James declared that Mark had chosen to follow the Lord's calling elsewhere, and they'd sure miss him. The board and congregation threw Mark a farewell reception, complete with a slide show of his various works at the church.

At the party, they'd handed him a guitar case. Not his. This one had no stickers or beat-up edges. The accompanying card read,

*Please accept this small token of our thanks in appreciation for your years of service.* The envelope included pages of handwritten notes and signatures from church members.

Mark opened the case and found a Martin guitar inside. The caramel wood gleamed, promising a sound deeper and richer than any he had ever played. He'd wanted a Martin for years, never believing he'd have the money to pay for one. Speechless, he tripped over his thanks.

"We're only sorry you won't be playing it for us much longer," one man said. "But we know—wherever he takes you—the Lord'll use it to his glory."

Then James had a wedding conflict. It just so happened he'd be performing a ceremony on the other side of town, at the exact time of Mark and Amanda's scheduled nuptials. A happy coincidence, and one that freed James from any whiff of a scandal.

"Sorry, buddy," James told him. "Been set for months, you know." He lifted his palms, a busy servant of the Lord overwhelmed by the flock's incessant needs. "Can't make last minute changes. You need me to make a call, find someone else for you?"

*Can't make last-minute changes. Except about your entire future. Buddy.*

"I'll manage, thanks." Mark heard the message loud and clear. He ended up asking his childhood pastor to perform the ceremony, much to the thrill of his mother. Marianne had voiced severe doubts about the Thompson family minister, and thankfully, Katy hadn't argued. She let her future son-in-law handle the "religious concerns," as long as she could plan everything else.

He hadn't laid eyes on Fred Wilburne, from Lubbock's Calvary Baptist, in close to ten years. He chose not to inform Fred of the early pregnancy, not willing to risk the loss of another official this late in the game.

He checked his watch.

"It's gonna be fine." Fred clapped a hand, heavy as an iron bookend, on Mark's shoulder. A long, dark robe covered the preacher's robust frame. His jowls flushed in protest of the heat. "Just fine."

"I know," Mark said. The only bright spot in this day, other than the scalding morning sun, would be the woman who'd walk down the aisle in a few minutes. He didn't want to wait any longer. He needed to be near her, to let her smile ground him and give him hope, even while all around him, inside him, chaos threatened.

"Let's get started," he said to Fred. "I'm ready."

"ANYBODY NEKKID IN there?" Ben Thompson's deep voice barreled through the old oak door.

"Just a minute, Daddy." Sweat tickled like devil fingers inside Amanda's wedding dress. She pulled a fragile handkerchief from her bodice, patted her face and chest, then stuffed it back into obscurity.

Standing in front of an oval mirror, she surveyed herself one last time. Something old. Check. The antique gown, handed down from Mother's side. Something new. Pure silk heels, pinching her swollen feet in a death grip. Something borrowed. Her friend's veil, a diaphanous fluff atop her head. Something blue. Her eyes, rimmed with red to match her nose.

She thought she'd be over the crying by now, but seeing herself as a bride tipped the emotional scale. *Inner glow,* she reminded herself. *You're a bride. You're pregnant. One way or another, you should be radiant at this moment.*

Sighing, she viewed her reflection sideways in the beveled glass. She straightened her back and smoothed the taut fabric. Not too bad.

A quick rap sounded. Mother.

Katy Thompson pushed inside. "Feeling better?"

"Yes, thanks, Mom. I needed a minute alone."

Her mother walked softly on thick red carpet and adjusted the tiny metal clasps in the back of the dress. "You look lovely." Her eyes met Amanda's in the mirror, and her own filled with moisture.

"Ohhhh." Amanda waved her hands fast in front of her face. "Stop, or you'll get me started."

"Hush. I'm the mother of the bride. I can if I want to." She squeezed the lace at Amanda's shoulders.

Ben Thompson thundered again from the hallway. "It's time, baby doll."

"Okay, Daddy. Come on in."

He rambled through, a bear stuffed in penguin clothes. His watermelon belly strained against the expensive cloth.

"All right. I'm ready." Amanda grabbed the bouquet she'd tossed on the baroque couch. A few stems of the mixed floral were bent out of shape.

She Mona Lisa'd her mouth and hung onto her father's arm, thankful for its familiar strength. The same arm that fished her out of the lake when she fell water-skiing. The one that kept her upright when she learned to ride a bike. He held her steady as they left the bridal room and waited in the wings.

Amanda lifted her bouquet to her nose. Fresh roses and stargazer lilies filled her senses.

At the end of the aisle stood her groom, substantial and real. More than his height or size, Mark's very essence sparked with bound energy, his shine unswallowed by the sanctuary's shadowy interior.

The aisle yawned between them, and her heart ached. Unbelieving that in just a few moments he would be entirely hers. That he wanted her, loved her, this wondrous holy man with the most tender soul she'd ever known.

He slid a hand through his hair and leaned over to whisper something to Fred. Amanda looked around, waiting for the cue.

Her minister lurked in the choir loft, having assured Presbyterian members of his presence at the ceremony to "guard the sacraments."

As if the Baptists would make off with the communion silver.

The organ started up a bombastic tune and, with a jump, Amanda realized it was her turn to walk.

Her daddy held her hand on his arm, patting it absently. "Let's do this," he murmured.

With a conjoined and muted rumble, the guests stood. Amanda and her father passed big lavender hats and blue-gray perms. An aunt in the second row shushed Amanda's cousin, a wiggly nine-year-old stuffed in pink ruffles. Dark suits highlighted peacock wives beside them.

Everyone stared, smiling.

At the altar, Mark took her hand from her father and gently squeezed her fingers. "You look," he whispered through her veil, *"beautiful."*

Before she could reply in kind, a West Texas drawl cut the thick air like a John Deere backhoe.

"Dearly beloved," bellowed Fred, "we are gathered here today . . ." No need for a microphone for Pastor Wilburne. His squinty eyes darted over the attendees, perhaps summing them up as future converts.

Fred waxed eloquent, loud and long through the traditional ceremony. Lots of preaching, prayers and hymns. Finally it was over. "You may now kiss your bride."

Mark leaned over and placed a kiss on her lips, cool as velvet lemonade.

"I present to you"—Pastor Wilburne paused for drama—"Mr. and Mrs. Mark Reynolds!" With a gentle nudge, he urged them to face the applauding congregation.

"As many of you know"—the preacher held up both hands, palms out—"Mark and Amanda have answered God's call in their lives." His voice swelled with pride. "Mark, after serving here in Houston as an associate pastor, now looks ahead to a new place in the Lord's army, wherever that may be."

The crowd clapped appropriately.

"Please add them to your prayer lists." He sniffed. "These fine young people." His voice breaking, he nearly shouted. "*Devoted* to following the Lord in ministry!"

Amanda flinched at the inflection and darted a look to Mark. His face was unreadable, but his eyes twinkled at her. They had a secret, together, and the knowledge tethered them with indivisible truth. They marched down the aisle, anointed by the cheers of the saints.

Outside the double doors, they stood alone.

"We did it." She didn't know whether to laugh or cry. "We're married."

Judging from Mark's expression, he didn't know either. Yet he pulled her close, squishing the bouquet even further. "You're mine," he murmured as the flowers fell forgotten to the floor.

"No, you're mine." She pressed herself full against him, hugging him tight. Behind them hung a life-size painting, Jesus calming the storm. The Savior's arms appeared muscular and strong, even as the disciples crouched terrified in the boat. She shut her eyes to the swirls of red and blue, losing herself in the freedom of loving her husband.

"*Harrumph.*" A tiny rat-faced man interrupted them with authority in spite of his size. Burton Lewis, the photographer, hired by Katy Thompson because he "does everybody who's anybody's wedding, darling."

"Picture time!" he sang, with all the enthusiasm of a Hollywood performer. "All right, you two. Over here." Outside in the garden area, he arranged them in front of a large stone fountain, where a naked baby with a fruit basket sprayed water into a shallow pool.

Grin, click, relax. Adjust. Grin, click, relax.

Burton arranged the wilted bouquet. Moisture, caught in a shiny mustache, clung to his upper lip. He struck the pose he wanted her to mimic. "Like *this*." His arms gracefully arched to an invisible groom.

A wave of body odor broke from Burton's brown suit and washed over her like a poisonous gas. She pinched her face away.

"Are you all right?" Mark whispered in her ear, rubbing her back.

"I'm okay." She bit out, clenching her teeth together.

The little photographer took his time, tsking over the broken flowers. "How about you hold it up here?" He placed her hand on Mark's shoulder. In doing so, he lifted his own arm, emitting an odor reminiscent of the monkey cages at the zoo.

Amanda reared her head back to the point of rudeness, blinked her eyes and pressed down hard with her toes. Hoping the pain from the killer slingbacks would stop the nausea.

"Do we need to go inside for a minute?" Mark tugged her waist. "Come on. Take a break?"

"Hmm-mmm." She shook her head, grinning like an ape for monkey man.

"No, no, not like that." The photographer grasped both sides of her face, the camera dangling around his neck on a wide band. "*This* way." He tilted her chin and smiled at her posability. "Wonderful."

*Whunderfuul.* His breath hit her dead on.

He must have had lox with his bagel.

The thought defeated her. She broke position. She shoved Burton away with all her might and hurtled toward the stone fountain. Gripping its side, in body-shuddering heaves, she threw up.

Click.

While still bent at the waist, she dug between her breasts for the handkerchief and dabbed the corners of her mouth. A delicate lady. A blushing bride. A perfect pastor's wife.

Bracing herself on the fountain's edge, she raised her head and pivoted on one excruciating heel. The first person she saw was Mark's mother. Her brand-new mother-in-law.

The Queen of the Baptists.

Dressed in yellow chiffon, with a rosebud corsage, she stared at Amanda. The woman's bird mouth formed a perfect O. Then she looked at her son.

Amanda followed the gaze. She saw what Marianne saw—Mark's reddening neck, his hands shoved deep in his pockets.

Shooting forward with Olympian speed, Marianne made it to Mark's side in nanoseconds. "Did you *know* about this?" Her voice floated over the onslaught of bridesmaids rushing to Amanda's aid.

Mark's reply was lost in the clattering of heels on ancient paths.

Just as someone thrust a glass of ice water in her shaking hand, Amanda heard the follow-up question. A low-voiced inquiry carried by an unlikely Houston breeze.

*"Is it yours?"*

# split

Mark refreshed his mother's coffee. It poured out like melted sludge, powdery grains stuck to the side of the Styrofoam cup. Marianne gripped it without drinking. "I just can't believe it."

In the church's parlor, he waited with his mother and new mother-in-law while the bridesmaids tended to Amanda in the bridal room.

Ben Thompson, after declaring a need for fresh air, had followed his old Aggie alumni buddies in a cloud of commiseration to the church back lot. Mark thought he saw the flash of a silver flask from behind a suit jacket, and wished he'd gone with them.

Better that than entertaining the ladies.

"How could you do this to me?" Legs akimbo in a mauve

Queen Anne chair, Marianne looked more frazzled than Mark had ever seen her.

"Excuse me?"

"Embarrass me like this. In case you missed it, your bride vomited in the fountain. *Morning sickness.*" She whispered these words in the same tone one might say *herpes.* "What must our friends be thinking? And Pastor Fred?"

"Not much, I suppose." Katy crossed her arms and stared out the window.

"What is that supposed to mean?" Marianne shot back.

"Only that he doesn't strike me as overly insightful." Not bothering to turn her head, Katy remained riveted, gazing at the gardens full of gossiping guests. "A boisterous fellow, but not too bright."

"I'll have you know, Fred Wilburne is one of the finest men to walk this earth. Why, when Mark was a boy, he—"

"Mom." Mark sank into the plaid couch across from her. "Fred's character really isn't at issue here."

"That's right." Marianne's bright eyes locked on Mark. "Yours is. Care to explain?"

"Not particularly." He loosened his tie and yanked it too hard, snapping the fine silk in the quiet room.

"But how could you let this happen?" His mother shrilled on. "Your career, all that you've wanted?"

"I still want those things." He didn't know if he meant it, or if by force of habit, he still played her game.

"Well, what did James Montclair have to say about this?" James held a second-place spot in Marianne's list of all-time favorite people, second only to Jesus.

Mark wasn't sure he'd even made the list. "He said that he wished us well."

"And?"

"And that I need to look for work elsewhere."

"*Oh my God.*" Marianne's taking the Lord's name in vain testified to the fullness of her devastation.

Katy finally picked up on the conversation. She turned from the window. Her eyes, a steelier variation of Amanda's blue, nailed Mark where he sat. "You mean to say you're without gainful employment?"

"For now. I have a severance package."

"Severance?" Marianne's lace handkerchief muffled her sobs.

"You've married my daughter"—Katy pointed her manicured finger at him—"and *you don't have a job?*"

"I'm working now. They're giving me two months to finish up. Until they find a replacement for me." *Until Amanda begins to show.* "But I've got some feelers out."

"Feelers? What kind of feelers?" Marianne raised her head, eyes puffy. "Where?"

"Some places here in Houston. Ad agencies. I'm thinking of getting out of the ministry."

At this, Katy joined them in the seating area. "That's an excellent decision, Mark." Dragonlady, as he'd taken to calling his mother-in-law in private, actually smiled at him. She patted his knee, her bejeweled fingers like sparkly claws.

He watched the glitter, the spark of old money and ironclad rules, and felt the room get smaller.

"I've got some great contacts," Katy said. "I can put in a word, get you started on a meaningful career."

"*Ad agency?*" Marianne looked horrified, as if Mark announced plans to pursue a career as a male stripper. "But what about your calling, Mark?"

"To tell you the truth, Mom," he admitted, "I'm not hearing it so loudly right now."

Yet, he remembered when he was called, as if it were yesterday.

At Calvary Baptist Church, in Lubbock, Texas. Mark sat in the deep red church pew, fourth row on the right, with his mother.

Wind whipped through the trees outside the stained-glass windows. Shadows of the slender limbs bowed and strained toward the church's white one-story cross.

He was twelve, skinny and fatherless. Doyle Reynolds had chosen to leave his marriage of seventeen years for Mona Torkman, a junior sales associate at Southwest Pharmaceuticals. She was married to Mr. Torkman, Mark's seventh-grade science teacher.

Doyle had loaded up his charcoal gray El Camino, shabby suitcases and cardboard file boxes stacked high under the camper, and left town with Mona. He never came back.

Mark became the man of the family before he became a teenager. He skipped adolescence and moved right on to adulthood, stepping into the role of sole emotional supporter for his devastated mother. At night, he'd lie in bed with his stomach clenched and endure the waves of her tears wafting through the duplex's tissue-thin walls.

Until the saints at Calvary Baptist came along.

They invited Mark and Marianne to church picnics, his mother to ladies' groups, Mark to weeklong campouts. He watched his mother's shoulders lift after months of crying into her pillow. And the burden from his own shoulders grew lighter as potlucks filled their empty evenings.

He first heard about his need for Jesus at camp, around the crackling campfire with other sweaty twelve-year-olds. Like the rest of the kids, he held a broken tree branch and listened spellbound to his new hero: Kenny Keisling, camp counselor.

"Boys, it's a decision only you can make. The Word says, 'For all have sinned and fallen short of the glory of God.' That means you've missed the mark, fellas. You ain't perfect, ain't never gonna be. You can try all you want, but if you want forgiveness, if you want to be good, you need the Lord." Kenny waved his well-worn Bible in the air.

*If you want to be good.* Mark thought of Mr. Torkman, a gangly man who wore corduroys and button-downs with wrinkled collars. How his former favorite teacher wouldn't look at him in class, how the other kids snickered like rats all around. Then the relief when Mr. Torkman took an extended leave of absence, and eventually moved away, leaving whispers in the hallways like ghosts of shame.

"It says right here"—Kenny poked an ivory page—"that the 'wages of sin is death, but the gift of God is eternal life through Christ Jesus, our Lord.'"

To Mark, the camp leader looked like a gladiator, some kind of warrior.

"So, what's it going to be, guys? Will you take the gift?" Several boys were already nodding. Kenny waved a knotty branch in the air.

One by one, Mark watched his peers throw their sticks in the fire. A sign encouraged by the camp counselors to show they'd given their hearts to Jesus. The ceremony ended with a rousing rendition of "I Surrender All," each of the four verses sung a cappella, and with much emotion.

Mark kept his stick, the rough places hurting his palm where he gripped it so tightly. He mumbled through the song and stared at his tennis shoes, clumped with mud from a week in the outdoors.

But later, just before the start of eighth grade, on a day when the wind threatened to split the trees in two, Mark heard it. The call. Not from the red face and passionate voice of a younger Pastor Fred Wilburne, but somewhere deep inside. He walked forward on heavy feet, down the plush scarlet liner, and knelt at the altar. He read the chiseled words on the light oak table—THIS DO IN REMEMBRANCE OF ME—just before he closed his eyes.

He didn't listen to the prayers over his head or the choir singing praises. All he heard was the quiet of his own pleading voice, "Please, God, I don't want to be like my dad. Make me good, Lord. Please make me good."

He stood to face the congregation. They clapped and smiled at him. His mother's tearstained face shining with pride. Mark's heart swelled. He'd done a good thing. He *was* good.

But when he grew to notice girls, doe-eyed in pink sweaters walking next to him at school, he feared the taint of his father's bad blood ran thick in him.

He wanted to be saved from that, free from the "like father like son" curse. The one that left people wounded in its wake. He tried to walk the straight and narrow, fighting his desires. But still he fell. Fell hard, his sophomore year, with a buxom cheerleader named Macy. Found out what he'd been warned against all those years in Sunday school, and that he liked it.

He felt sure his church friends would read it on him, a scarlet *A* scripted on his forehead. But they didn't, and Mark discovered an inner division to his soul. That a righteous man could sometimes dance the crooked path, teasing fate, dabbling in temptation. *Let not your right hand know what your left hand is doing.*

So he led a split life. Right versus left. Right against wrong. He read Paul's lament a million times. *I do that which I do not will to do.* The flesh and the spirit at war. He lost more times than he wished to count.

Then the saints at Calvary Baptist hallelujah'd his decision to go to seminary on Graduation Sunday and helped raise tuition through bake sales and craft bazaars. They sacrificed, pledged and sent prayer cards. "We're behind you!" they cheered. "Praying for you daily," they promised. Their faith in him shamed him for his failures and thrilled him all at once.

Some of these same folks from Calvary Baptist drank punch around the fountain today when his beautiful bride announced to all, by accident, that she was with child.

His child.

Right hand met left, his divided worlds collided. Leaving broken pieces of his pride, for everyone to see. The truth he'd suspected all along.

He wasn't good at all.

# god's green earth

Dust particles danced in afternoon sun, filtered through the windows of the apartment. They rotated and spun to an unheard song, then gathered, clinging to the photo in Amanda's hand.

She blew them away, soft as a southern breeze. Slick fax paper captured the blurry image of the fetus, black-and-white swirls promising new life. She traced her fingertip over the curves. Followed the tiny length of legs and arms. Lingered over the head and heart.

A medical font pronounced the mother as *Amanda Thompson*, along with the date and baby's measurements at ten weeks. Just before the wedding.

Two months had passed, and Amanda's stomach could no

longer be hidden under superstrength girdles. She'd never felt right about them anyway, for fear of squishing the baby.

Since Mark's tenure ended last week, she didn't have to worry anymore. No more false sunny appearances on Sunday mornings, doodling on her bulletin and counting the minutes until the charade was over.

James Montclair had the nerve to ask about her health on their last Sunday. Not caring who saw, she rubbed her midsection and grinned a Cheshire smile. "Just fine, Jimmy. Just fine."

Amanda got up from the nappy apartment carpet and stepped carefully over her list of thank-you notes from the wedding. Piled all around her lay crystal bowls and heavy linens, priceless china and the few oddball gifts. A nacho warmer. A set of hand-knitted pot holders. A hideous clock with pigs cavorting on it. From Mark's side, she had no doubt.

She changed the radio to something bouncier, to get in the mood for organization. Her decaf iced tea melted, so she dumped out the huge plastic glass and made a new one with fresh mint from her window box.

Settling herself back in the one circle she'd managed not to clutter, she picked up the picture again, postponing the tedious art of writing thank-you notes. Choosing instead to dream. *Little One. Half-pint. Two Bits.*

Not knowing the sex of the baby was killing her, but she and Mark would find out in a few more weeks. She'd go back to Dr. Hoffman's office, lie down on that vinyl green "lounger," and stick her feet in the freezing stirrups. She'd do it cheerfully, because she'd get to hear the baby. To see the baby.

At the first appointment, she'd felt so nervous she'd been afraid she might pass gas right there on the table. The thought gave her the giggles. Mark's exasperated look couldn't squelch her laughter, but the chill from the clear gel sobered her.

Lisa, the technician, a skinny girl with long permed hair and puffy bangs, seemed perfectly at ease poking around her most private areas.

Amanda kept her eyes glued to the screen, a small monitor to the side. She couldn't really make out the lima bean shape but uh-huh'd knowingly as Lisa listed off her baby's critical parts.

The heartbeat, big rhythmic booms, had been so strong it startled her, like heavy orange basketballs thumping in practice in a high-school gym. That sound, the hugeness of it, made it all real.

Amanda met Mark's eyes as hers filled at the sound—the external proof of the internal. Her baby's music.

Mark slid his gaze away and focused on the screen. Wordless. He hadn't made the leap to expectant fatherhood yet, not quite in the way she'd hoped. But he would. He just needed more time. After all, they'd gone through so many changes already.

When the communications firm had cutbacks, she'd agreed to a part-time position to preserve her job. Now, with Mark out of work, the financial strain became evident in the hours he spent at the kitchen table, brooding over the bills and job listings in the paper. With the pregnancy and lack of money, their dancing dates had waned away. Even finding time for movie nights at home proved difficult, with Mark on the computer for hours. Polishing his résumé. Searching for opportunities.

But she knew, when Mark found another job, and especially when the baby came, things would get better. Easier.

Like they were before.

Amanda replaced the sonogram photos in her memento box, an old cardboard boot box she hoped to replace with something prettier. Pregnancy tests, doctor receipts and prenatal brochures spilled out. Her baby stack grew as fast as her stomach.

Digging through the pile, her hands found an oversize album easily. She'd bought the Beatrix Potter baby book at Hallmark.

Fell in love with it at first sight. With no regrets, she handed over her Visa.

When she showed the treasure to Mark, proud of her purchase, he said it was too expensive. He obviously didn't share her unbridled enthusiasm for whimsical flowers and little mice. Not to mention flagrant disregard for their strict financial plan.

"I've got no job, Mandy," he'd reminded her. "We're on a shoestring. This severance isn't going to last forever."

So, she hadn't started using the album in case she had to return it. But the baby book had a spot ready for the sonogram photo, outlined with ivy petals and impish critters. She itched to go ahead and paste the picture in, but she was trying hard to be a good wife.

She'd wait until he forgot about the purchase, and do it later.

After all, how could she possibly return her baby's first keepsake? She imagined looking through the album with her child, reminiscing about first teeth and birthday parties.

Besides, she didn't have time to worry about it, not that she was much of a worrier—she had a hundred thank-yous to write.

The phone rang, she dug behind a pile to find the cordless.

"It's me," Mark said.

"How's it going?" She loved when he called her during the day to check in. She never tired of hearing his voice. "Have you interviewed yet?"

"No. There's about ten guys in the waiting area. They all look pretty much like me. Younger, though. More professional."

"No such thing. You'll be great. Call me when it's over. Better yet," she put a sexy spin in her tone, "come right home."

"That, *Mrs. Reynolds,* is a promise." They still got tickled calling each other Mr. and Mrs. Reynolds.

"Good luck." Smiling, Amanda leaned to hang the phone up. A sharp pain hit her side, almost like a cramp from running.

Massaging the spot, she stood upright.

"Little one, we've overdone it, I think." Thinking to lie down, she headed for the garage-sale couch in the living room. The cheap fabric covering she'd made already pulled away from the burnt orange velvet underneath. *I should really sew that up. It won't take but a minute, and I can sit down when I do it.*

Changing direction, she headed for the laundry closet to get her sewing kit. But she didn't make it down the hall. The pain returned, slicing through her entire abdomen like a scythe.

A sound, shrill—between a scream and a whisper—escaped her as she crumpled to her knees.

*Oh no. Oh no-no-no.* She held her stomach with her hands and prayed. *Oh, God, please, no.* The cramps hit harder, twisting her insides around. The pain skewered her, held her helpless. *Oh, little one, little one. You're okay. Please be okay. I need you to be all right. We're all right.*

Trying not to hyperventilate through the spasms, she crawled to the phone. She squeezed her thighs tight together and continued encouraging her unborn baby to hang on. She paused between shuffles to cry. To breathe.

The phone book weighed a thousand pounds as she tugged it off the counter, still on her knees. Where was the interview? Which office? Mark no longer had a cell phone. The church paid for their old account and apologetically confiscated Mark's phone upon his "resignation."

They hadn't had the money yet to get another one.

She turned pages, her leg muscles shaking from the strain.

She had to control her breathing so she could talk. She misdialed once, then twice. Trying to calm herself, so they would understand her.

*Please let them understand me.*

A pinched voice piped through the phone. "Good morning, Davis Enterprise. How can I help you?"

"Mark Reynolds," Amanda whispered. Then, with more strength, "On an interview this morning. The ad department." She couldn't help the sob that escaped. "I need Mark. Please get Mark."

"One moment, please. I'll put you through."

The line clicked to hold, and Amanda listened to the Muzak. An instrumental of "Walking on Sunshine," she guessed, while she waited for Mark, and her baby died inside her.

THE PAPER-COVERED pillow crinkled as Amanda turned her heavy head toward Mark. He entered the hospital room well, with the appropriate air of someone bringing both empathy and hope to a sad situation.

*He does this so well. He would have made a good pastor.*

As he stepped close to the bed, she saw he wasn't as pulled together as she first thought. His green eyes now bloodshot, red around the edges, and glassy. He had that line on his forehead, that crease telling her he'd been worried or angry. Maybe both.

But he smiled at her, gentle and sad.

She hadn't seen that smile before.

"Come here." Her voice sounded thick to her own ears, like the walls of her throat caved in on themselves. Like her uterus had caved in on her baby.

Women had babies every day of the week. Carried them, strong bellies round and triumphant. Yet she had failed. Failed herself. Failed Mark. And failed her child.

She reached for Mark and pulled his head, his precious head to her. "I'm sorry. I'm so sorry. I tried to hang on. . . . The baby—"

"Mandy, no. *Shhh.* It'll be all right."

She buried her face in his hair, not caring if her tears or nose or anything else ran over him in the process. He was hers, and she could cry on him if she wanted to.

His smell comforted her, spoke to something deep inside. He smelled like safety and hope and a future. She drew it in as deep as she could. She cried harder, letting herself dissolve into his scent. He bent over her, curving around and above her like a shield.

Holding her, but he did not cry.

He accepted her tears and stayed strong for her, and a tiny shadow in her heart hated him for it.

When her sobs waned into deep breaths, gasping for a calmer rhythm, he pulled away. He smoothed her hair with long fingers. They tangled and it hurt.

Making more crinkly sounds, he leaned to the side of the bed and pulled a tissue from the rollaway cart. He handed it to her and she blew her nose loudly, inelegantly.

"Amanda." His voice had the thick sound too.

She looked into his eyes, still bright with unshed tears, and saw it written there. She knew what he was going to say.

It was tangible, like the awful pillow and the grainy tissue and the hollow pain in her womb where the baby used to be.

*Don't say it. Please don't say it. Oh, God, don't let him say it.*

He squeezed her hand, reassuring. "I know this is a terrible thing. I know how you must be feeling. I'm hurting too."

Her doubt of his intention stirred. She didn't see the hurt in him. She didn't see much feeling at all. Then anger, displaced rage at his wholeness, while she lay in a million pieces, reared hot and lashed inside, a loosened tether whipped free.

*There's no way on God's green earth you know what I'm feeling. Have you ever had your insides scraped out, Mark? Have they taken out your very heart and called it a "simple medical procedure"?*

She lay there waiting, knowing what would come. She only

hoped she could stand up against it, and not melt like wax before the fire.

Mark's fingers wiggled a little, betraying him, but his voice came out strong, sure. "Mandy, I just can't help thinking that maybe this was for the best."

His face had nothing "best" about it. He looked like ashes stuck together, his green eyes dull against the mottled gray.

"That God knows best, and it's his will for us." He finished with another squeeze of her hand, a stranger to her in this intimate moment.

So it fell, like a tombstone on her soul, pushing, knocking away her breath and hope in one sweeping motion.

## CHAPTER 8

wise men

Mark stepped into the hospital hallway. He wished for a quiet place to hide, to pray, for the fluorescent light above his head to stop buzzing.

*Her face. My God, her face.* He leaned against the wall, the tile behind him cool against his palms, and closed his eyes. Trying to forget the sights of the day. Amanda in the fetal position balled on the apartment floor. Begging him to help her and save the baby.

He'd never felt so inadequate. So helpless. Never had he felt so far from God. Crazy thoughts raced through his mind, hymns and verses jumbled together. *Nothing but the blood of Jesus. How precious is the flow that makes me white as snow.* The red against the white of her thigh. Sin and sacrifice, paid for in blood.

Her face, in the hospital, paler than the pillow. The checks from her gown dancing in front of his face. Dark circles shadowed her eyes. Copper hair twisted around her.

*I am looped in the loops of her hair.*

He'd asked, "How are you feeling?" A stupid question.

Two single tears began to flow out her eyes, taking on speed and strength to course down her cheeks. She didn't brush them away and they pooled, sacred springs of sorrow wetting the sides of her temples.

She held his hand like a lifeboat line, thin and slipping, holding so tight her knuckles whitened.

Then he heard the words come out of his mouth. *God's will. Best.* They tasted like bitter death on his tongue, and he watched them fall on her. Making the darkness in her eyes grow, as if way in the back a light had been extinguished.

He'd meant to soothe her. To put a balm on the hurt. Instead, he fouled the room with his presumption, poisonous and painful.

She rolled to her side, slowly, heavily, a ship tipped over in deep waters, and she didn't look at him again.

The tap of his dress shoes had sounded his defeat as he left the room to seek sanctuary in the too bright hall.

He imagined he appeared to be a grieving father, leaning outside her room, industrial bulbs highlighting him like a halo. Only he knew, he was a man afraid of the darkness in himself, of that tiny part glad this happened. Wicked, evil relief that the path to his own desires, his own will, had suddenly become clearer.

A nurse passed by with a squeaky cart and Mark wanted to hush her. To tell her people were sleeping, and could she keep that racket down? He glared after her, following the squishy steps until his gaze stopped abruptly on an incongruous sight.

James Montclair, his tie askew, drinking coffee in the waiting room. He must have sensed Mark's stare as he looked up from the magazine in front of him and put the drink down.

Standing frozen, Mark watched as his best friend, his mentor, his enemy, stood to meet him. The stifling atmosphere of the hospital unable to contain the glory of Pleasant Valley Baptist Church's senior pastor.

Mark thought at that moment he might truly hate James Montclair for coming here, now.

"Hey, buddy," James called out, striding forward. A nurse's aide watched with appreciation as he passed her desk.

"Hey." Mark felt like he'd been run under the tires of an eighteen-wheeler for about four months now, and couldn't help but feel James had done the driving.

"How is she?" An ID tag dangled from James's neck. The caption, printed under his photo, stated LIVING IN GOD'S GRACE.

"Not good," Mark said. "What're you doing here?"

"Hospital rounds. You know, the usual. Saw your name on the board, thought I'd wait. They wouldn't tell me anything. What's going on?"

Mark didn't even try to pretend. "She lost it."

"I'm sorry." James lifted an awkward hand, as if to pull Mark for a hug, but patted his shoulder instead.

"It's okay." Mark shrugged away. "God's will and all that." Punishing himself with the words. He looked at James. "Frankly, I've got no idea what God wants. From me or anybody else."

To his credit, James didn't appear shocked. "I know how you feel." He shoved his hands in his pockets, a study in rumpled elegance.

Mark raised a brow at him.

"Sarah lost one, three years ago."

"I didn't know." *You never said.*

"Yeah, it was pretty rough. On everyone."

They sat in silence a few minutes, contemplating the name board on the wall. So many people, in little rooms. Bright pink ribbons with bears dangled on some doors. Mylar balloons proclaiming IT'S A BOY! on others. And a few plain, like Amanda's, where no tiny cries echoed inside. Just pain—a silent flood, building, threatening to spill out onto the antiseptic hall and over the joy of the surrounding patients.

"Hey, I've got something for you." James withdrew his wallet. He produced a folded piece of paper, upon which his neat handwriting spelled out a name and number.

"'Ervin Plumley'?" Mark read it aloud.

"Old friend of mine. Played ball for him in college. He's running a church in the Panhandle. Small, community-type. Needs an associate, and I told him about you. You might give him a call." James gestured toward Mandy's door. "When you're ready."

"I'm not sure I'll ever be ready," Mark admitted. "I'm thinking about getting out of the ministry altogether."

"I'm sorry to hear that," James said.

Mark fiddled with the note in his hands. He looked at James. "Does he know?" He indicated the paper. "Did you tell him about the baby?"

"That's not my place. Just think about it."

Mark put the number in his suit pocket.

"Listen," James said. "Can your former pastor give you one last bit of advice?"

Mark nodded.

"About God's will. It's as much a mystery to me as anybody else. But I can tell you this . . ." James looked Mark full in the eye. "God knows what it is to have a child die." He paused, giving weight to his words. "And I don't believe he'd wish that on anyone."

James Montclair did pull Mark into a hug then. The preacher

gone and the mentor's arms around Mark, his friend. "Take care, buddy. Take care."

IN THE THOMPSON garage, Ben Thompson, immense gut hanging over faded Levi's with the loops popped off, stirred the boiling pot like a tobacco-chewing wizard. Flames from the out-door cooker, a wrought-iron instrument attached to a propane tank, cast a rosy glow to his complexion. "Come here, Mark. Need your help. It's time for the malt."

Mark rose from his position on the dusty Coleman cooler. Amanda slept inside, Dragonlady hovering over her, with the men relegated to the outdoors. Or the garage anyway.

Obedient, Mark got the big plastic spoon, and stood at atten-tion next to Ben.

"Now stir fast, try not to let any stick to the bottom. It'll burn if it gets stuck. Don't want a charcoal taste." Ben poured the thick caramel-colored liquid into the unfurling steam. "Smooth and steady, there you go."

Malt dissipated in the water, making a rich brown liquid. "Smell that?" Ben sniffed theatrically, the aroma like hot, sweet cereal. "Amber ale. Gonna be a good one. Ready in time for the season opener. Nothing better than a cool one and a kickoff."

Mark murmured his agreement, still stirring.

Ben shuffled over to the garage refrigerator, a nonreturnable olive green that Katy had deemed "horrid" upon delivery, accord-ing to family lore. The door opened with a *shlooping* sound when the airtight seal popped, and refrigeration poured out like fairy frost. Bottles tinkled in a mismatched melody as Amanda's dad dug for a specified brew.

Back at the pot with two bottles, Ben used his key chain to pry off the lids then handed one to Mark. He paused to take a deep sip and Mark did the same.

"How's the job search?" The folding chair groaned under Ben's weight.

"I've got a few more interviews lined up next week. Katy's been a big help," Mark said.

"I bet. Her web knits far and wide through the greater Houston area." Ben gestured with his drink, arcing from corner to corner, invoking a horizon image.

"I wouldn't have these contacts without her. My résumé doesn't exactly scream *ad exec.*"

"You know"—Ben stared into the bubbling pot—"you don't have to go where she tells you."

Mark bristled. "I'm not. I think the agencies would be a good start for me. And when Amanda gets well, maybe she can go back full-time."

"What about that job in the Panhandle? With Ervin whatshisname?"

"Plumley. Ervin Plumley. In Potter Springs."

"That's the one. Ever call him?"

"Just to check it out."

"Nice guy?"

"Ervin? Yeah. Seems like it anyway. Retired coach, real enthusiastic. Said he needs somebody pretty soon. Before the board changes their mind about the position."

"How's the pay?"

"Okay. But they'd give us a house, and the cost of living's low."

"Sounds like a pretty good deal." Ben accentuated this observation with a hearty belch.

"Maybe. But it's too far. And Mandy . . ." Mark looked at the house, his wife hidden inside like some sort of a wounded Rapunzel. "Like I said, I'm making a change."

"I don't know about you," Ben said. "But me, I'd take my bride and get the heck out of Dodge. Make a *real* change. Start your own lives. Away from"—he stared at the screen door—"outside influences."

Mark thought of Amanda, ensconced inside her pink ruffled room, Katy running interference and keeping him at bay. He wondered when he'd get to bring his wife back home. The tiny apartment they could no longer afford as his severance dried up like rain in the Houston heat. "You trying to get rid of me?" Mark took another drink.

"No, son. Trying to help you. Besides, aren't you from the Panhandle? Lubbock, right?"

Not technically the Panhandle, but close enough. "Yep."

"So, in a way, it'd be like going home."

Home. To windswept plains and broad fields of dancing yellow grass. Sky wrapped around the earth like a quilt, thin and high. Weather riding up like a herd of horses, clouds thundering in, seeing lightning from forty miles away. A land where sunsets were gifts brought from afar in colorful and glorious splendor.

No city smog, no traffic, no mother-in-law or failed ministry. A new start.

With no history. No credentials.

Mark shook his head, the idea too overwhelming to be tempting. "I can't think about moving right now. I've got enough on my plate getting Mandy better. Finding a job."

"In advertising."

"Yes."

"Sales and things."

"Along those lines."

"Sounds fulfilling." Ben revealed no hint of sarcasm. "Really working with people."

Mark's heart twitched. A whisper of the call tickled his spine. He felt no call at all to advertising amongst the slick and shiny. But maybe that's what he'd been doing all along.

He sighed. "Enough already. I'll call Ervin, see if the job's still open. But I'm not promising anything."

"I'm not the one you owe your promises." Ben creaked out of the chair to check the simmering brew. "She's inside. And she needs you now more than ever."

# goliath

"Here, put this in on the side." Ben Thompson grunted, sweat streaming from his forehead as he jostled the bed frame up the U-Haul's ramp.

"Don't you think over there, where there's more room?" Mark gripped the other end, the metal pinching his palm.

"Nah, this'll work." Ben gave a mighty shove and the bed frame tugged a tear in the corner of the couch. "What else we got?"

"That's about it." Mark looked away from the fresh gash in the furniture. "One more lamp, I think. Honey, do you have anything left inside?" Mark called to Amanda, who sat with Dragonlady under the shade of a magnolia tree. He couldn't hear their words, but the women's postures crackled with tension.

For all Mark knew, Katy was orchestrating a last-ditch effort to keep Amanda in Houston.

Thankfully, it didn't look like it was working.

"No, just my purse. I'll go get it." Amanda stood with effort, looking none too steady.

He hated they had to leave so soon, without the luxury of time that Amanda needed. But with the apartment lease up, and Ervin Plumley raring for their arrival, postponing the inevitable seemed foolish. They'd have to pay more to stay, and Mark figured he could take care of his wife just as well in Potter Springs as in Houston. Maybe better, without Dragonlady hovering, ready to strike.

"No, let me." He halted Amanda's progress, squeezing her shoulders. "You say good-bye to your parents and we'll head out." He went inside and made a final check of the apartment, then locked the door behind him. Holding her purse in one hand, he balanced the lamp and a fake plant under his arm.

In the parking lot, Ben embraced Amanda. Great tears rolled down his face as he hugged his daughter tight.

She kissed his cheek, her own eyes dry, and whispered, "Bye, Daddy."

After closing the back of the rig, Mark started the U-Haul and blasted the air-conditioning. He retrieved Mr. Chesters' carrier and shoved it in the small space behind the seat, and received a heated hiss in response.

Clearing Amanda's side, he set her new atlas on the console. He'd bought it at Wal-Mart for five dollars, a little treat for the road. He had wandered in the store—what do you give a woman who leaves hearth and home to follow you out west, to chase after your dream when hers died in a hospital in Houston?

He sensed something had broken in her that day, had flowed out with all that blood. She couldn't seem to shake her sorrow and Mark didn't know what to do to help her. He forged this crazy plan and hoped a change would spark her spirit.

Instead of flowers or candy, or even a piece of jewelry, he bought her a map. Something to look at, to navigate by. To see they had a future, and it was real.

When Amanda parted from her father, Mark held the door open and ready. He helped her inside, lifting her tenderly onto the cushioned seat. He paid extra for the deluxe cab model, and when she sank into it, he sensed a gratefulness that he had done at least this one small thing right.

Holding her close, he caught a scent of copper pennies. "You all set?" The tired in her eyes made his voice catch.

"Ready." She clicked her seat belt into place.

Ben came up to the side of the truck and patted it as if it were a thoroughbred. "Got that Toyota latched tight. Shouldn't give you any problems."

"Thank you. For everything." Though Mark had refused financial help from Amanda's parents, Ben's simple advice had made the difference. A catalyst to snap him out of his fog and see the truth.

*She needs you now more than ever.*

They shook hands, and Mark took his place in the driver's seat.

Katy came around for her good-bye, poking her frosty blonde hair through Mark's window.

He braced the steering wheel. "Thanks for every—"

"You take care of my daughter, Mark."

Her voice was so low he barely caught it.

"You hear me? Take good care of my daughter."

She didn't smile when she said it.

"I plan to," Mark replied. He gunned the motor and, with his bride secure in the passenger seat, left imaginary skid marks on Houston.

*       *       *

TUMBLEWEEDS CHASED EACH other over the highway like long-legged spiders dancing in ghost ribbons of red dust. Under the wheels of the U-Haul, the lifeless branches fragmented, pieces spiraled behind them in a sharp-edged wake.

For the greater part of the trip, Amanda sat silent, perched atop a mountain of maxi-pads. She shifted only to change the radio, and to alleviate pressure on her tender parts. Mostly she looked out the window and watched the trees thin as the landscape grew flatter and the sky grew larger as if it would swallow her whole.

"Mandy?" Mark turned down the radio, speaking loudly over the U-Haul's incessant roar. Wind whiffled through invisible spaces, making conversation difficult, if not impossible.

"Hmmm?" Amanda didn't look up from her new atlas. On the map, Potter Springs looked flat and ugly, with no green hatch signs for trees, no blurry browns for mountain ridges. Just thin black and blue lines, like varicose veins, weaving sparsely through a sea of white.

"You getting hungry at all? There's a town ahead, about forty more miles. We can get gas, take in the scenery."

Since leaving South Texas, the landscape had bleached to a burnt gold color, dotted with panting cows and divided by fencing. As if the poor beasts had strength enough to wander.

Amanda knew Mark sought to coax her from herself, to fill the growing gap between them. She wanted to reach him too, but everything within her seemed to fold in on itself, curling up, trying to heal. She just didn't have the energy to do more.

"No, I'm not all that hungry." The stale smoke smell in the rented truck made her nauseous, and the toast from this morning sat in her stomach like two slabs of cement. To be nice, she added, "But a break sounds good."

"Okay, then." He smiled, as if pleased with her effort, and the sound of the road reigned again.

In the flat expanse, the vegetation itself seemed to struggle for refreshment. For life. Each dot on the map proved to be a wasteland of peeling houses and junked-out farm equipment. Trees tilted sideways and old grocery stores boasted boards instead of windows.

Amanda looked for mile signs like oasis markers, hoping they'd enter Mayberry country soon.

They hadn't spoken much since The Big Talk. The one where Mark laid out possibilities for their future, plans that included leaving Houston, her job and her family for a new position at a rinky-dink church in the middle of nowhere.

Maybe it was the painkillers, but his vivid descriptions about the high plains and the wide, open spaces had worn her down. That old connection tugged at her. Her lover, her mate, imploring when reason argued otherwise. She'd never been reasonable when it came to Mark, just instinctual. Stepping in time to his music, naturally matching the rhythm of his heart.

And now, when her own heart beat slower, duller, wrapped in a cloak of pain, she simply trusted him. To make the decisions when, for her, rising out of bed seemed a daunting task. They would go to Potter Springs, together.

Just the two of them.

Like it used to be.

Somewhere south of nowhere, an eighteen-wheeler lay flat on its side like a vanquished Goliath, felled by the mighty invisible wind. Sparkly blue paint shot reflections as they passed. The trucker stood alongside the rig, scratching his head.

"Should we pull over?" Amanda stared as they whizzed by.

"No, a cop'll be along any minute. He's got a radio for help. And we're supposed to be in Potter by dinner."

Sure enough, the next mile brought the flashing lights of a state trooper. *Probably by now,* Amanda thought, *another trucker was already there.* She hoped so anyway. The man looked so lost.

"How much farther?" she asked, even though she could see for herself on the map.

"Not too much," Mark answered. "A few more hours, after we stop for gas."

She bent over to find her flip-flops, feeling a warm gush between her legs. She straightened and rubbed the small of her back, hoping with every hope in her body that Potter Springs would be the refuge she needed.

A place to heal.

POTTER SPRINGS, TEN MORE MILES, read the sign. Mark saw Amanda shift straighter in her seat. He snapped off the radio and rolled down the window, letting the town's breath roll into the stagnant U-Haul.

The minutes passed slowly, the landscape still yellow and flat. They rode in silence, with only the music of the rushing wind and the occasional roar of an oncoming car or truck. The road narrowed and dipped down, and the landscape turned greener on either side.

He glanced at her to see if she noticed the green. Green, he knew, was important to her.

WELCOME TO POTTER SPRINGS! announced a hand-painted placard with a cow on it. POPULATION 10,927. Tended shrubs grew at the base. No trash cluttered the embankments leading into town.

They passed a few truck stops and twenty-four-hour coffee shops. In town, a sixties-inspired post office threatened to take off for outer space at any minute. Mark eased the U-Haul to a halt at a light in Potter Springs' downtown square.

Their new hometown.

The courthouse, with red-brown brick and a towering steeple, dominated the four surrounding streets. Manicured trees and a statue of a man on a horse decorated the grassy area around the building.

Slowly Mark circled the corners. An old movie marquee proclaimed two evening shows of last year's blockbuster. In front of an ice-cream shop, customers lounged on wrought-iron chairs, visiting and swatting at flies. A mother shared a vanilla cone with her baby, pushing the stroller back and forth with her foot.

An antique shop displayed a rusty tricycle and a wide-eyed doll in a wicker carriage. The banner overhead, DOWNTOWN MINI- ALL, had a faded place where the M for *Mall* must have been. As if the owner preferred the more inclusive title and left well enough alone.

"Need anything?" Mark pointed to the eclectic store. "They've got it 'all,'" he punned, hoping to cheer her with bad humor. Hoping she didn't hate this small town on sight.

This elicited a small smile from her. "No."

"Let's do it then." He turned down a long street, where they passed a Dairy Queen, a tire shop and an orange building with *B-B-Q* painted in bold black letters.

They veered left again, to a neighborhood with pastel houses with large front porches. Decades-old columns strained against pitched roofs like strongman Samson from the Bible. Some yards had dogs tied on long metal chains, and too many cars parked out front. Windows looked like mismatched little girls in various shades of curtains. Not the elegant wood blinds of their Houston apartment, in muted tones of bone and alabaster.

Katy Thompson, he knew, would hate this neighborhood.

On their new street, Mesquite, they turned right. About halfway down, trucks, minivans and people crowded around a yellow house with green trim and a bright red door. The garage yawned open, empty save for folding chairs and coolers beside tables with checked cloths.

Mark slowed even more and they pulled into the driveway, narrow and cracked as an old woman's face. He killed the engine, wondering what his bride thought of this strange threshold. "Ready?"

"Yes."

She looked terrified.

Katy Thompson would despise this house. Dragonlady, no doubt, would sneer at these people.

But would her daughter?

# CHAPTER 10

# potter springs

Amanda had never seen a religious authority's naked legs before. Not counting Mark's anyway.

Ervin Plumley's legs looked like chicken limbs fresh out of the plastic bag. Pinkish white and plucked, with saggy skin around the joints.

Over a barrel-shaped torso, he wore a monogrammed knit shirt tucked into coach's shorts. The emblem on his shirt read LAKEVIEW COMMUNITY CHURCH. Sweat stains soaked through the underarms in spite of the Panhandle's cooler temperature. What he lacked in appearances, he made up for in enthusiasm.

"Howdy . . . howdy . . . hi!" he shouted up to the U-Haul. Pearly teeth shone through his beard as he waved a tanned forearm.

Several women started up from folding lawn chairs in a circle on the driveway. A brunette smoothed her skirt over slender hips. An elderly grandmother type scuttled to a folding table and adjusted some serving pieces. One lady pulled a compact from her purse and checked her lipstick.

Amanda realized they looked as nervous as she felt, and found strength enough to unbuckle her seat belt. She stepped down to the cracked driveway and leaned in to get Mr. Chesters in his traveling cage, covered with a towel to keep him from going ballistic. A bewildered mewl sounded from inside. The cat's weight shifted, tilting the carrier in her hand.

Mark came around the truck and took the box from her. "We can do this."

"I know. I'm okay." She wasn't okay, but he tried so hard. He'd handled everything from the planning to the packing, taking care of her along the way. Pulled all this together, not just for himself, but for her too. They both wanted this move to work, and she would do her best to see that it did. After all, she'd signed on for the long haul. For better or for worse.

Looking at her new life, at a group of complete strangers, she couldn't tell which end of that spectrum she faced.

"You'll see," Mark whispered. "It'll be fine. Hang in there." His lips came soft against her hair. He faced the small gathering. "Well, we made it!" After setting the case down, he threw his arms wide. The triumphant traveler.

A spattering of applause ran through the group, a few men in cutoffs and Wranglers came up and clapped Mark on the back.

Amanda freed Mr. Chesters, coaxing his shaking form from the shadows near the back of the cage. She wished, for an instant, she could trade places with him and hide in a small, dark place.

"Quite a rig you got there." A tall man with a wide Western belt smacked the side of the U-Haul. "What kind of mileage she get?"

"Eight to ten."

The man whistled through his teeth, low and long. "At least it's a one-way trip," he reasoned. "I'm Joe Don Wexley."

"Mark Reynolds. Good to know you."

"Well, we're not paying for the return drive, so I guess you're stuck with us." The chicken-legged man edged close to the U-Haul and pumped Mark's hand up and down a few times. "Good to see you again, son."

The interview process had been mostly by telephone, but Ervin and Mark held a meeting in Dallas, a halfway point, to shake hands and discuss particulars while Amanda recovered in Houston. She didn't know what excuse Mark had used for her absence at that final interview, but the miscarriage wasn't part of the dialogue.

"No need to air our problems," Mark had said.

Our problems. She understood. James Montclair hadn't told, and the new church didn't know about the baby or the miscarriage. It would be Mark and Amanda's secret.

The new job depended on it.

Mark's boss smiled at Amanda. "Ervin Plumley. Glad to finally lay eyes on you."

Ervin turned back to the house. "Hope y'all like it. We've tried to get her shipshape for you, but if there's anything you need, just let us know."

The house looked like an unruly toddler who'd just had a scrubbing. Freshly painted trim brightened uneven brick, a new cedar swing hung from the tiny porch. Flowerbeds wound around the edges of the house. Plantings of yellow flowers with big, dark eyes bobbed in the wind, nodding hello to the newcomers.

Joe Don hooked a thumb in his belt loop. "Me and the boys got down under the house for you. Plumbing's sound. Wiring's covered, no termites. That's the thing about pier and beam, you can figure out what the he . . ."—Joe Don shot a guilty look at Ervin—". . . eck's going on without having to get a jackhammer."

A small woman with dark eyes stood on the edge of their conversation. "Pansies." Her soft voice in the midst of the deeper tones drew Amanda's attention.

"I'm sorry?" Amanda put Mr. Chesters down, and he darted to the side of the house, his tail splayed out like a toilet brush. She hoped he wouldn't go far.

"Pansies. They're only annuals—so if you don't like them, you can take them out." The woman bit her lip, looking at the cheerful beds. "Do you like them?"

Dirt formed semicircles on the tips of the gardener's nails as she twisted the end of her T-shirt.

"Yes," Amanda decided. "I'm Amanda Reynolds."

"Of course." The woman raised her hand, then noticed her soil-stained fingers and did a quick retreat. "Oh!" She settled on a short, flappy wave. "Yes, hi. Um, I'm Missy Underwood. That's my husband, Jimmy."

Jimmy was bent over digging in a cooler, so all Amanda could see were jean shorts riding dangerously low on a flat behind.

"You can meet him in a minute." Missy's face reddened and she focused on the flowers again. "We weren't sure what kind you'd want, or even if you garden. We went with something seasonal that would last. With fall coming on, they should make it through winter."

"I don't know much about gardening, really." At Missy's crestfallen expression, Amanda added, "But I do want to learn."

"Oh, I'm no expert either." Missy's words fell over themselves like eager puppies. "But I can tell you about pansies. I planted some at my house, and they're going gangbusters." Missy shoved her hands in the deep pockets of her culottes. "I don't mean to sound like I'm bragging."

"No, not at all." The smell of the cut grass and new paint wrapped around Amanda like a comforter, even as the ache resonated through her inner thighs to the bottoms of her feet. She hadn't stood this long in a while.

Ervin's drawl to the men overrode their conversation. "Joe Don here runs a farm way south of town, and he's a handy fella to know when it comes to fixing most things."

Joe Don shuffled his left boot under this great praise.

"He's the one who did most of the work on the house for y'all," Ervin said.

"Thank you so much." Mark shared a glance with Amanda. "I can't tell you how much we appreciate being able to move right in."

"Well, we want you to feel like Potter Springs is home." Ervin clasped an arm around Mark's shoulder. "We're glad to have you, son. So glad to have you."

The preacher turned to Amanda. He wasn't very tall, so she didn't have to crane her neck to look at him. His eyes were brown and opaque. He took her hand gently, not a shake really, but a hand-holding. "And you too, little miss. Welcome to Potter."

Amanda pulled away first. "The house looks beautiful. Thank you."

"My gosh." Ervin slapped his forehead. "Here I am yapping at y'all, and you're probably dead on your feet. Peggy, come on over here and help these kids inside the house."

Peggy radiated competence as she marched up to the group in soft-soled nurse's shoes. She stood four inches taller than Ervin and outweighed him by thirty pounds. She wore a shiny floral shirt over stretchy pants. Her short curly hair had more than a few specks of gray twisted in it.

"I'm Peggy, Ervin's wife. Been married twenty-eight years, and he's hauled me all over the state of Texas, and some other places too." She didn't shake hands but grabbed Amanda immediately into a crushing hug. "I know just how you feel, honeygirl."

"Oh, I'm all right," Amanda murmured into the polyester folds. "A little tired."

"It'll get better," Peggy assured as she patted Amanda's back in a soothing rhythm. As if she'd known her forever, or was kin somehow. "And you'll like Potter Springs too. Maybe not now, but it'll grow on you. It's like a fungus that way, but a good kind."

When Peggy released her, Amanda realized she'd been hugging the woman back.

The men circled around Mark, talking, asking him questions. He looked for her over their shoulders, and she nodded to him, *I'm okay.*

Nonverbal marital permission. *Go ahead and play with the boys, I'll go crochet with the womenfolk. My heart isn't broken, and I can't wait to exchange cookie recipes.*

Mark went back to whatever story he was telling. As Amanda followed Peggy across the driveway, she heard the men's laughter and knew he had them in the palm of his hand already. Golden-boy.

Peggy ushered Amanda through the bustling one-car garage and shooed the welcoming women out of the way. "Y'all get back to the truck and start bringing the little stuff in. Amanda here needs to sit down a minute, and she don't need y'all pecking around her like a bunch of hens."

"Who's calling who a hen around here?" In the kitchen, a rosy-cheeked woman with oversized pot-holder mittens took a steaming casserole out of the oven. "I'm Shelinda James," she announced, shoving the oven door closed with one skinny hip. Placing the dish with care on the stovetop, she grinned at

Amanda. "Hope you like King Ranch. We've got this for your dinner and a few more frozen besides."

"Thanks so much, you didn't have to—" All the faces, the sincere smiles, combined to overwhelm Amanda. She couldn't arrange her own expression in an appropriate response.

But no one seemed to notice, or mind in the least.

"It's nothing. Really, we're just busybodies and wanted to be the first to get a good look at you." Shelinda laughed and covered the casserole with foil. "If I get to vote, I think you'll do just fine." She pointed a spatula. "And don't you talk her ear off, Peggy. We want her to *like* us."

"Shelinda, hush now and get on out to the truck." Peggy flapped her arms. "You can start with the kitchen things."

"She's bossy, but good as gold, Mrs. Reynolds. I'll catch up with you later. Maybe have coffee or something."

The woman's easy manner and offer of companionship pulled at Amanda. She sensed a future friend here. "Please, call me Amanda."

"Amanda then." Shelinda nodded with a smile. "Welcome home." The ruffled lace curtains on the back door fluttered as she stepped out into the garage.

Home. She sat in a cool metal card chair in the quiet of the empty den. The house wasn't much bigger than a cracker box, but the voices outside remained thankfully muted.

Peggy's pants made scratchy sounds as she seated herself next to Amanda.

Red and orange streaks filtered through the high windows from the backyard. Leaves swayed, making cutout pictures of light. *A tree. My backyard has a tree.* She'd taken trees for granted in south Texas. Not anymore.

Potter Springs hadn't been quite the Mayberry she'd hoped for. But not as bad as she'd feared either.

Dusty on the outskirts, flat all the way through. But green in town, just like Mark had said. Their postage-stamp lawn, the tree, the shrubs here and there. Green meant someone took the time to water. To nurture. Making green must take a long time in the Texas Panhandle.

Amanda wondered if she'd ever be green again.

Soft hands covered hers and squeezed. Peggy shifted on the chair to get closer. "Now, tell me, honeygirl. How was the trip? How are *you*?"

And to Amanda's surprise, waves of unshed tears rushed from her eyes and made dotted patterns on Peggy Plumley's polyester pants.

CHAPTER 11

brother's keeper

The church resembled a Monopoly house with four square sides and a low-pitched roof. A slender steel gray steeple drove up into the sky like a solitary fence post, and variegated bushes surrounded a brick sign with LAKEVIEW COMMUNITY CHURCH etched into deep grooves.

Mark climbed out of the passenger seat of Ervin's white double-cab pickup. A pungent aroma wafted from the blacktop parking lot. All around the brown building, prairie flowed like a gentle pond. Long grasses fluttered like cattails in the breeze. The plains were dry as stacked hay, without a lake in sight.

"Lakeview?" Mark asked.

"No lake," Ervin confirmed. He nestled a wooden toothpick between his teeth. "But you gotta admit, it's quite a view."

81

A bird called high above, soaring under the wisps of clouds. A tractor far down the road turned off the main route. The grinding machinery puffed dirt in its wake.

Ervin tossed a set of keys into Mark's chest. "For your office. And that." He pointed to a small pickup, blue with white lettering. LAKEVIEW COMMUNITY, it read, with a stylized lake and tree on the side. "For running around in," Ervin explained. "Smokes a little, but it'll get you from here to there."

"Thanks." Mark shoved the keys into the pocket of his khakis.

They entered the building through a side door with a metal frame and handle. Ervin pushed easily inside.

"Not locked?"

"Nah. Not during the daytime anyhow. We don't have much worth stealing. They want it bad enough"—the door squeaked behind them—"come on in and get it."

The interior smelled like an old school library, of books, dust and gathered bodies gone stale. "Down here's the sanctuary." Ervin disappeared through double oak doors. Mark followed.

Inside, pews lined straight across with an aisle dividing them. No stage, but a simple oak communion table had the familiar words on the side: THIS DO IN REMEMBRANCE OF ME. It had been a long while since Mark had seen an altar like that.

"It's not so fancy, I know," Ervin's voice echoed in the sanctuary. No elegant Muzak filled the silence. "But we're doing a fall fund-raiser, to spruce up the place a little. Get some greenery. Peggy says we need more greenery." At this, Ervin placed his hands on his hips, an old coach surveying the playing field. With his belly pushing the elastic of the coaching shorts to maximum support, his white legs encased in tube socks and tennis shoes, Ervin couldn't look any more opposite James Montclair if he'd tried.

Mark didn't guess that Ervin tried much, as far as appearances went.

"You'll be wanting to see your office." Ervin led him down yet another hall, another door. Seated at a small desk, a gray-haired woman in a violent polka-dot dress attacked a typewriter with a vengeance.

"Hi, Letty!" Ervin called above the *rata-tat-tat* as if greeting a long lost friend.

"Hello." Letty scowled, her fingers frozen above the keys.

"This here's Letty Hodges. Letty, meet Mark Reynolds, our new associate pastor."

"Mr. Reynolds." Letty nodded in greeting and adjusted Coke-bottle glasses farther up her pinched nose.

"You can call me Mark." He offered a hand. For the briefest of instances, he thought she'd refuse. But then she grasped it, brief and cold, leaving behind the distinctive odor of Ben-Gay.

"You may call me Ms. Hodges."

"Miss Letty's my best gal Friday," Ervin said. "Actually, my only gal Friday. Been working here long 'fore I ever showed up. Came with the building, I think."

For this, Ervin was rewarded with a one-sided sneer, which might have been Letty's excuse for a smile.

"She'll work for both of us till the board sees fit to throw us more money for another assistant. She's more'n glad to help out, though. Aren't you, Letty?"

"I'll do my best." She shuffled papers on her desk and heaved a great sigh.

"I won't add much to your load," Mark offered. "I'm pretty self-sufficient."

"Just make sure you give me notice." Letty sniffed. "I've got plenty to do as it is. And I don't make coffee."

Mark thought a retreat at this point might be his best strategy. "Nice to meet you, Ms. Hodges," he lied.

She made no reply, but the typewriter roared back to life.

Ervin laughed at her rudeness. "See you later, doll!" He yelled to Mark over the noise, "Let's go see your office!"

They stopped in front of a putty-colored door with a small sign, JANITOR'S CLOSET. From inside, sounds of a deep bass thumped under a steel guitar. The music drifted out in patterned bursts.

"Is this . . . ?"

"No, no. I just want you to meet Benny. Benny!" Ervin pounded on the door. "Benny, it's me, Erv. Open up!"

The knob rattled and a skinny teenager holding a half-eaten bag of Chee•tos answered. Benny wore a black T-shirt that read SMOOTH. He wiped his fingers on it, leaving orange streaks like snail trails. Behind him, the closet contained shelves of industrial cleaning supplies, a stack of black rubber trash cans, a dusty vacuum and a portable stereo. "Yeah?"

"Benny, meet Mark Reynolds, our new associate. Mark, this is Benny Ripple, one of our junior custodians."

Benny tossed his greasy hair in a gesture of greeting. "Hey."

"Hey," Mark answered in kind. "Cool shirt."

A flash of respect crossed Benny's pockmarked features. "Thanks."

The closed door muffled the thumping music again, and Mark and Ervin continued on their way. As they walked, Ervin explained, "Benny's a good kid, but he's had a hard run. Him working here is . . . a favor for a friend."

Mark nodded. *A favor for a friend.* He remembered James Montclair handing him the number in the hospital and wondered if he was yet another favor from Ervin Plumley. At this point, he didn't care. He needed the job.

The associate's office was tucked around the corner from the janitor's closet. The door had no nameplate, or even a number. In fact, nothing suggested it wasn't a restroom or an extension of Benny's hangout.

"Used to be a book room. Storage for the library," Ervin said. Inside, a teacher's desk and two plastic chairs completely filled the space. Wallpaper, printed with a faux paneling design, peeled away at the corners. On the right hung a city map of Potter Springs. An oversize calendar, torn to September, covered the warped wood desk. The only decorations consisted of fresh ivy in a daisy pot and a FARMERS FIGHT coffee mug full of sharpened pencils and blue pens.

"The plant's from Peggy." Ervin indicated the container. "Greenery."

"Tell her thanks for me."

"Don't have a computer yet. Got a line on a used one, though. Should be here by the end of the month. Until then"—Ervin yanked hard on one of the drawers—"you'll have to make do with these." He lifted a stack of yellow pads.

Mark thought of his state-of-the-art computer in Houston. His executive mahogany desk. "That'll be fine."

"Why don't you try it out?" Ervin pulled back the plastic chair with great aplomb.

Mark obliged, arranging his long legs under the desk. If he stretched his feet far enough forward, he'd be able to kick his door shut without leaving his chair. He pulled a pad of paper to the center and scribbled his name on it. "Works great!" He felt like an idiot.

Ervin stood at the bookcase. "There's plenty of room for your things, and, hopefully, we'll get you a stipend to buy whatever else you might need." He ran his hand down the metal shelves, the corner of which edged up to a woven shade. "What's this?" Ervin tugged at the tweed fabric, which had to be thirty years old. Dust flew as the shade curled up.

"Well, I'll be!" Ervin looked like he'd just discovered pluto-nium. "Didn't know this room had a window. Maybe we should swap offices."

Outside was a view of the parking lot and a rusty Dumpster with paper cups spilling out of garbage bags. Blackbirds scattered like cockroaches at the noise from the window.

Not quite the wall-to-wall windows from Mark's former office, with the breathtaking view of downtown Houston.

"Oh well." Ervin sighed at the unappealing sight. "Can't win 'em all."

Mark watched the birds descend again, scavengers on the trash. Their ebony feathers shone, as if they'd pomaded them before making their daily rounds.

"Listen," Ervin said. "I've got someone else I want you to meet. Dale Ochs, chairman of our board. Sells house policies when he's not hanging out up here. Kind of the king of the overseers as far as the deacons go. Takes his job real serious." Ervin winked. "Mighta taken yours too, if he'd been the one deciding. We'll do lunch on the square, at JoJo's Steaks 'n' More. You'll find it. It's next to the jail."

AT JOJO'S, MARK sat at a shellacked pine table and ordered iced tea from a paper menu. Nearby, farmers with weary eyes and tall boots thickened the air with cigarette smoke. Apparently, the smoking section entailed all the windowed areas, with the center reserved for nonsmokers. *A handy system,* Mark thought, wiping his watering eyes.

Ervin entered, hollering hello to several patrons who waved

back. Next to him stood a short man in stacked boots. The man had tight curls at the nape of his neck and a proud, beakish nose. He held his arms about four inches away from his torso, and after approaching the table, nearly crushed Mark's hand with the strength of his shake. "Dale Ochs, glad to meetcha."

All three men ordered prime rib, the daily special. The steak arrived well done, covered in dark gravy and mashed potatoes. Mark eyed the brown meat, knowing full well he'd ordered his rare. He'd never seen prime rib served with gravy in his life, but decided not to push it. He finished his salad, pure iceberg with slivered carrots, preslathered in ranch dressing.

"Dale here's done a great job with our board." Ervin scooped some gravy from his dinner plate and dribbled it on his salad. "Set up a new system for communion to the shut-ins and snow-plowing in the winter. Beats anything we've done in the past."

"I'd like to hear about it." Mark tried not to watch Ervin as he chomped the now tan-colored lettuce.

"Sure," said Dale. "I'll do you one better. Come on to the next meeting and we'll sign you up a spot. Put you on the communion rotation. That is, unless you don't want to get your hands dirty." Dale set his iced tea down. A gold pinkie ring twinkled at Mark.

"Not at all." Mark forced himself to be pleasant in the face of the man's obvious baiting.

"Communion's not hard," Dale commented. "Basically, we air out the faithful geezers, pour a little juice down their throats, lead them in a prayer or two." Dale's silverware scraped through the overcooked meat as he sliced in precise squares. "After a couple of rounds with me, you should be able to keep up."

"Thanks," Mark said. "I'm sure I can wing it."

"James Montclair says this kid's the real deal." Ervin puffed up, a coach landing this season's star recruit. "Got the passion, got the know-how, got the goods."

"That right?" Dale speared a bit of steak. "So," he asked, chewing, "how come a city boy like yourself left that big old church in Houston, come all the way out here for this?" He waved his fork at JoJo's clientele and the quiet square outside.

"Needed a change in scenery, I guess." Mark kept his voice pleasantly level. A trick he'd learned in seminary. "Following the Lord's will you know. Never can tell where it'll take you." Safety in platitudes.

Dale sipped his tea. "I find, sometimes people move 'cause they're running. Got something to hide." He wiped his hook nose with a paper napkin. "Not always, but sometimes."

"How interesting." Mark gave a bland smile.

"Like me!" Ervin interjected. "Got outta coaching 'cause I couldn't stand the hours. Sure do miss the games, though," he added wistfully, gazing out on the main thoroughfare as if a team might be warming up there.

"One of my spiritual gifts"—Dale made no acknowledgment of Ervin's reminiscence—"you might say, is discernment." He focused intently on Mark. "Telling truth from a lie. Comes in handy with the board, restoring the flock to the right order. I consider it my life's work."

"I thought you sold insurance." Mark refolded his napkin.

"Sure does!" Ervin enthused. "Got the biggest office in Potter, his name on a billboard and everything."

"Insurance is my livelihood," Dale agreed. "But ministry, leading the righteous in spirit and in truth . . ." He took the check from the aproned waitress. "I'll get that, sugar."

Dale signed the bill, then continued. "*Righteousness,* now that's my passion."

"I'll keep that in mind." Mark tipped his tea glass.

"See that you do." Dale's teeth flashed as he signed the bill. "And we'll get along just fine."

"Two peas in a pod!" pronounced Ervin, a coffee stain growing on his cotton shirt.

"Closer than brothers." Dale stopped smiling. "And I don't mind being my brother's keeper. At all."

CHAPTER 12

the price is right

A deafening car commercial poured from the television and filled the small living room where Amanda sprawled with Mr. Chesters on the couch.

On screen, a scrawny salesman sat with his four grandchildren in the back of a used double-cab Chevy. "Putter to Potter, to Hemp's Used Motor-way. Where the prices are low, and the people are friend-lay!"

The doorbell rang, and Amanda muted the jingle she'd heard so many times. Unsettling Mr. Chesters, she peeked through the miniblinds. Wanda Zimmerman. Again.

"Hi, Mrs. Zimmerman." Amanda held the door open a crack and the autumn sun poured inside.

"My, you've got it awfully dark in there." Mrs. Zimmerman's

eyes fairly danced over the interior of the house. Waiting, no doubt, for an invitation to come inside. In one hand, she held a black poodle, in the other a Tupperware dish.

"I was napping." Amanda didn't soft-soap her response, knowing it wouldn't matter if she said she'd been performing open-heart surgery.

"Oh, I'm sorry." Mrs. Zimmerman craned her neck for a closer look down the hallway. "We sure hate to interrupt you."

The woman didn't look sorry at all. Her hair was freshly teased from the beauty parlor and today's culottes were a sassy lime green. Spiffed up to go a-calling.

"I've brought this soup over for you, cream of mushroom. Mark told me how much he liked it last week, so I made extra."

Amanda believed Mrs. Zimmerman had a crush on Mark, in spite of their forty-year age difference. "Thank you so much." She took the bowl, still frozen solid as if Wanda had whipped it out of the freezer on a whim. A good excuse to pop in on her favorite next-door neighbor.

"Thought you might have it for your lunch. He should be home soon, right?" Wanda patted the puffy sphere atop the dog's head.

"About a half hour or so. I'll tell him you came by."

"Oh, don't worry about it. I'll probably be out walking Princess, and catch him when he pulls in. It's a lovely day. Have you been out?"

"Not yet." As if the woman didn't know already. With a picture window covered only with sheers, and supersonic telescopic hearing, Mrs. Zimmerman had the inside track on virtually everything.

"Well, I'll see you around the yard, I guess." She waggled Princess's paw in good-bye.

*Not if I see you first.* Amanda closed the door and returned to her show.

A dizzying pattern flashed above the host's coiffed head. "And it's back to you, Tammy. What will be your bid on this beautiful white sofa bed?"

Amanda sipped her coffee, bitter from hours on the burner after Mark's early departure for church, and watched the contestants hop up and down while the audience screamed numbers.

*Come on, Tammy. Go for the undercut and bid a dollar.* She put the mug back on the antique chest next to her breakfast remains, an empty carton of yogurt and crooked bone crusts from cinnamon toast.

Flopping back on her own couch, she ran a finger over the unraveled edge. She never got around to fixing it. Maybe she should get to a furniture store today and look around.

Or maybe not.

She tucked the frayed part into obscurity and readjusted the fleece blanket over her legs. Her movements twisted the waistband on her pajama bottoms, borrowed from Mark's dresser. She slid a hand under her cocoon to adjust the worn cotton.

Her stomach was still squashy, like a layer of bread dough. She didn't dwell on it. She was tired of dwelling and tired of crying.

The cordless phone buzzed on the antique chest and interrupted her self-evaluation. Picking it up, she read the caller ID. Ben Thompson. *Sorry, Mama, I just can't.* Setting the phone down, she sent silent apologies in the general direction of Houston.

The machine kicked on. A loud beep, then her mother's voice. "Amanda. Amanda, baby, I know you're there. You're probably lying on that wretched couch watching television." An audible intake of breath, a phone-call smoke under way.

"It's all right if you don't want to talk to me. If you're too *busy* with your new life up in Potter Springs." The heavy guilt tone seeped through the phone line like toxic gas.

Amanda nestled farther into the cushions. Her new life. Where she dodged invitations from Shelinda for coffee. Avoiding "How are you, honeygirl?" phone calls from Peggy, and hiding when Missy delivered a welcome basket to her door.

Amanda told herself she was just settling in, but she didn't believe it.

"Anyway"—an exhale—"you might call your father sometime this week. He's worried about you. I tell him you are *just fine,* but of course he doesn't believe me. And I don't know why he should, it's not like I've *spoken* with you this week, to know for sure."

Her mother let that marinate a moment or two.

"Well, that's all I have, baby girl. I'll talk to you soon." Katy Thompson hung up without a good-bye or *I love you*, as was her tradition.

Amanda pushed a button, amplifying Tammy's delirious screams, drowning out the silence.

"Miss Tammy, tell me this . . . how would you like to win . . . a NEW CAR!" Bob said the magic words, and Tammy launched into an ecstatic explanation of how winning this ice blue seven-passenger minivan would be an absolute answer to prayer.

The phone rang again, interrupting Tammy's enthusiasms. The church number came up, *Lakeview Com* broken off at the top. Mark. Amanda cleared her throat. "Hello?"

"Amanda?"

She always thought it funny that Mark asked. As if some other strange woman would answer their phone in the middle of the day.

"Hi." She tilted the phone to the side and coughed again, to expel the morning frog.

"You feeling okay? Sounds like you're getting a cold." Concern filled his voice.

Since the baby, Mark had tiptoed around her health. He never mentioned the miscarriage, just made vague references to her general well-being.

Maybe he feared if he mentioned *baby,* she'd come apart like a rag doll. That she'd spill lumpy grief on him, exposing her unpretty insides.

"No, I'm good," she lied. Knowing he didn't want the truth. He wanted her to hurry up and get over it, so for both their sakes she would pretend that she had. "Just lazy. I slept in a little this morning."

"Oh. Well, that's okay. You probably need the rest."

"Probably." She eyed her open journal on the floor next to the couch. Instead of Mark's shoulder, she cried on flat pages. Gushed out stored sorrows in a muddy flood, ugly words written in a spiral notebook. She wrote letters to the baby, tried out names.

Amanda believed, in her heart, that her baby had been a girl. She would have named her Grace.

"How's work?" She changed the subject to a safe topic and picked up a pen.

"My computer came in. It's a total dinosaur, but I've got my office all set up. I'd love for you to come up here and see it. When you're feeling better."

She doodled on the empty page. Daisies, shooting stars, and the name Grace Reynolds, over and over.

Grace would have had Mark's fair hair and long fingers, and would have been naughty and funny and wonderful. Grace would have filled Amanda's days with coos and cries and diapers.

Maybe with Grace, Amanda would feel a connection to this place—the place where her baby would be born. She'd push the carriage through the square, like the other moms, and share a melting ice cream with Grace. The sweet cold would touch perfect rosebud lips and she'd watch her baby's eyes sparkle.

"Listen." Mark's tension cut through her silence. "They've got a women's social coming up soon." He softened his voice with an encouraging lilt. "Their fall kickoff, a kind of a getting-to-know-you thing. It'd be a great chance for you to meet more of the women. There'll be a luncheon, maybe a speaker. What do you think?"

*That I'd rather have a root canal?* "Oh, I don't know, Mark. I'm just not sure if I'm ready."

If Amanda had Grace, she would be eager to make friends instead of staying home on Sundays, each week's excuse lamer than before. They'd throw her a shower with flowers and ribbons and balloons. Precious things for baby Grace. She'd fill in her book, put Potter Springs, Texas, on the space for place of birth, and would laugh with her daughter about how it had no spring. She'd love this town and these people because of her baby.

But there was no baby. And there never would be.

The day she checked out of the hospital, when the doctor came in with his starched coat and cold eyes, he'd told her. Gave a fancy name that meant your womb is no good. *Close to impossible,* he'd said. Made condolences, shook Mark's hand and left.

Mark, holding her clumsily as she sat stunned in the hospital-issue wheelchair, telling her everything would be okay.

But it wasn't okay. Their baby had died, and so had her dreams. They would never have a family and now she was stuck in this town with no friends and no desire to make them.

"It's just that, well, everybody wants to meet you. There are some really nice people here."

"Like Letty? Or Dale?"

"No. There are others, believe it or not. Like when we moved in. A whole congregation full. You'll like them, I promise."

I promise. She'd heard them before. *It'll be better in Potter Springs. We'll get through this, Mandy. I'm here for you. Always.*

I promise. *To have and to hold. For better and for worse. In sickness and in health.*

*Till death, do we part.*

I promise.

She didn't comment on Mark's promises, just watched Tammy race to place gigantic price tags on tables holding electric toothbrushes and vacuum cleaners.

When she didn't say anything further, he offered, "I understand if you need more time."

He didn't understand at all.

"Amanda, I'm trying here." He lowered his voice as if Letty Hodges lurked just outside his office door, ready to snatch up marital gossip and run. "I'll give you all the room, all the space you need."

But she didn't want room. Or space. Or time. She wanted her best friend, her only friend, to climb into the darkness with her and hold her. Cry with her. Rail against fate with her and talk about what could have been. Grace.

To come into this cave and bring some of that light he shone so bright.

If he knew about the cave, he didn't say so. And the walls were so cold, the air so heavy, she could hardly breathe to tell him. To scream out to help her, for God's sake.

But Mark was elsewhere, for God's sake, she reasoned. She felt pretty safe in the cave, used to the coolness. The security of the prison. She wasn't sure she was ready to leave its confines to the wide, open spaces of Potter.

"I'll tell you what. Just think about it, okay?"

"Sure," she managed. The hope in his voice nearly crushed her. "I'll think about it."

"Great. So, I'll see you in a little bit?"

"See you then. We've got more mushroom soup from Mrs. Zimmerman."

"Lord, help us." Mark sighed. He hated mushroom soup.

Amanda clicked the phone off as Tammy wrapped stubby arms around Bob's neck and planted a fevered kiss on his face. She'd won the van.

Amanda checked the wall clock. Eleven-thirty. She had just enough time to hop in the shower and clean up her breakfast mess. With a little lipstick and a fresh outfit, she'd be ready. She rose from the couch, ran her hands over the buckled fabric, and padded down the hall toward the shower.

Her husband was on his way home. Cave or not, she'd put on a happy face for him. Because raggedy dolls always wore smiles, and she wasn't about to disappoint him.

CHAPTER 13

∽

shady springs

At Shady Springs Nursing Home for the Aged and Infirm, Mark followed the clipping boots of Dale Ochs down the flecked tile hallway. They traveled deep into the nursing home's labyrinth, past the decorated waiting room into the abyss that actually held the patients. The stench—urine and feces blended with warmed-over cafeteria vegetables—nearly knocked Mark over.

"Mrs. Weatherby," Dale called, stepping into a small room that held two beds and a recliner. Heavy curtains closed over a single waist-high window. The television, a seventies model with bent rabbit ears, blared at top volume. Dale snapped it off.

In a corner, a white-haired woman sat like a withered bird in her cage, a steel wheelchair with thin rubber tires. She was slumped over, but straightened at the click of the television's manual dial and ensuing quiet.

"Hello." Her vowels drew out like gasps and she formed a smile around toothless gums. She wore a pale dressing gown, buttoned to the neck. Terry cloth slippers peeked from under the hem. Her toes poked out, revealing sparkly polish. A different color for each thickened nail.

Another woman lay on the bed, her mouth open wide, eyes rolled to the back of her skull. She rasped like a leaky balloon, clutching the daisy-print bedspread around deflated breasts. Her hands clawed the pilled polyester.

"She's not one of ours." Dale pointed to the sleeper and made no effort to whisper. "We're here to serve you the body and blood of our Lord Jesus Christ!" he hollered at Mrs. Weatherby.

"*Ayesm.*" Spittle ran out the corner of Mrs. Weatherby's mouth.

"It's time to prepare your heart to receive this great blessing, and I will pray for you," Dale announced.

Mrs. Weatherby nodded. Dale arched a look at Mark as if to communicate, *Listen closely to how it's done. You might learn something.*

Mark cocked an eyebrow. *Go ahead, big boy.* He stayed by the door.

"Our Heavenly Father Great Almighty Jehovah God," Dale bellowed in one breath. "We are gathered here today in this thine most holy day, the day of the Sabbath, to join in communion of the body and blood of our Lord Jesus Christ. We lift up to thee at this time the heart and soul of this grave sinner, Mrs. Ruby Weatherby, and ask that thou wouldst forgive her for her trespasses, which are many, and cleanse the blackness from her evil heart."

Mrs. Weatherby tilted forward in the wheelchair and, for a terrifying second, Mark thought she might fall out. A low snore escaped her.

Evidently, Dale was used to such wily actions as he thumped a hand on Mrs. Weatherby's fluffy head, rousing her from her doze.

Startled, she made another unintelligible sound and looked at Mark. He put his palms together and closed his eyes to remind her, *We're praying, Mrs. Weatherby.* He winked and a wide grin spread over her features as she followed suit. She giggled like a naughty girl in Sunday school, her wrinkled lids squashed shut.

Dale pursed his lips, then barreled on with the praying. "Thy word doth say that if we confess with our mouth that Jesus is Lord and believeth in our hearts that thou hath raiseth"—he stumbled a little on all the *th's*—"him from the dead, we shall be saved!" He took a deep breath, worn out from his own drama.

Dale thumped Mrs. Weatherby's fragile crown again. She made no sound. "Mrs. Weatherby receives this bounty of thine true sacrifice, the Holy Lamb of God, slain for her sins, and she doth pray she might be made worthy of such blessings." Dale opened his eyes and surveyed Mrs. Weatherby, clearly doubting such worthiness might occur anytime soon.

He dispensed the crackers and pop-top cup of juice with clinical formality. She might have been taking her afternoon vitamins.

The purple liquid dribbled down her chin as Dale ignored her, checking the chart for the next shut-in requiring communion.

Mark knelt in front of the wheelchair and drew a snow-white handkerchief from his pocket. He wiped the juice from Mrs. Weatherby's face, her skin like tissue drawn thin. He took care not to pull the creases and smiled into her cataract eyes. "Jesus loves you, Mrs. Weatherby."

She nodded and began humming. Mark recognized the tune. A child's singsong favorite. *Jesus loves me, this I know, for the Bible tells me so.*

"That's right, Mrs. Weatherby." Mark patted her hand, gentle for the swollen veins there. "We'll see you next week."

But by then she was already asleep.

MARK WAITED IN the lobby while Dale met with the nursing home's office manager. A bowl of potpourri sat on the table, contributing to the more pleasant smell in the waiting room.

After serving communion to six more residents, Mark wanted nothing more than a steaming shower. Whether to cleanse the nursing-home stench from his skin, or the experience of ministering with Dale, he wasn't sure.

He'd give the man five more minutes. Leave him and his "you wait out here" control issues and walk home if he had to. He wished he'd driven the church pickup rather than depend on Dale for a ride.

If only he had his jogging shoes, he'd be back on Mesquite Street in ten minutes flat.

"You must be Mark Reynolds." A Southern voice poured over his right shoulder.

But he'd smelled her before he heard her—a musky perfume that reminded him of magnolias. Strong enough to overpower Shady Springs' *eau de toilet.*

He turned and saw an attractive woman carrying a large basket, briskly headed his way. She balanced just fine in three-inch heels as she clicked up to his vinyl chair.

Mark hoped the stink from the nursing home didn't cling to him like a demon aroma. "Yes, and you are?"

"Courtney Williams, president of Lakeview Community Ladies' Guild." Setting down her basket, she tossed her long blonde hair and offered a manicured hand. "They told me all about you. My!" she exclaimed as he stood. "You *are* big! Football, right?"

"No, heredity. But I did play some." Mark smiled and shook her hand. "Nice to meet you." He briefly wondered if the rest of the guild looked like this. Christie Brinkley in the *Uptown Girl* phase. Big hair, lots of makeup, stunning in a shiny kind of way.

"Serving communion with Dale?" She made it sound like fighting for world peace, a truly heroic deed.

"Yes, as a matter of fact."

"That's *so* nice of y'all. You don't see many people up here. Not even on Sundays." She crossed her arms over a fitted top, knitted from several sacrificial bunnies.

"Are you visiting someone?" Mark thought Courtney looked more ready for a photo shoot than an afternoon at the nursing home.

"Ruby Weatherby. Did you meet her?"

At Mark's nod, she said, "She's my Gran. We have a date every Sunday. Girlie day." Courtney pointed to an array of polishes in the basket.

The twinkly toes, Mark remembered. "I bet she enjoys that."

"She does." Courtney smiled. "It's the simple things she likes now. We have a little lunch, a makeover, sing some songs. Sometimes she participates, sometimes I feel like I'm flying solo. After meeting her"—Courtney shrugged—"you can imagine. Still," she said brightly, "she's my Gran."

"I'm sure she appreciates you."

An old man squeaked by in a wheelchair, his back curved in a permanent comma. His bare legs stuck out like hairy Q-Tips, cotton socks puddled at his ankles. He stopped his wheels about a foot away from Courtney and cricked his neck up at her. "You wanna see my possum?" he invited, clawing at his bathrobe.

Without batting an eye, Courtney replied sweetly, "No, thank you, Mr. Pierson. Be good now and go on to your room." She twirled his wheelchair, pointed it down a corridor and gave a solid push.

Over his shoulder, Mr. Pierson glared at Mark. Clearly judging him a rival for Courtney's affections. The old man wheeled away, muttering.

"Listen." Courtney brushed Mark's arm for a bare instant.

The magnolia scent tickled his nose again. A good kind of tickle.

"I'm sorry I didn't make it out to the housewarming party when you moved in. I'm a teacher at the elementary, and we had a prep day."

Mark noticed for the first time Courtney's apple earrings. "Don't worry about it. Although I'm sure my wife, Amanda, would be happy to meet you." He thought of Amanda at home, probably still in his pajamas, covered in blankets on the couch. Wool socks instead of heels, soap instead of heady perfume. No dynamo outfit, no glossy smile. He pushed the comparison away.

"I know you're just getting settled, but she really should come to the Ladies' Guild kickoff luncheon. I can introduce her around," Courtney offered. "I know just about everybody."

"Thanks, I'll tell her." Mark felt a surge of gratitude for Courtney's diplomacy. Not once had the woman asked, *Where in the world has your wife been?*

"Good." She nodded, as if sealing the deal. Courtney bent to pick up the basket.

Mark tried hard not to linger on the deep V in the front of her sweater.

"And Mark"—she straightened—"may I call you Mark?"

"Sure." He blinked.

"Well, Mark, if you need anything at all, just anything, you let me know." She turned to leave, her pencil skirt snug over her backside. "Oh," she called. "And Amanda too."

He watched her go, her heels tapping cheerfully.

"I see you've met our fair Courtney." Dale stood at Mark's elbow.

He hadn't heard the man approach, even in his stacked cowboy boots. Dale had slithered in without sound, like a prairie snake just before the rattle.

Mark couldn't help but wonder when he'd get bitten.

"You ready?" Mark was beginning to dislike the president of the board with an intensity he could taste.

Dale made no sign of moving. "She's divorced, you know. No kids. Does just about everything at the church."

Down the hall, Courtney stopped at Mrs. Weatherby's door and fluttered a hand at the two men staring at her.

"Yep." Dale jingled his keys. "You two'll be working together quite a bit. Should be cozy—what with her being so easy on the eyes."

"Really?" Mark said. "I hadn't noticed."

getting to know you

"The ladies *need* you." Mark swung the doors on an armoire at Barry's Fine Furniture. "What do you think of this one?"

"Cheap. See how it's split already, in the corner?" Amanda thought they might never find what they needed, in all of Potter Springs. Barry's boasted plenty of powder blue velveteen and oak veneer, but they had yet to light on the perfect dining set. Let alone bedroom pieces. "And no, they don't need me."

"Are you finding everything all right?" Barry himself trailed behind them, in gray polyester slacks and a Looney Tunes tie. Apparently ecstatic to have real-live customers on a Tuesday afternoon. "That's a fine chifforobe right there. You can stick clothes in it, or a television. See the holes in the back, for the plug?" He made a punching thumbs-up gesture. "Versatile!"

"Thanks, we're just looking." Amanda led the way to the dining sets, away from the owner's eavesdropping.

"Peggy can't be there," Mark continued, once out of Barry's earshot. "Her aunt's got shingles, so she's gone to Talukah."

"I know. I got her message."

As Ervin's wife and unofficial director of women's ministries, Peggy would normally be in charge of the luncheon. "You can do it, honeygirl," the older woman had promised on the answering machine, right before Amanda pressed delete.

Mark lifted the price tag on a dusty dinette. "This one's in our price range."

"It's *chrome.*"

Barry hollered from behind the counter. "That style'll last you forever." He jabbed his thumb in the air again. "Classic! I can come down on the price, but only 'cause you're friends and all."

Amanda had never laid eyes on Barry before today. "Do you know him?" she whispered.

"Thanks," Mark called in return, and pulled Amanda to the rear of the store. "Barry sings in the choir. Gave me his card a month ago and asked me to come by. I've been promising I would." He stopped in front of a pillow-top mattress. "Honey, about the luncheon. Somebody from the staff, or staff family, should go. And it's a women's function."

*So, because I have ovaries, I'm subject to an afternoon of horrible food and small talk?* Amanda sighed and sank down on the bed. "How long will it last?"

Mark grinned in victory. "Just a couple hours. You'll know some of them already from the move-in."

"There's no way I'll remember their names." Moving day was a blur, but a few stood out in her memory. Of course, crying all over Peggy wasn't something she'd soon forget. But Ervin's wife seemed the forgiving sort, especially since she hadn't even pressed for an explanation. "Hardly anyone will know me."

"But they will, once you go. I'm sure there'll be name tags. And you'll meet Courtney Williams, the president of the Ladies' Guild. She said she'd show you around."

Barry appeared out of nowhere and bounced on the edge of the mattress. "Feel that support? Come on, give it a try. Comes with a lifetime guarantee." He gave a flashy grin. "Quality!"

"Oh, we're not really in the market for a new mattress," Mark explained. "But if we were, this sure looks like a winner."

Barry beamed.

Only Mark would take the time to soothe a furniture salesman's ego.

"If you don't mind, Barry, we need to discuss our options." Mark stroked Amanda's shoulder. "You know what I mean."

Barry nodded knowingly. "You and the little lady talk it over, we'll see what we can do." He retreated behind the counter and stared. Lip-reading, no doubt.

"Fine," Amanda whispered. She didn't see any way out of it. So far, she had avoided Sunday mornings entirely. Now she wished she'd gotten her feet wet before facing the masses by herself. "I'll do it."

Heedless of Barry, Mark pulled her close. "You're the best."

"No, I'm the worst," she told his neck. "But I love you, so I'll go."

Mark shook Barry's hand in good-bye and the man looked close to tears as they left the store. "Zero percent financing, and that's the best I can do!"

AMANDA MUTTERED CURSES of regret through her teeth as she entered Lakeview Community Church. A pink sign, announcing today's Getting to Know You Luncheon in the activity center, fluttered with the closing door.

A small stage and fake green trees decorated the church's activity center, aka gym. Gingham cloths and cutesy centerpieces adorned circular tables. Women's chatter filled the area, high and low voices blended with various perfumes and tea light candles for a distinctly feminine mix.

Amanda shuffled in, hoping to be unnoticed, and looked for a seat in the back. Not one woman stopped her. She must be as invisible as she felt.

She'd battled anxiety that morning, trying to decide what to wear to an arm-twisting. She settled on her favorite black pants and a light blue sweater set. Thankfully, she hadn't underdressed for the occasion. Most of the women wore stretchy pants and colorful tops.

A quartet sang onstage. Two ladies sat on stools with their legs propped daintily on the rims, long floral skirts flowing to their pumps. The other two, wearing pantsuits, stood and made passionate hand movements, like gospel divas. They sang with eyes closed and full-throttle voices.

*It'll be fun, you'll see.* Mark's promise echoed in Amanda's mind as she found the most remote corner possible. To her relief, she recognized a face. It went with a name tag. Missy Underwood. The pansy gardener.

The woman's eyes widened as Amanda approached. "Hello! Oh, you're *here.* Come sit down . . . if you want. Everyone will be so happy to see you!"

So happy they hadn't stopped their conversations to make time for a quick hello? Or had they seen her? "Thank you." Amanda hung her purse over a chair. "This seat's not taken?"

"Not at all. I try to sit in the back in case I have to slip out to feed the baby."

The baby. Emptiness blossomed in Amanda's womb. Pain petals unfurled and snatched her breath away. She fought it, sucked in some air and forced herself to smile. "The baby?"

"Taylor. He's ten months old. And a hearty eater." Missy unconsciously brushed her breasts as she spoke. "The nursery has to pull me from time to time 'cause he gets so ornery if I'm not there to feed him."

"Do you have other children?" *Breathe deep. Be normal. This is normal, two women having a conversation about children.*

"Yes, a four-year-old girl and an eight-year-old boy."

"You're pretty busy, then." Amanda parroted clichés, her mouth moving at random.

"It's not bad. I get to stay home with them, so that's a blessing." Missy fiddled with the sugar packets on the table as the quartet finished to enthusiastic applause.

A tall blonde in fitted pants and heeled sandals grasped the microphone. "Good afternoon, ladies of Lakeview Community Church! For those of you who don't know me, and I don't think there are many, I'm Courtney Williams, your Ladies' Guild president." The women clapped politely. Courtney brushed her hair from her shoulder and let the applause continue before she spoke again.

"We've got lots to talk about, starting with our fall activities. But before I get into that, I want to introduce you to a special guest of honor whom you might not have met yet. In fact, I'd begun to wonder if she existed at all! But I'm told she's here and we're glad to have her."

The burn started up toward Amanda's face. She willed serenity, in spite of her pounding heart. *I am cool. I am calm. I am the pastor's wife.*

"Amanda Reynolds—wife of our own precious Mark Reynolds!" *Amanda Reynolds, come on down!*

Courtney peered into the shadows. "Amanda, would you stand up for me, please?"

Amanda stood and waved to the women, who stared at her.

"No, I need you to stand up!"

Laughs all around. More unadulterated fun in the form of short jokes.

"Y'all be sure and give her a hug after the program. Introduce yourselves and make her welcome. Now, for our announcements . . ."

Having performed to expectations, Amanda tuned the speakers out and started in on her lunch. Thinking as soon as she finished, she could leave.

Next to Amanda, Pam Hart, according to her marks-a-lot name tag, shifted forward in the plastic school chair. "So, Amanda. How do you like our fair town so far?" Pam chewed on a tortilla rolled with cream cheese and olives, and intermittently dipped it in a bowl of salsa. Double dipping.

"I like it," Amanda answered, almost honestly. Driving to the church this morning in her Toyota, the crisp breath of fall whipped through her open windows. The air cleansed, cut through her in a way that Houston breezes never did. She'd even turned on the radio and sang through her nervousness to the latest Alan Jackson coming through her tinny factory-edition speakers.

It wasn't until she hit the church's parking lot that she wished, with overwhelming urgency, that she'd never agreed to come.

Still, she must make an effort. Her cave's darkness had covered her for so long. If she didn't try, she'd stay inside forever. Baby steps.

After all, she was here to get to know the women. That, and to try to consume dry chicken and lukewarm green beans without choking to death.

"Tell me about your sweatshirt." Amanda pointed to Pam's brightly colored top.

"Oh, my goodness! Can you believe that?" A hot sauce trail dribbled over the puff paint sweatshirt. Pam smacked it with a paper napkin. Paper balls peeled off the napkin to stick to the wet spot. "Not fifteen minutes into the meal." Pam blushed her apology. "Such a mess."

"No, you're fine. It hardly shows." Amanda hid a smile.

Pam heaved a sigh and set the blotter down. "It's a gift from my daughter in Chitapee," she explained. "Works at the high school over there. Voted teacher of the year. That's hard to do, you know."

"It must be nice to have family close." Amanda salted her rice pilaf, which held all the flavor of shredded cardboard. "Your daughter enjoys your company, I bet."

She'd ached for her own family, even as she gave her mother assurances she was fine. Lasting only minutes on the line with her daddy before breaking down, his gruff voice telling her he loved her. She missed them, flaws and all, with a palpable longing.

Almost as much as she missed Grace. Her little flutters. Even the sickness, the sleepiness.

"Sometimes," Pam agreed. "Now, don't get me wrong. I'm so proud of my daughter I could burst—she's got two young-uns . . ." She pulled a well-worn photo of chubby toddlers from her voluminous purse. "They drive me bananas, but they're my heart. Strange, that your heart can run around outside your body like that, on two legs."

"I know what you mean." Whispers of hurt, the petals stirred inside Amanda.

She missed her pregnancy dreams, the ones where she could almost see her little girl's face.

Amanda woke some mornings, even after the miscarriage,

with the words aching on her lips. *Turn around, Grace. Please turn around and let me see you.*

But Grace never did. And now Amanda didn't even have the dreams anymore. Still, she wondered what Grace would have looked like, dancing and running outside her heart.

"Anyway," Pam chattered on, "it's good to have a little distance. Oh"—she interrupted herself and shot out of her chair—"game time!"

Chair legs thumped against the industrial carpet as the ladies rearranged themselves into small groups.

"Amanda!" After an excruciating game involving pillowcases and stockinged feet, Courtney grabbed Amanda's upper arm in the exact spot she hated most to be touched. The woman pulled her near enough that Amanda smelled Courtney's coffee from dessert.

"I'm Courtney! Ladies' Guild president," she added, as if Amanda possibly needed further clarification on that point. "I teach at the elementary, Mark probably told you?"

"No." Mark hadn't said much about Courtney Williams at all. Taking in the woman's good looks, and obvious familiarity with her husband, Amanda wondered why. An unpleasant sensation reverberated in the back of her neck.

"That stinker!" Courtney shook her head.

*Our own precious Mark Reynolds . . .*

"Then you probably don't know I'm also an independent beauty consultant for LeFleur Cosmetics. And you, Amanda, are in danger of premature aging."

Amanda refused to flinch.

"I'm not kidding. Your kind of fair skin ages the worst in our climate. The worst! The dry heat, the wind. You'll be shriveled up like a raisin before you know it!"

How was it that the prospect of Amanda's withering skin made

Courtney even cheerier? Amanda fought the urge to pull away, or at least back up from the coffee-breath zone. Space invasion of the multitiered marketing kind.

"You have to guess how old I am. Come on, just guess." Courtney released her grip on Amanda's arm to frame her golden face with her hands, dramatic director style.

Looking over Courtney's fitted sleeve, Amanda eyed the departing women with envy. Some carried the luncheon center-pieces out with them, colorful house-shaped planters with ivy cascades down the side. She hoped to snag one, but the odds diminished by the moment.

"Oh, I really couldn't say," she murmured.

Undaunted, Courtney rushed forth with her pitch. "I'm telling you, these products are amazing. You won't believe what they'll do for you. Even with those freckles."

In incredible detail, Courtney outlined the benefits of utilizing a multifaceted skin care regime, starting with exfoliation and ending with skin moisturizing illuminators. "I'd be happy to schedule a makeover and skin diagnosis appointment." She whipped out a Day-Timer and flipped it open to a full page of highlighted appointments.

"I'll let you know. We're just getting settled," Amanda stalled. "I should get home to Mark."

"Oh, I gotcha." Courtney winked. "Newlyweds." She pressed a wad of brochures and some samples encased in Pepto-Bismol–pink plastic into Amanda's hands. "Just think about it. You could host a beauty party and win free LeFleur products!"

"Maybe."

"Well, you don't have to decide right this minute. I'll call you. 'Kay?"

*Don't call me anything.* "Sure, that'd be great."

At home, Amanda tossed the handouts in her white wicker

bathroom trash can and examined herself in the mirror. A newly-wed. An aging newlywed. From the inside out.

Splash stains from Mark's shaving blurred her reflection in little circles. She got out the ammonia and wiped the streaks away.

# more mashing

The three of them sat around the dinner table. A dying mum bouquet served as the centerpiece. Mark had brought the orange and yellow flowers home for Amanda last week. Their decay cast a slightly musty smell.

He'd throw the flowers away for her later. Buy her some new ones. As many as it took, for putting up with his mother.

"That was an *excellent* meal, Amanda. Wonderful. The potatoes could have used a little more mashing . . . perhaps a tad more butter . . . but other than that, outstanding." Marianne Reynolds dabbed the corners of her mouth. "Don't you agree, Mark?"

Amanda twisted her fork in a small mountain of potatoes, eyes downcast at her half-eaten meal.

Mark slid his chair back and patted his stomach, full in Friday-evening flannel. "You did a good job, hon. On all of it." He tilted his empty plate as evidence and she quit the twirling, her shoulders easing a bit.

With a weak smile, Amanda stood and collected plates from the heavy wood table, a recent purchase from Barry's Fine Furniture.

They'd ordered it from one of Barry's specialty catalogs and the financing had gone through "like poop through a goose," according to Barry.

The salesman had informed the choir all about it and showed them the pictures. Now several other ladies had the same table on order, each hoping to match the Reynolds with their big-city tastes in time for Christmas.

Barry declared business had never been so good, and put a rush delivery on Mark and Amanda's table for free.

Mark was just thankful it arrived before his mother's visit, so she'd have one less thing to criticize.

"Oh, we'll get those dishes." Marianne fluttered from the table and shooed Amanda like a fly. "I know you've been tired lately."

"I'm fine." Amanda's soft voice slid through the clinking plates.

"We-e-ll," Marianne drawled, "I couldn't help but notice all the naps you've been taking."

"Today, I guess, but it's not like . . ." Amanda set the stack on the counter and smoothed a wild curl behind her ear. She looked to Mark.

He shook his head. *Don't worry.*

His mother missed the silent exchange. In the three days since her visit started, they'd done an excellent job of conducting entire conversations with body language and eyebrow movement. The small house and reverberating hardwoods didn't allow for more verbal discussions.

"I'm doing this, and that's final." Marianne shifted the plates closer to the sink and opened a drawer for a dishrag. "You go put your feet up, Amanda." She cast a sweet gaze at her son. "Even though Mark's worked hard at the church all day, I'm sure he can muster up some energy to help."

Mark shrugged. "Sure. We've got it, Mandy."

"Besides," Marianne added over her shoulder, "it's not like there's much to wash, with just those two side dishes."

"You still hungry? There's plenty more." Mark stared out the kitchen window at the dark fall sky and wished his mother would quit smiling as she stabbed his wife.

"You know I like to keep my figure." Marianne tapped a slender hip.

Mark guessed she'd been the same size forever. Same size, same conservative dress, same hair.

"You can't let things slide, no matter how comfortable you get. Oh!" A guilty hand flew to her mouth. "No offense, Amanda."

Same cutting remarks.

Amanda hadn't lost all the weight from the pregnancy, and her thickened waist had caused more than one weepy morning. Her shoulders stiffened ramrod straight, and Mark thought for an instant her old fire might have returned. That she'd give his mother what-for.

Instead, her eyes filled, a familiar sight. Mark left his post at the counter. He gathered her to him and stroked her side.

*You look good to me,* his hand whispered. *Your body is mine and you are beautiful and my mother is a crazy witch.*

She rubbed her forehead against his shoulder. *Thank you,* her warmth answered back.

Marianne started the hot-water tap. "Where's your scrubby brush, Amanda? I find a good stiff brush is essential for dish-washing. Do you have one?" Without waiting for a response, she dug under the cabinet. "My goodness, this *is* an older home. There's some water damage under here, Mark. You might have some of the church workers take a look at it."

He wondered if her entire body would fit into the cabinet if he gave her a quick shove.

"Here's a sponge, I guess this will have to do." She pivoted triumphantly, waving the yellow cleaner. "Go on now," she ordered Amanda. "We can take care of this."

"You sure?" Amanda spoke low to Mark.

"You could use the break." He rubbed the small of her back. "Go get some quiet. I'll keep her busy."

"Thanks."

A few minutes later, he heard the water running in the bath-room. He hoped she'd take her time and soak the stress of his mother's visit away. Watching her wring her hands under the table during dinner made him want to start his mother's Buick and send her back to Lubbock.

"You know, if you used a little no-stick spray on your cook-ware, it'd clean easier." Marianne's elbow pumped back and forth as she scrubbed.

"Just soak it. I can finish in the morning." He'd get up early and do the housework before anyone stirred. He found peace then, in the quiet. Thinking as his wife slept that today would be the day she would rise with a smile, one that would last. He prayed for it each dawn as he tidied their home, as if the work of his hands might make the difference.

"Oh. Do you think Amanda will still be tired then? In the morning too?"

"She's fine, Mom. It's been a hard move."

"Have you thought of *other* reasons she might be fatigued?"

"She's not pregnant." His words came out harsher than he intended. Defensive at his mother's prying. "It's too soon." *It might be never.*

"Humph. I never said she was and I wouldn't dream of asking. That's much too personal. You don't owe me that kind of information."

"It's all right."

"I didn't mean—" she insisted.

"Forget it." He counted to five. Then ten. "It's okay. It's been tough for Mandy to be away from her family, her friends. But she's adjusting."

"Yes, I can see that. Why, I think she might have put away that stack of laundry I washed two days ago."

"Cut it out, Mom." He could only play nice for so long. And he found as the days passed, his patience with his mother grew shorter.

"I'm sorry. I just had different ideas for you. For who your wife would be—"

"I know, and I don't want to hear it. I've heard plenty."

"One of the girls from seminary," Marianne continued.

*Not listening. She never listened.*

"Or even our home church. I know of at least two myself who still burn a candle for you."

*Burn a candle? Who says that?* "I think you overestimate my appeal, Mom. Regardless, I love my wife."

"I love Amanda too. You know I do. She certainly had a . . . a certain *spark* when you were dating. *Darling* girl." Marianne pulled a dripping pan from the steamy sink and wiped it with a towel. Handwashing.

Mr. Chesters crunched his premium-brand cat food in the kitchen's corner, glaring warily at Mark.

Finished for the moment, the cat thrust his white paws forward, arched his back and yowled. Mark understood the command. He opened the kitchen door and watched Mr. Chesters slink off into the night.

Cool air washed over him. He smelled a fire burning. On the porch next door, Mrs. Zimmerman called softly to Princess, and her television poured noise and flickering glare into the empty night. Another cat meowed a greeting, or a warning, to Mr. Chesters. Mark left the animal to fend for himself, and went back inside.

Marianne cocked her small head sideways, contemplating. "Does she support you, honey?" Her soft brown eyes searched his, her expression pleading. "In your profession, I mean? This church, your opportunities here. You could go so far, be anything you want to be." She shook her short brown curls. "Imagine, you'll have your own church before long. Think of it."

Penny loafers clicked against the linoleum as she moved to put the pan away. No stacking in a pile for Marianne Reynolds. You wash, you dry, you put away. Relentless in her busyness.

"But without a helpmate to stand beside you, it just can't be done." She lowered her voice. "You'll never be greater than an associate pastor without a more visible wife."

"I'll be as great as God allows, Mother. And whether or not my wife needs some transition time shouldn't have much effect on a life's calling." He stepped on his anger before it ran away from him.

"Besides"—he breathed the tension out—"she'll find her legs here. Get friends. She just needs a niche, is all. She might be in a slump right now, but with more time, everything's going to be better."

"Of course it will. Yes, you're right. If you say so, then it must be the truth."

She had the gall to tap him on the head as she passed him on her way to the pantry. "Still, I wonder. How much time will it take? And do you have enough left to give her?"

CHAPTER 16

# what i need

Suspicious, Amanda crossed her arms. "Tell me again."

"The ladies specifically *asked* for you," Mark repeated. "By name. They want you to ride with them on the way to the retreat." Mark sat on a kitchen chair, retying his shoelaces after a Saturday-morning run through the neighborhood.

"They did not." Amanda taped a black-silhouetted witch to the window. *My name.* She wondered what they called her. Mrs. Reynolds. She shuddered, thinking of Marianne.

Mark's wife. The preacher's ball and chain. She dug into the plastic Wal-Mart sack for the matching cat.

Or had they said Amanda? She remembered Shelinda, with her easy laugh in the kitchen with King Ranch casserole. Shelinda called her Amanda.

She squelched the beginning of hope, flat as a June bug in September. Not liking its unfamiliar creep in the shadows of her heart.

Hope left when Grace died.

Securing the cat with Scotch tape, Amanda slapped the cutout next to the broom.

"Did too." Mark stepped over the grocery bags and picked up her newspaper tornado, rumpled and forgotten in front of the couch. As he gathered, he folded the sheets into conformity before sitting down to read it himself.

Following him, Amanda mimicked his nonchalance. She didn't care. She placed a chubby ghost candle on her paperback bookshelf and plugged in an electric jack-o'-lantern on a side table. Examining its blinking grin, she asked over her shoulder, "Who?"

The newspaper rattled as Mark turned the page. "Let's see. Pam Hart, Missy Underwood. They remembered you from the luncheon." He added, "Course, Peggy'll be there. And, whatshername? Courtney Williams, the one who does everything."

Fantastic. She'd be cornered for hours by the effervescent *LeFleur* saleswoman. "Did you bring it up, or did they?" She imagined him sidling up to a chattering pack on a Sunday morning and tossing her name among them. An awkward, deflated volleyball. *Thunk.* They'd have nothing to do but pick it up. "You arranged all this, didn't you? You. Not them."

Leaning forward, Mark rested his elbows on his knees. "Forget about who did what. The important thing is the church is paying for the trip. Well, maybe that's not the most important thing," he corrected himself. "But the point is, they're footing the bill since I'm . . . *we're* on staff. It'd be rude for us to turn them down. A weekend in the mountains of Colorado. How could you say no?"

"*N-o.* It's not that hard, Mark. It's called taking a stand. You don't have to do everything they ask you." She knew she was being petty. Digging her heels in. But she wanted to lash out, to make some sort of a point she couldn't even define for herself.

"A stand about what? A women's retreat?" Mark went back to the kitchen and fumbled in the pantry for his postrun protein drink. He slammed the door, impatient. "It's not a political statement. It's called a vacation. And I thought you could use one." The spoon clicked against the glass like a clock on speed. *Ting ting ting ting ting.*

"I don't need a vacation." She poured candy corn in a ceramic pumpkin bowl. Her thoughts tumbled forth, caught by ambivalent porcelain.

Telling him without sound, wishing he could hear. Watching the sweets fall.

*I need my husband at home and not sitting beside every grieving widow inside Carson County.*

Sugar niblets cascaded in slow motion, clattering against the sides, spinning in a crazy dance.

*I need my partner not to interrupt our dinners with church phone calls, calming down a deacon while the gravy gets cold.*

Triangles of white, yellow, and orange candies piled together, blurring into a muted peach.

*I need Sundays for us, a lover's Sabbath, not waiting for hours while you schmooze with the tithers after church.*

She picked the broken pieces out. Ones missing the pointed white tip, or cracked in half. These, she ate. But their sweetness spread bitter on her tongue.

*I need to talk about our child. The one who died. Let's use words like* loss *and* grief *and* heartache *and admit our lives aren't anything like we thought.*

But unspoken sorrows had fermented to anger. Acid, just

below the surface. Amanda feared the sputtering bile would burn them both, should she crack that lid.

"I need," she started, the words choked inside her. Their sharpness hung on the sides of her throat. Fresh burrs on tender flesh. "I don't know what I need."

"Come on. It's all set up. A chance to get away. You've been so . . . unhappy." A protein mustache covered his lip. He looked like an oversize boy. Lost and bewildered.

"So, why would I want to get away? To be unhappy with people who don't even know me?" She didn't wait for him to answer. "I'm sorry if I've been a burden—"

"I can't stand seeing you like this." His confession strung an invisible banner in the late-morning air.

She played with it in her mind. Folded the streamer into new shapes.

*I can't stand seeing you like this.*
*I can't stand seeing you.*
*I can't stand you.*

It tried to tangle her, this twisted string. Knotted up, she closed her eyes and prayed for freedom. The sun touched her face through the screen door, but not enough to warm her.

"Although"—Mark took a heavy swallow of the thick drink— "I'm glad you're taking an interest in the house." He glanced uncertainly at the glow-in-the-dark skeleton, kicking his heels up on the front door.

"This is your solution? Sending me to Colorado? So you don't have to see me like this?" She stared back at him, not caring about her red eyes and inflamed nose. He should be used to them by now.

"Stop. You know that's not what I mean."

"I don't have a say in this at all, do I?"

"No. *N-o*, Amanda Reynolds. You have no say-so." Surprising her, he set the glass on a nearby table without a coaster. His tennis shoes squeaked on the hardwood floors.

He folded her in his arms. She smelled the salt on his skin, the sweet of the drink on his lips. She folded herself into him, wishing she could disappear.

"See, I can do it," he whispered. "I'm taking a stand. You need to go to Colorado."

They stood in the doorway, embracing. Appearing, for all the world to see, like snuggly newlyweds.

"For both our sakes, you need to go."

THE WOMEN ARRIVED for Amanda nearly a week later, early Thursday morning. They swarmed out and grabbed her bedding from the entryway. A few waved to Mark, as an afterthought, but mostly they buzzed around his wife like a prize pie at a summer fair.

Amanda stood as if frozen, not showing her panic. Mark sensed it, though. A silent, high-pitched alarm. An impending warning.

Mark rubbed her arm. "Mandy, you remember Shelinda James, from moving day? And here's Missy Underwood and Pam Hart. You might not know Kendra Sue McAllister. She leads Bible studies at the church." He gestured to a woman with glasses and mousy brown hair.

"Hello." Amanda stayed stock-still.

He wished she would give them a chance. Give *him* a chance. He missed the dazzling Amanda, the one who lit up a room with her presence. Her fire. Her laughter. The spirit that made him soar.

If he saw her glimmer again, even just for a second, it might give him the strength to carry on.

Maybe he hoped for too much. Maybe this was all a huge mistake.

Shelinda tugged Amanda's sweatshirt sleeve. "Don't look like that. We're fixin' to have some fun!" The woman laughed at Amanda's dour expression. "Just wait until we have our evening celebrations. The ones where we cut the heads off live chickens! Course, that's after the public confessions and ceremonial cleansings. I'm telling you, it'll bring you close to the Lord!"

Mark didn't find Shelinda's gentle terrorization of his wife remotely funny. Then he caught a hint of Amanda's smile as she followed the others to the bus-size SUV in the driveway.

*God bless Shelinda James.*

Mark loaded Amanda's suitcase in the roomy luggage area. He rearranged sleeping bags and hanging clothes in a more efficient arrangement. Finished, he quizzed Shelinda. "I'm assuming you know the way?"

"Sure do," she sassed back. "Colorado's what, west of here?"

"Oh." Frosty breath exited in a puff of anxiety. Mark attempted a chuckle, but it sounded more like a hiccup or a wheeze. "Do any of you have a cell phone? Just in case?"

To the chorusing yeses, he nodded, approving. He walked Amanda around to her side. Kissing her brow, he whispered, "I'll miss you."

"Me too." She clenched his shirt, tight.

"And I love you." He tugged her fingers away, squeezed them and let go.

"Me too." She turned to stuff her pillow in the car.

The door, larger than the entire broadside of Amanda's Toyota, closed and latched. Sealing his wife's future for the next three days.

Maybe his as well.

They scraped away, running over his morning newspaper. Mark waved until he couldn't see them anymore. Precious cargo.

His day stretched before him, the pink light just touching the oak next door, brushing on its pointy leaves.

The house looked at him. Empty.

Her car sat in the open garage, dust covering the faded red paint.

An idea struck him with pleasure. He got the keys and started the Toyota with a clinking hum. Backing it out, he found the floorboard full of muck and the seat seams stuffed with crumbs. The interior would need a full cleaning too, but he'd start with the exterior.

The water from the hose splashed cold on his hands, liquid ice. He relished the sting and the soapy bubbles, caressing the hatch-back's dinged panels, washing at the rust. The sun rose higher and warmed him at his work. He whistled through the easy labor.

He needed to do this for her. He needed to show her, without words. A small thing for the woman of his heart.

He only wished he could do more.

# retreat

The bell above the Toot 'n' Totem jangled when the five women entered. The convenience store greeted Amanda with the distinct smells of coffee and hot dogs. Fresh doughnuts shone in a gleaming case.

"Hey, girls," a familiar voice called from a side booth. "Y'all headed out for the retreat?" Dale Ochs sat with a group of men gathered over ceramic mugs.

"Yessir," Shelinda said.

He waved them over, but Amanda pretended not to see. Instead, she wove her way past boxes of paper towels and found the women's restroom, wondering what she'd gotten herself into for the weekend.

The stall next to her clicked shut. "I like your shoes," Kendra Sue complimented.

"Thanks." Amanda wore her most rugged style, hiking boots that Mother hated. Mountain shoes. "I like yours too."

Kendra Sue had on Birkenstocks with rainbow fleece socks. "They're my traveling shoes." She did a little tap dance on the floor, and Amanda laughed. "Got to be fashionable, you know."

"You got any extra toilet paper over there?" Pam called from the other side. "I'm out."

Amanda passed some under the divider. "Here you go."

She finished up and washed her hands. Missy stood by the sink, and the hot-air dryer whirred behind Shelinda. "I always add chilies to my cheese grits," the taller woman was saying. "It adds that little bit of pep."

"I've heard blue cheese is good too," Missy said.

"Chocolate," Shelinda announced as she followed Amanda into the shopping area. "We need chocolate."

Dale Ochs and his cronies had left. The women loaded up on candy bars and diet Cokes. Girl food. Pam bought a fried burrito and Missy sipped a blue Slurpee.

"Just don't spill it on the seats," teased Shelinda.

Next to the register was a plastic bucket with a picture of a child's face on it. *Help send Lou Bell to Houston for chemo treatments!* read the handwritten paper. *God bless you!*

She was a beautiful girl, with a front tooth missing. Her smile spoke of innocence and hope.

Amanda put money in and took her bag from the cashier. The bell jingled again and she found her spot in the Suburban. They hit the highway at top speed, leaving the Panhandle behind in a great golden river.

Shelinda drove while Kendra Sue rode shotgun in a dual role

of navigator and conversation starter. In the second row, Amanda and Pam presided over the snacks. Missy sat in the third row of seats, stuffed in with the jackets and extra blankets.

Time flew as steadily as the Michelins over the asphalt as they talked nonstop, pausing only to sing along to songs pouring out of Shelinda's CD changer.

Kendra Sue flipped a page in her book of questions. "All right, here's a good one. 'When you were a child, what did you want to be when you grew up?'"

"Children!" Pam perked up as if she'd waited the whole ride for this precise moment. Dressed in a vibrant pink and green running suit, she made a violent *swish* sound as she twisted toward Amanda. "I hope you don't mind, but I've just been *dying* to ask—when are you and Mark going to start?"

The blood rushed from Amanda's head. The highway whirred outside as vertigo blurred her vision.

Kendra Sue winced. "You know, Amanda, you don't have to answer *all* the questions. We just want to have fun. Not be . . . well . . . nosy."

"Nosy yourself! I'm a grandma. It's not nosy, it's natural." Pam was undeterred by the gentle rebuke. "My daughter in Chitapee started right away. Didn't want to be hauling toddlers around when she's forty-five. Not like *some* women do these days." She wrinkled her nose at such thoughtlessness. "So, when?" Pam urged a response.

"That's a good question," Amanda stalled. Her voice sounded like it came from someone else. "Our parents wonder the same thing."

"Now, that's no kind of an answer." Pam's face took on a bull-dog quality. "Why not start now? Mark's got a good job, y'all have that adorable little house. What's holding you back?"

"It's not that we're holding back, exactly."

"Aha! Next year maybe? It'll be so much fun. We can have showers, I'll host. You won't want for a *thing*—"

"We're not supposed to." Amanda blurted the words out, a short burst of gas from the cesspot. She clamped her lips shut, forbidding any more to escape.

"Not *supposed* to? Not supposed to what?" Pam's face contorted into shock, then compassion. "Oh, Amanda. You poor thing! What you and Mark do in the bedroom is all *right*." She patted her knee. "It's the Lord's *design*, you see. For the man and woman to come together. Tell her, Kendra Sue. You taught that study on marriage. Tell her about the leave-and-cleave."

"I don't think that's what she means." Kendra Sue set a soft gaze on Amanda. "Let's talk about something else."

"Wait a minute. Why in the world shouldn't she be supposed to? Other than adultery, fornication"—Pam numbered off sexual immoralities like a grocery list—"lust, lewdness—unless you just flat-out *can't*." She appraised Amanda's figure. "Some sort of a condition?"

Amanda wished a large hole would open up in the bottom of the Suburban and she could roll to safety, or get crushed by an oncoming car. Either way, she didn't mind, as long as removal from Pam's presence was part of the package.

Flipping through the question book, Kendra Sue burst out, "I know—how about another question?"

Amanda twisted her pillowcase until the flesh of her fingers turned white. She stared at its floral folds as if she'd find a different strain of conversation wrapped around the dark green vines.

"Found one." Kendra's announcement released an iota of tension from the now confining quarters. "Pam, your turn. 'Who is the person, living or dead, you most admire?'"

Pam moved on from her impromptu interrogation to wax

eloquent about her ancestors, children and, of course, Jesus. Amanda prayed instant and numerous blessings on her new best friend, Kendra Sue.

A small pressure fell on Amanda's shoulder. Light as a leaf in October, a touch to get her attention. Missy, quiet in the back.

"You've lost a baby," she whispered.

It wasn't a question. The truth. Uttered and made real.

Amanda hadn't told. She'd held fast to the unspoken promise. Loyalty to Mark, to her own integrity, had built an ugly, stucco facade. Slapped together with pain and hypocrisy, the weight had nearly suffocated her.

"Yes." A slab of moldy plaster fell away. Amanda wiggled her seat belt to turn backward.

"I'm so sorry. My goodness." Little fingers grasped hers over the seat back. Strong and dry and warm. "I'm just so sorry."

Narrow beams of light streamed into Amanda's cave, bringing fresh air and hope. She breathed it in deep. "Thank you." Not knowing what else to say, Amanda simply tightened her fingers and held on.

"I've had two," Missy said. "Miscarriages, I mean."

"You? But you've got the baby, the other children. And they're all—"

"Healthy as can be. Doctor said one in four is a miss. Can be genetic, can be a fluke." Missy wiped her watering eyes with her free hand. "Didn't feel like a fluke at the time, though. Felt awful."

"I know." And Amanda's wasn't a fluke. Her body was the fluke. Her womb, a failure. *Close to impossible,* the doctor had said. His eyes as cold as his hands.

But she couldn't reveal that part. Not to Missy. Not to anyone.

"It took a long time for me to even get back to church." Missy looked down. "See, we'd told everybody, and then when I wasn't pregnant anymore, I just didn't know how to face them."

Amanda couldn't tell if her car mates were oblivious to the conversation, or were allowing privacy for kindness' sake. Sound traveled strangely in the Suburban. Hard to be sure. Still, she took comfort in their discretion, even as she kept her voice low. "How did you?"

"Do what?"

"Start facing people?" Amanda wondered if she'd ever be able to face people again. To be herself and not the person hiding behind the stucco.

"Oh, it started small, I guess. The ones who came to the house after I lost the baby. The friends who cried with me, who let me talk about it. And then, of course, God helped. But not for a while. Right after it happened, I didn't want anything to do with God. Too hurt, maybe." Missy's voice ran in a rush. "I know that's not the spiritual thing to say, to the pastor's wife and all."

Amanda shook her head and nodded at the same time. "No, it's okay. Go ahead."

Missy's chin thrust out. "It's true. I was mad at God, and I didn't want to pray or go to church or hear about his blessings at all. 'Cause the way I saw it he'd stolen my blessing away. Coulda stopped it, but he didn't."

"So how'd you . . . you know . . . get over it?"

"I don't think you ever get over something like that."

Amanda's heart shrank. *Not ever?*

"I guess I just learned to get *through* it. Crying makes it better."

"I can't seem to stop crying," Amanda confessed. "Over everything."

"Talking helps too. That's how I started up with God again,

realizing he hadn't forgotten me after all. He sent those women, girlfriends, to walk me through it."

"I haven't been able to. Talk, I mean. The dates"—Amanda met Missy's gaze and risked honesty—"they don't add up right. For a pastor's wife."

Missy chewed on her lip for a minute. "Jimmy and me, ours are that way too." She blushed. "I won't say anything. You can trust me. And if you ever want to talk about it . . ." Missy tipped her head toward the other women, now belting out show tunes from *Oklahoma*. *"Oh, the cowman and the farmer should be friends . . ."*

"Other people will understand too. If you give 'em a chance. You might be surprised."

Amanda eyed her fellow carpoolers. Yes, they might surprise her. Yet, life had taught her, she mused over the next few hours, not all surprises were good ones.

THE COLORADO RETREAT center resembled an old-time log cabin village, nestled amidst pines and mountains. The air thinned, and emerging from Shelinda's Suburban, Amanda felt lighter too. The late afternoon sun blazed high, yet the heat didn't seem to reach the parking lot. Amanda hugged herself against the cool, and drank deep of the scent of wilderness.

"We're here!" Pam announced to no one in particular, unfolding from the vehicle.

Kendra Sue dug in her book bag. "I think they've got us bunked in the main cabin." She pointed to a larger building.

"I hope we're roommates." Missy trailed alongside Amanda, juggling her pillow and a duffel bag.

"I'd like that." They stepped into the warm hallway, already filled with women ready for the retreat. Some smiled and said hello to Amanda as they walked past.

"Oh, here's mine. I'm with Kendra Sue." Missy smiled an apology, waved bye and disappeared across the hall. Next door, Pam informed Shelinda that she needed the bunk by the bathroom as she had severe diarrhea that morning and would most likely be up all night.

Amanda found her room—two matching name tags announced that her roommate would be Peggy Plumley. A nice surprise.

Shelinda shot a look and mouthed, "Wanna trade?"

Amanda grinned and shook her head no. Inside, she put her suitcase and pillow on the bed closest to the door. A picture window framed the soaring mountains outside. Atop each single bed, covered in patchwork quilts, lay school-type paper folders. Hers was green.

Inside, a stack of inserts detailed the weekend's activities. She skimmed through the lists of sessions, meal schedules, and noted the free time to go hiking or take a nap.

One sheet featured a caption, DRAW NEAR TO GOD, AND HE WILL DRAW NEAR TO YOU. Underneath it read, *Welcome to Lakeview Women's Retreat. Start your special time here by writing a letter to yourself. What do you want from this weekend? What are your hopes and prayers? What are you feeling, right now?*

The rest of the page was blank, left empty for the answers. Except Amanda didn't know the answers, and this felt like homework, so she shut the cover and lay back on her pillow.

*You need to go,* Mark had said. *For both our sakes.*

She cracked an eyelid and stared at the mountains. "But I don't want to," she said aloud.

The mountains made no reply, so she sat up and opened the folder. After locating a pen in the nightstand drawer, she kicked off her shoes and crossed her legs.

*I feel . . .*

The paper looked so white. The pen so dark. The loops of her handwriting naked against the page.

*I feel . . . like an idiot.* She stared at that, then scratched it out. *I want . . .*

She figured she could keep it light, and no one would know the difference. *I want to lose five pounds. I want my hair to look halfway normal.* The ink flowed freely while she scribbled down her thoughts, her handwriting worsened the faster she wrote. *I want to not have to sit near or talk to Courtney Williams. I want to have a good time.*

*I want to go home.*

*Home.* The word gave her pause, and she thought of Mark, waving in the driveway as they pulled away. Planning this for her, making the effort.

*I want to be a better wife.* She used to be a good wife, she thought. They used to be so great together.

She paused, remembering. The earlier days when they flowed, connecting like hot honey and butter in a delicious, decadent swirl.

When she could laugh, or make a face, and he knew her heart, her spirit. She didn't have to explain herself. A time when neither of them had to try so hard.

Her chest tightened and she slowed her breathing, the pen hovered over the page. She thought of his tenderness. The little things he did for her, hoping she would notice. How he rattled around in the mornings, cleaning, driving her crazy as she tossed in the sheets.

His puttering made her nervous, sensing he wanted to clean her up too. To make her all better. But, try though he might, he couldn't. And she didn't know how to do it for herself.

The one thing she really wanted, she couldn't have. She saw no use in putting it down on paper, to mock her. *I want a baby. I want my baby.*

She considered the page again, picked up her pen and wrote one last entry. *I want to get better.*

It was the first time she had thought that. The words swam before her and she put the pen down and let her tears run free.

The door opened and Peggy Plumley pushed inside with a suitcase the size of Dallas. "My Lord! Those stairs were a killer! How are you, honeygirl? Make the trip all right?"

She nodded and brought quick fingertips to her eyes, brushing away the moisture.

Peggy unzipped her shoulder bag and tossed a small package of Kleenex to Amanda as if it were the most natural thing in the world to find her roommate for the weekend in tears.

Of course, given their history as friends, the woman had every right to believe "in shambles" as Amanda's most natural state. She unwrapped the package, revealing pink tissues that smelled of powdered flowers.

"Isn't it great we're together?" Peggy hung her shirts, nearly identical to the one she already wore, in a neat row in the closet. Finished, she heaved herself on the other bed and squished the folder there. "What's this?"

"Some stuff we're supposed to do before the sessions." Amanda folded her letter and sealed it in the envelope.

"I can get to mine later." Peggy stood, smoothed her top and braced her hands on her hips. "What do you want to do first?"

Amanda thought about it. Stay behind, have solitude, finish reading through her curriculum for the weekend. Maybe cry a little more. *What do you want?*

Laughter rang down the hall, and a succession of knocks sounded at the door. "Mandy! We're hungry . . . let's go eat!"

Shelinda peeked in. "Oh, hi, Peggy. Y'all wanna check out the cafeteria?" Missy and Kendra Sue stood behind her.

"Well? What do you say?" Peggy made for the hallway.

*I want to get better.*

She must start small, and do her part. If she had bootstraps, she'd tug them, but instead she retrieved her lace-ups from the floor and smiled. "I'm in."

CHAPTER 18

a big surprise

Mark checked his appearance in the mirror one last time before going to the dining room to wait. He smoothed a wayward cowlick, huffed his breath in his hand to check for odor and swiped Chap Stick across his lips. He hoped for plenty of kissing later on. Among other things.

A big surprise waited for Amanda's homecoming, and he figured some been-away-from-home, you're-the-most-amazing-husband-in-the-world loving was headed his way.

When she called Friday, her voice had been giggly, girlish. Through the spotty reception, he detected something he'd almost forgotten—happiness.

"Are you having fun?" He was almost too afraid to ask.

"Oh, Mark. We had to do these skits tonight. Skits! I haven't done that since church camp. Shelinda played a policeman, and I was—I was"—she broke up laughing—"a dog!"

"Sounds hilarious," he teased her. When was the last time he teased her?

"Well, I guess you had to be there," she admitted. "But I've been having the best time. The sessions are so good, and the mountains . . . it's just incredible. So beautiful."

"Are you glad you went?" He couldn't help prodding.

"You have no idea. I know you want to hear it, so I'll just say it. You were right."

"You didn't have to say that." He tried not to sound smug.

"I did too, and wipe that grin off your face. Yes, I'm having a great time, and yes, you're the best."

"Miss me?"

"Yes," she breathed. Emphatic.

He liked the sound of it.

"In fact, when I get home, there're some things I want to talk about. And things I want to . . . well, you know . . ." She lowered her voice an octave. *"Do."*

Heat raced through him at her tone. "I can't wait." But he had to. Two more long days, watching the pigs twirl around the living-room clock. He checked the map again, figuring they should arrive within the hour.

Thirty minutes later, Shelinda's silver Suburban pulled into the cracked driveway. Women piled out like clowns from a Volkswagen, dropping pillows and purses and Lord knows what else. Mark made pleasant small talk, and tried to keep his hands off his wife.

"Here she is, safe and sound." Shelinda grinned at the group. "Toldja we'd make it."

"I never doubted you," Mark lied.

Warmth and cinnamon filled his senses as Amanda ran at him,

her hair flying into his mouth. Scratchy wool encased his neck. "I missed you."

His arms twitched in thankfulness.

"Ahwooo, lookee there! We need to let you two lovebirds alone!" A singsong voice shattered his desire fog, and he backed an inch or two away from Amanda. But not more.

Pam Hart, in an eye-popping sweat suit, winked widely at the rest of the ladies. "Shoo, shoo, y'all. Get back in the car. We're not needed here."

They collected themselves, took turns hugging Amanda and left in a cloud of perfume and fluttering hands.

Shelinda's rear bumper scraped heavily on the inclined drive. *Honk, honk, honk,* the horn sounded a strange beat, like a feminine Morse code, as they turned the corner.

Women.

"I have so much to tell you. So much I want to talk about." Amanda practically hopped up and down in front of him. "Good grief, it's cold. Did a front come through? Come on." She tugged his hand. "Let's go inside."

He let her pull him close, dipped in to taste her willingness. He folded her in his arms, pressing her as close as possible without being naked.

She held the back of his neck and ran her fingers, restless, through his hair.

Across the street, a door slammed. Mark realized they were in the front yard, in full view. The preacher and his wife necking on the lawn.

He fought the urge to toss preparations and order to the wind and whisk her to the privacy of the bedroom. But, rationally, he wanted the evening to unfold slowly. Delayed gratification.

He'd waited months for her to come to him like this. He figured he could handle a few extra minutes.

More surprises waited in the house—roses, music and new candles. The domino effect, to fall according to plan, needed a push. The first gift.

He pulled away, while he still had the strength. "We'll go inside." He brushed her lip with the pad of his thumb, touching the swell there. "In just a sec. I want to show you something first."

After gathering her coat from the top of the heap, he explained while she shivered into it. "It's a . . . a kind of surprise. A big one." He delivered his much-practiced sell line, "For now, and for the future."

She didn't seem particularly impressed with his wording, just smiled up at him, blowing into her hands.

Guiding her to the garage, they crunched across brown grass, narrow shoots dead from an early freeze.

He'd planned this all out, had the electric door opener in his palm. His hands felt slick on the plastic, and he hoped she didn't notice them shaking.

The creaky door, solid wood warped with time, groaned open with the speed of a turtle. Inside, glossy green paint sparkled in the setting sun. Mark slung an arm around Amanda, taking in the view.

Perfect. He'd timed it just right.

A gigantic red bow graced the sloping hood. The minivan filled almost the entire garage, barely leaving room for Mark's bike and the washer and dryer. He spent all day yesterday clearing out junk to make room for it.

She stood so still under his arm. Not moving, or jumping up and down, like he'd imagined. Just staring.

"I know what you're thinking." He had no idea, but took a stab at it anyway. Anything to fill the void. "That it's too much. But with low interest rates and a long-term plan, we could swing it."

She said nothing.

"I figured it all out," he continued, unable to stop the projectile explanations. "I've got the paperwork . . . I still need your signature to make it final . . . plus my math inside." Why wasn't she *saying* anything? "I can show you down to the penny. It'll work, hon."

His stomach cramped in the silence.

"Where is my car?"

He didn't think he heard her right. "What?"

"My car. What have you done with my car?" Her voice rose to new heights with each syllable, ringing in the twilight.

He glanced at the neighbors' houses, wondering if sound traveled farther in cold temperatures. "*Shhh.* You're right, we should go inside. We'll talk about it inside."

"No. We'll talk about it *now*. What have you done with my car?"

Her old fire had returned, he noticed. His eyebrows might just be in flames. "I'm sure this isn't the time or the place to bring this point up, but technically, it's *our* car—"

"The car I worked through high school for, the car I drove in college—"

"I cleaned it up for you." He wanted her to know that part. "And then I realized how banged up it was. The high miles. It was time."

"Banged up? High miles?"

"We needed a warranty, and this one has unbelievable safety features and a super *Consumer Reports* rating."

"I know every tic and joint to that car. And it was . . . *is* . . . *mine!*"

"I traded it in." To compensate for her volume, he made his extra quiet.

"Traded it in? *Traded it in?*"

More shrieking. Piercing, almost.

"To get a lower payment."

"You traded in my car? My car?"

She sounded like a parrot. He thought he might hear her in his dreams. *My cahr, my cahr, my cahr.*

"Yes."

"Where? Where is it? Who did you give it to?" She looked around wildly, as if he'd hidden the hatchback in Mrs. Zimmerman's landscaping.

"The dealership. Hemp's Used Motorway. You know, the one on TV? And I didn't *give* it to them. I *traded* it. Worked for hours on a good price so we could get this. Like I said . . . I don't think you were hearing me . . . this one has a *warranty.* It's only one year old. All you have to do is sign."

"Tell me, Mark. Who are you expecting to ride around in all these seats? What is it, a six passenger?"

"Actually, seven, 'cause there's this little half seat in the back—"

"Mark!"

"I thought it'd be good for . . ." he hesitated. His perfect evening had dominoed, all right. But in all the wrong directions. He didn't want to upset her any more, but she expected an answer. "For ministry," he finally admitted. "Since you'd met the ladies and hit it off, I thought you might jump in with the youth. We need some sponsors." He scuffed his shoe against a broken piece of driveway.

"A youth sponsor. You bought this"—her fingertips, red from cold, pointed at his gift to her—"because you want me to be a youth sponsor?"

"In a nutshell." *Anything in a nutshell. Let's stick it all in a nutshell so we can go. Inside. Now.*

"Not for any other reason?"

Her lips had that quiver. *Not tears. Oh, Lord, please, sweet Jesus. No more crying.*

"Just what is it that you want me to say?"

Mr. Chesters twisted around his legs, purring violently. No doubt the animal wanted Mark to stoop to pet him. To get him close enough for a good clawing. But Mark had learned the cat's games long ago, and ignored him.

"Family." Amanda scooped up Mr. Chesters, and he slumped like a contented infant in her arms. Leering at Mark. "Children. That you wish we could have children."

"Oh, Mandy." He watched her face crumple. "I didn't mean—"

"Of course you didn't. Wonderful Mark Reynolds, *precious* Pastor Mark would never mean to." She hiccuped and buried her face in Mr. Chesters' fur. "Because *that* would bring up the topic of *babies* and we can't talk about that because ours was too early and not in your timeline, and *what will the good folks at Lakeview Community Church say,* but then, as luck would have it, she died."

The full force of her anger fell, and he found himself pushing back. That she would mock him, even in hurt. "If you want to read all that into it, fine. Take it how you want. I only thought you'd like the van, and it'd be a good surprise." He clung to that tenet, for fear of having to look elsewhere.

"I can't do this. I can't *do* this." She dropped a squirming Mr. Chesters and went in the house, slamming the screen door. Leaving Mark and the bags in the chill night air.

Alone. Again.

"Evidently, I was wrong," he told the cat, who stared at him, switched his tail and climbed over the fence with amazing grace.

Next door, Mrs. Zimmerman's porch light came on. She peered out, clasping a terry robe to her throat and balancing Princess and a cordless phone. She held the glass screen open with one hip.

Pink rollers filled her hair, a sight she normally wouldn't have allowed. Curiosity must have overcome her.

"Did she love it?" Her face shone with night cream.

"She was . . . surprised." He couldn't fake a smile.

Mrs. Zimmerman lifted the receiver from her chest and whispered to whoever was on the other end. "She didn't like it."

Mark's hand ached from gripping the remote, the warmth in his palm had long since cooled. He pressed the button again, watching the great mouth swing shut, then headed inside to deal with the mess that was his life.

# welcome home

The hollow moon lay over Amanda. Unlit candles, freesia and vanilla, scented the darkened bedroom. Deep red roses on her dresser appeared black in the shadow. The buds, cut before full bloom, drew tight together like a kiss. The small card beside the vase, in Mark's fluid handwriting, simply read, *Welcome Home.*

The sound of the water running stopped, bathroom drawers slid opened and shut. Quietly, with no banging or slamming. The silence of resignation. Not wanting to upset her while she slept, but she didn't sleep at all.

Her suitcase, still packed, slumped in a corner full of dirty clothes and her folder. The letter was no longer tucked inside. She'd handed the sealed envelope to the session leader this morning, to be mailed back in one year. "You'll see how far you've grown," the elderly woman promised. "How your prayers have been answered."

Leaving emotions of hidden hurt, which weighed a thousand pounds, Amanda flew home on wings. Yes, she'd left some heaviness behind, but what had she taken with her? Back in Potter Springs, the same difficulties, the repressed anger, had grabbed hold of her before she could breathe.

*I want to get better.*

She stared at her suitcase, the shape of leaving, until her eyes burned. She closed her eyes and saw the brilliant sun in Colorado, the bright blue sky. She'd felt so high and near to God, truly on a mountaintop, seeking answers for wisdom and direction and healing.

One morning, under the privacy of a towering tree, the poetry of the Psalms voiced a promise to her, clear as a lover's song. *Weeping may last for the night, but joy comes in the morning.*

She grasped it and made it hers. She would see morning, she believed it. Her gifts from the retreat had been new friends, and a new perspective. That she might find hope, if only she kept going. She just didn't know how long her night would last.

Mark slipped in the sheets beside her, damp from the shower. He settled his large frame, not disturbing her as she curled on her side away from him.

She heard loneliness from the curve of his back, and it called to her. He deserved so much more than she gave him. His heart was precious to her, even if his actions made her crazy.

She unwound and turned to him, smelling his neck, his body, the steam and the stillness. Sliding her arms around his chest, she kissed his bare shoulder, and wondered at the weight he carried there.

He'd been so strong for her, for so long.

*I want to get better.* Effort thickened her voice. "I'm sorry." The hardest thing to say, but a place to start. "I hurt your feelings . . . about the van . . ." She would not say the words *my car* again.

"It doesn't matter." He spoke to the wall.

But it did, the straightness of his spine said. The links of his vertebrae arched together, lined up against her. She traced a finger along the bumps and felt his involuntary shiver. In the tender spot at the base of his back, the place tension coiled, she pressed with her thumbs and rubbed. His muscles bunched, then separated, smooth as glass under her hand.

She said the words. "I missed you."

He turned on his side to face her, one arm supporting his head. "You did?" His breath smelled like mouthwash. The moonlight caressed him.

"I did." She nodded, and brushed away the hair on his forehead. He needed a haircut. She hadn't noticed it before.

His hand spanned her waist, smaller now through sit-ups and walks. Soreness hummed in her legs, strained from hiking in Colorado. She welcomed the tightness in her thighs. Hoping he felt a renewed firmness in her body. Her muscles, her strength, returning.

"How much did you miss me?" He dragged her across his chest so she lay full atop him. His pajama bottoms warmed her bare legs.

She tangled her toes in the flannel and tugged down, her calves restless. Her sleep shirt bunched against her hips and he gathered it up farther, rubbing as if it were silk and fine. Calluses on his fingertips feathered her legs, her ribs, the curve of her breasts.

He freed her from the cotton. "How much?" he asked again.

As he kneaded her flesh, she slid kisses along his neck, burrowed her face against his chest. "Much." She pulled away to look at him.

Meeting her gaze, his eyes spoke of longing and hope. Her tangled hair pooled around their faces, a makeshift canopy, warm and safe. Hidden from the outside world, from the gray moon and the darkened flowers.

"I love you," he said.

"Me too," she whispered back.

A ghost of a smile crossed his lips. "Show me."

SHE WOKE LATE, as usual, and after throwing on her robe, found Mark already dressed in the yard fooling with the weed-eater. "Good morning."

"Morning." He grinned with all his facial muscles. The look of a truly happy man.

Sleep still fogged her brain as the sun stung her eyes. "Don't you have work?"

"No." He shook his head. "I took the day off, thought we could spend it together."

A small miracle.

"I like that." She watched him. His love language to her, doing things around the yard, picking up the house. Not with words, but with actions. *Show me*, he'd said.

And she did.

"I left bacon for you on the counter." He crouched over the coiled tubing. "There's fresh coffee too. I got that dark roast you like."

"Thanks."

Mrs. Zimmerman walked Princess on the other side of the street. The dog stopped on a neighbor's immaculate lawn, bunched in a triangle shape, and pooped. "Good girl!" cooed Mrs. Zimmerman. She waved at Mark and Amanda, and continued on her walk.

No doubt several other neighbors would be recipients of Princess's little presents before the morning was out.

Amanda yawned and jammed her hands in her robe pockets, her toes curling from the cold driveway. "Maybe after breakfast I'll get dressed and we can head down to the dealership."

"The dealership?" He looked at her.

"You know, the van. So I can get my . . . the Toyota."

He stiffened, then concentrated on a tangle in the coil. Saying nothing.

"We're going to, right?"

"I thought you might think it over for a few days. Before we do anything rash."

"I don't need to think about it. I want—"

"Tell you what." He'd gotten the snag undone. "I'll finish the yard, and you can go down to the dealership." His tone was light, conversational.

"But why don't you—"

"Mandy," he said gently. Squinting into the brightness behind her, he rested his forearms on his knees. "I want the van. I like the van. And if you don't, then maybe you need to work this out for yourself."

"Fine." Irritated, she accepted the challenge. She dressed quickly, poured coffee in a travel mug and drove the minivan to Hemp's Used Motorway. It wasn't hard to find. After all, she'd seen the commercials a bazillion times, and knew the address by heart.

Faded pennants strung across the sales lot like a tired fiesta. Amanda scanned the rows for her Toyota, but didn't spot it anywhere. Sighing, she executed a turn to a dead stop in front of the sales office. Scavengers hovered on the stairs, no doubt tossing a coin over who'd get the next sale on the lot.

Greasy Mustache won, sliding his hand over an impossibly

black pompadour. He smashed his cigarette, straightened his tie and advanced toward the van. "Name's Donny." His handshake was as vigorous as his breath. "What can I do you for, little lady?"

Amanda adopted her best Katy Thompson impersonation. "I need to speak with your manager. Right away."

"Now, now, hold it there." Donny wheezed and held up both hands. "Lemme see if I can help you."

"No. Thank you, but I need immediate assistance from someone in charge." Amanda stared him down.

"Allrighty," he conceded. "I'll get the top man for you." He shuffled toward the oversize windows with a shrug.

A few minutes later, a hefty man in a silver Stetson strode out the double doors, leaving them flapping in his wake. The friction from his waddle could have started a fire. "Steve Boyd, Hemp's used-sales manager. Can I hepya?"

"I hope so. There's been a mistake on a trade-in. I need to get my car back."

"Which car is that?"

"A Toyota hatchback. Red, two-door. Tan interior. My husband traded it. For this." She motioned toward the hunter green minivan. "Awaiting my signature. I'm afraid I won't be signing."

"Now, that van's a real peach. . . ."

"But I'm not interested in this *peach*. If you would please return my car, I can be about my business." She dangled the minivan's uni-key.

"Well, it's not that easy, Mrs. . . ."

"Amanda Reynolds. Mark Reynolds arranged the paperwork."

"Oh, thassright. Nice guy. Not too many husbands'd do a thing like that. Get a new car for their wives, a surprise and all." Steve Boyd regarded her.

Amanda refrained from comment and ignored the guilt whispers. She did not owe the used-sales manager an explanation.

"Told me he's in the ministry, and y'all needed it for the Lord's work." He cocked an eyebrow. "Guess the Lord don't need no more helpers?" Huffing, he opened the door.

She followed Steve up a short stack of stairs to an office. Shiny posters filled the walls, portraying misty forests at dawn and determined joggers on the beach, with captions like STRIVE and IMAGINE.

"Lessee here." He filtered through papers, shuffling them like a Las Vegas dealer.

Amanda sensed a scam coming on. Steve Boyd had a loaded deck, and she knew it.

"Here we go." He grabbed a sheet with scribbled math figures and whistled through his teeth. "Gosh, I'm almost glad you came in. Nearly *gave* that baby away." He chortled, shaking all the way through his belly, where cheap white buttons threatened to pop.

Amanda didn't join his laughter. She sat on the edge of her seat and waited for the torture to end.

Skimming the paperwork, he shoved on a pair of glasses. "Hmmm. Seems there's a bit of a wrinkle."

"Problem?"

"A small kink." He peered at her over plastic amber rims.

"How small?"

"Well, this here deal on your van?" He wiggled the sheets. "Was what we like to call a lock."

"But without my signature it *can't* be a lock," she pointed out. "Legally speaking. Right?"

Steve Boyd rolled his eyes at the mention of legalities. "Your husband told us your Hancock was a done deal."

"It's not, though. Because you need me to sign and I'm not going to."

"I'm beginning to understand that, *MizReynolds*. However, it seems"—he tapped the paperwork—"one of our junior salesmen's already loaned out your Toyota. To some potential buyers. A beginner's mistake."

"Who has it?" she asked through clenched teeth.

"Can't tell you that."

Steve Boyd, keeper of great secrets. And small imports with high mileage.

"Now, don't hold me to this." He shifted his weight in the swivel chair, which emitted a low groan. "But we *might* be able to get the Toyota back in the morning."

Amanda noticed he didn't say *your car*. "I should think so, since it doesn't belong to you."

He flinched. "We can handle the exchange then. That is, if you haven't fallen in love with that peach out there by tomorrow."

Aha. The classic bait 'n' switch. She'd learned car talk at the knee of a master, and no low-rate dealer from Potter Springs was going to pull a fast one on Ben Thompson's daughter. Amanda scooped up the detested key and pushed back the chair. "I *will* see you in the morning, Mr. Boyd."

Driving home, she fought tears of frustration. The good old boy network. Jerks. Success eluded her, and she wanted to weep in Mark's arms. Or have him do something primal, like go beat up every last salesman on the lot.

Then she remembered—she'd left on a tense note this morning. And it was her fault. However misguided, he'd done a nice thing in buying the van for her and she'd overreacted.

How did they ever get this far apart? She wanted to throw herself at him and start anew, to holler, "Do over!" and have the past months erased, shaken clean like a brand new Etch-A-Sketch.

At home, Mark met her in the kitchen. He'd been waiting.

Looking downright adorable, in sweatpants and running socks, standing on the vinyl tiles.

No sense of victory graced his brow. No crude championship from his stance. He didn't even check the driveway to see what she'd driven back from the dealership.

On the table between them sat fresh sandwiches and glasses of milk, with cloth napkins folded just so. Some of the neighbor's garden mums filled a mason jar. An indoor picnic for two, ready and waiting.

"Hi." She took the first step. "That looks great." Tossing her purse on the floor, she prepared to tell all. To commiserate. To love and let him love her back.

Then she noticed the ashen cast to his face.

"Your mom called while you were gone. From the hospital in Houston. It's your dad."

CHAPTER 20

minutes on the hour

M ark sat next to the uneaten sandwiches and tepid milk, in awe of his wife's cyclonic fury. Since she'd hung up the phone after a terse exchange of information with her mother, he'd never seen her move so fast. An auburn whirlwind.

She pulled clothes from the dryer, cotton tangled in denim. Her hands shook as she packed the pile, still knotted, into an open knapsack. She dug a few things out of her larger suitcase from the retreat and transferred them to the smaller bag.

"Can I help? Is there something I can do?"

"No." She tossed in a few books and her journal.

"Let me call the church. Get Ervin to cover my rotation. I'm coming with you." He ran a hand through his hair and stared at

157

the phone. He thought of his father-in-law, Ben. Tobacco and beer, sharp eyes and wide girth. He couldn't imagine the level of pain it would take to fell such a giant.

"No. You stay. You're needed here."

"Don't *you* need me?" He followed her to the bathroom. They both hardly fit in the tiny room, the towel bar braced into his side. The edge of the bedroom carpet tickled his heel.

She stuffed toiletries and his toothbrush in a large plastic bag. He didn't tell her she picked the wrong one.

"Of course I do." She placed a dry, fleeting kiss on his cheek. "But I'll have Mother. And I've got to get to Houston as soon as possible. By the time you arrange everything with Ervin, I could be there." She shut the medicine cabinet.

"Are you sure?" he asked her in the mirror.

"I'm sure."

Back in the kitchen, she dug in her purse, leaving wrinkled receipts on the table. "If things change, either way, I'll call you. We'll find out what's going on. How bad it is. Later, when we know more." She hefted the knapsack, zipper open with a pink bra strap hanging out, over her shoulder.

Mark took the bag from her, zipped it shut and carried it to the van.

Outside, he tugged her coat closed and buttoned the top toggle. He held her a minute longer than she held him. "I love you."

"Me too. Take care of Mr. Chesters for me." She started the engine and pulled away. The minivan disappeared down the street, turning out of sight.

Mark stared at the empty road, imagining himself racing down its length and reaching her. Yet, the rift seemed so wide, he didn't think he could ever cross it. No matter how fast he ran.

\*     \*     \*

AFTER INQUIRING AT the information desk, Amanda found the ICU waiting room on the fifth floor. Once there, she merely followed the smell of smoke and an orderly hightailing it down the hall.

Katy Thompson looked worse than Amanda had ever seen her. The designer, color-wheeled clothing was gone. Her naked lips wrapped around a cigarette. She wore plaid stretchy pants with a floral sweater and slip-ons. No hose.

"Ma'am." The hospital worker halted in front of her mother. "May I remind you, *again,* this is a *no smoking* facility?"

Not wanting to get in one of her mother's quarrels, Amanda hid behind a magazine rack and waited for the storm to blow over.

"Yes, Bryan, you may." Like an amused high schooler, Katy took another long drag and blew the smoke in artful swirls.

"I'll have to ask you, again, to please refrain from smoking. You are welcome to utilize our *outdoor* receptacles." Bryan had a slight lisp. *Pleath, sthmoking, retheptacleth.*

"All right." Katy puffed deeply, nodding.

"And, as we've discussed *several* times today, you must put the cigarette out *immediately* or I will be forced to notify . . . security." His frustration formed a beautiful hard *s.*

She fizzled the butt in her makeshift coffee cup ashtray and smiled sweetly. "Those are the magic words."

"Really." His disgust gave him a lecturing tone. "You are endangering our patients. Other families. You should have more respect."

"And *you* should realize your patients are in plenty of danger already. A little second-hand smoke isn't going to make one iota of difference. But as for me"—she rubbed her temples— "you do *not* want to encounter me on a nicotine low. Now, *that's* dangerous."

Bryan stomped away and disappeared around the corner, warning, "I'll be back to check on you."

"I'm counting on it," Katy called to the empty corridor.

"Hi, Mom." Amanda came out from her hiding place.

"Oh, honey." Dark circles marred Katy's porcelain complexion, as if the deep blue from her eyes had leaked down to tender skin and stained it. She appeared ten years older since the last time Amanda saw her.

The day they left Houston for Potter Springs. When her daddy held her in his strong arms and he cried. He'd smelled like Old Spice and humid summertime and he whispered in her ear, "I love you, baby girl."

Amanda blinked the memory away, fighting to keep herself together. She pulled from her mother's thin embrace. "How's Daddy?"

"Holding on. You know your dad." Katy sat down again on the bench seat. She twisted a stir stick as she spoke.

"Can I see him?"

Her mother checked her slender Rolex, the hot sparkle of diamonds out of place in the astringent room. "Not yet. We've got a while before they'll let us back in."

"What happened?"

"I'm not sure, exactly. One minute, he was working on the car, and the next I heard a loud crash. He knocked his tool chest over when he fell. It was early, just past breakfast. I wasn't dressed yet."

This was not a revelation. Amanda's mother, barring any critical social engagements, sometimes stayed in her cashmere robe and slippers until well past the noon hour.

Amanda nodded and moved a magazine so she could sit closer.

"And he just lay there, on the garage floor." Katy wrapped thin arms around herself, as if the cement from the garage had chilled her too. "Wrenches and metal things all over the place. Splayed out like he'd been run over, looking at me. For help. He couldn't talk." She ran her hands through golden blonde hair. Grease smudges spoiled her French manicure. "The *look* on his face. My God, if I live the rest of my life, I never want to see that look again."

"Is he going to be okay?" Amanda repeated her question. She'd first asked it hours before, frantic on the phone after Mark told her the news.

Katy, between uncharacteristic tears, had told her she didn't know, but to get to Houston as soon as possible. That she might not get to see her father alive again if she didn't hurry.

So she had, knowing as she turned the minivan's key that she'd made a deal with the devil. Steve Boyd, through circumstances outside his control, had sold her the metallic green beast.

Crying as she crossed the county line, Amanda was unsure if her tears fell for her marriage, her father or the loss of her car. Maybe all three.

"The paramedics said it was a heart attack," Katy explained. "A failure. Blood pressure, poor diet, obesity. Your father hit all the high points."

"Who knows? Maybe this'll be the wake-up call he needs."

"Sure it will." Katy rubbed the back of her neck, stretching from side to side. She squeezed Amanda's hand. "Thanks for coming. Was the ride all right? Did your car make it?"

Eleven hours at breakneck speed, eating prepackaged gas-station food and arriving in Houston's crawling masses after dark. "Piece of cake," she lied.

"I bet." Katy pulled a cigarette pack from her purse and dug for her lighter.

"I got a new car," Amanda added. "A minivan actually."

"Really? How interesting."

If Katy had been in top form, she might have run further with this information.

"Have you eaten anything?" Eyeing the unlit cigarette in her mother's hand, Amanda hoped to ward off another confrontation with the staff of Houston Memorial Hospital.

"Some crackers. Coffee."

"Let's go get something," Amanda said. "I saw a cafeteria downstairs. Is it all right to leave?"

"The next visitation's not for a while. I get to go in every hour, for about ten minutes." Katy stuffed the cigarette pack back in the tapestry handbag, pulling it to her shoulder. Miraculously, the accessory almost tied her mismatched ensemble together.

*Amazing,* thought Amanda. *Only my mother.*

"It's crazy." Katy led the way down the bright hallway. "You live your whole life with a person, and when they think it's the end, they'll only give you minutes on the hour."

The silver doors slid shut and Katy pressed the button for the first floor. "Minutes on the hour." She applied bloodred lipstick in the elevator's mirrored sheen. Gazing at her reflection, she murmured, "And that's not enough."

∽

# wonderland

"Heckuva job, Mark. Heckuva job." Ervin Plumley, in a curly wig and painted face, held an oozing chili dog in one hand and nearly tore Mark's arm off with the other.

The church's gym smelled of dirty socks and cotton candy. Children darted like fireflies, their rolling laughter echoed through the crowded area. Fall Festival, at full capacity.

"Thanks, Ervin!" Shouting over the din, Mark returned the handshake in the West Texas palm-crushing tradition. "I didn't do it by myself. You, the deacons—everybody—deserve the credit. Your work on the setup, especially."

Mark had enlisted an army of helpers, charming the Ladies' Guild and sweet-talking the board. As a result, his vision had

163

evolved into the biggest carnival Lakeview Community Church had ever hosted.

"Shoot." Lakeview's head pastor wiped spilled chili off his arm. "Wasn't no step for a stepper." Ervin took another bite, then darted a look around. "Oh, Lord. There's Peggy. I'm fixin' to be in trouble." He crammed the tail end of the dog in, poking the bun with blunt fingers. "Not good for the cholesterol," he confessed through chipmunk cheeks.

"Ervin, I see you!" Penny marched up in a Mother Hubbard costume. "Just how do you expect to sleep tonight with all that chili? Not to mention candy!"

Ervin flashed a guilty look, his speech stunted by processed foods.

Peggy put her hands on her hips. "Don't think I haven't watched you put away more sweets than the Easter Bunny. It's gluttony, Ervin. Sheer gluttony. Save some for the children." She kissed him on the cheek and slapped his belly, largely hidden inside the clown jumpsuit.

"Hello, Moses," she greeted Mark. "Where'd you get that outfit?"

He lifted the robe's hem from the floor. "From the children's supply closet. I think it might be left over from a pageant." Mark scratched his face under the gray beard. Holding up two arched cardboard tablets, he added, "I made the commandments myself."

"Well, it's a fine party," Peggy praised. "You've done a wonderful job, our best yet. Although, you might check the booths. I think someone's made off with the rings for the bottle toss." After patting Mark's shoulder, she strode away.

Leaving Ervin to digest his junk food, Mark found the missing rings and mixed among the masses. Children ran wild in costumes, carrying bags full of candy and prizes. They bounced in the inflatable castle, discarding tennis shoes and cowboy boots outside the plastic door. They ate corn dogs and cupcakes, and raced delirious on a communal sugar high.

Mark crossed his arms over his long brown tunic and nodded, satisfied.

Happy children equaled happy church members.

Pick-a-Duck, judging by the waiting kids snaked around the corner, reigned as the favorite booth. The zigzag line almost blocked the balloon dart display. For safety's sake, Mark corralled the partygoers into a more uniform order.

"Every duck's a winner," called Courtney Williams over the throng.

Shaking his head, Mark wondered why she had requested to host the Pick-a-Duck. That woman ran a mile a minute. She'd done huge amounts of work for the carnival. Getting Sunday schools to sign up in shifts, soliciting donors for the raffle and persuading women into baking for the cakewalk.

At the booth, plastic ducks bobbed in a toddler pool, their flat bottoms marked with a winning number, 1, 2 or 3. Children plucked dripping fowl from the makeshift pond, showing the hostess to get their reward. A great game.

The only problem was the wait. Squirming in line, a tired Cinderella wiped her nose on a glittery sleeve. "Is it my turn yet?"

"Just a minute, hon. You hang in there." In what looked like a custom fit Alice-in-Wonderland costume, Courtney appeared unruffled in spite of her booming business.

"My, don't you look pretty!" Courtney told the princess, brushing back a smooth lock of her own real-life Alice hair. She smiled, lip gloss gleaming.

Dazzled, the tot seemed prepared to wait an eternity for her chance at a duck.

"Looks like you've got a handle on this," Mark complimented.

"I hope so." Courtney laughed and waited on her next customer. "Two tickets, please."

"I can't thank you enough for all your help on this thing." He meant it. With her advice and organization, the carnival proved to be a whopping success.

"Oh, it's my pleasure." She reached behind her for a rubber snake and plunked it in the winner's bag. "Here you go, a black one."

The satisfied pirate showed gap-toothed approval.

"Are you set here?" Mark asked. "Have enough candy?"

"Let's see." She bent down to dig under the table, revealing a perfectly tied black bow on her narrow waist, long ribbons flowing over puffy Alice skirts. "I'm good on candy bars and snakes. Glow balls and erasers are running low, but I can make do."

"No problem. I'll get them for you."

"Thank you so much." She turned back to the game. "Number one. That's a glow ball. How's pink, you little cutie?" The toddler pulled a shriveled thumb out of her mouth to grab the toy.

"I'll put a rush on it." Mark grinned at Courtney's patience and headed for the supply closet. Luckily, he'd ordered plenty, not wanting a lack on his first watch as carnival planner. He passed busy ticket-sales counters. The lockboxes filled with dollar bills, and the ladies rolled out tickets by the dozens.

He couldn't wait to compare this year's grosses with last year's, and hoped to beat it by 50 percent.

A loud "Hey, Mark!" interrupted his mission to the storage room.

Jimmy Underwood, the owner of the gravelly twang, leaned against the brick wall with a cardboard bowl of jalapeño nachos. Beside him sat his dark-haired wife, holding a baby.

Mark ran through his memory, pulling up a mental file. Mail carrier. Deacon. Husband to Missy, Amanda's friend from the retreat. Keeping church members organized in his mind was a special gift, and useful. "Hey there, Jimmy. How's the route treating you?"

"Can't complain. Or I could." He snickered. "But since we're in church, I better not."

"Hello, Missy. Taylor's getting bigger by the minute." Mark squeezed a chubby little thigh. The baby gurgled at him, and Mark caught a scent of powder that teased the back of his throat like springtime allergies.

Thumping the infant's padded rear in a well-rehearsed rhythm, Missy agreed. "He eats like a horse."

"Where's *your* better half?" A gob of cheese glommed on to Jimmy's mustache.

In complete view, Missy kicked her husband with the toe of her boot.

Mark pushed a nearby chair under a table, clearing the walkway. "She's in Houston. You might remember her dad had a heart attack?"

"Oh, that's right. How's he doin' anyways? He gonna make it?" Jimmy licked his fingers.

"The doctors think so. He's at home now, but it'll take a while for him to get back on his feet." Using some discarded napkins, Mark wiped the spotless table.

"Been there awhile now, hain't she?"

For this astute remark, Jimmy received another swift blow to the shin.

"What the . . . ouch! Missy, what's gotten into you?" Rubbing his leg, Jimmy shook his head at Mark. "Must be the hormones."

Missy turned as pink as a glow ball.

"Recovery's complicated." Mark ignored the squabble. "They don't want to rush things. Mandy's a big help to her mother."

Noticing he'd unconsciously crushed the napkins in his fist, he tossed the wad, à la Michael Jordan, into a nearby can.

He missed.

"Anyway, Jimmy, you know church life." He retrieved the fallen napkins from the floor. "It'll keep you plenty busy."

"I heard that." The mail carrier grunted and swabbed up more cheese with a chip.

Balancing the baby on one hip, Missy stood and caught Mark's sleeve. "You call us if you need anything. And tell Amanda. Tell her that I . . ." She bit her lip. "That *we're* thinking of her."

"Will do," he said. "But as for me, really, I'm fine."

In the supply closet, the comforting smell of animal crackers and construction paper greeted him. He leaned his forehead against the door, shutting himself inside for a few treasured seconds. Composing his Pastor Mark mask before it fell off and revealed the crumbling man underneath.

Each day, he woke, and in the intangible moments before full awareness, he knew peace. A calmness, a feeling of safety. Then he'd remember. *Amanda is gone. My house is empty. My life is empty, and none of this means anything without her.* The sense of security ripped away, leaving him to grieve through his day behind the falseness of his smile. Precious Pastor Mark, always peaceful, always together. Perfect.

The only one who knew his imperfections was over three hundred miles away. And judging from last night's phone call, she had no plans to return anytime soon.

"When are you coming home?" A broken record, he played it nightly. In the dark of their bedroom on Mesquite Street, where his own vulnerability wouldn't disgust him.

"I'm not sure. I can't describe it, what it's like to see Daddy this way." Amanda paused. "He needs me here, I think."

*I need you too,* Mark wanted to plead. But he'd been on enough guilt trips, paid for by his mother, to try to manipulate Mandy to suit himself. He remained quiet, listening to the click of the floor furnace on the cool night. Keeping himself from begging. *When, Mandy, when?*

"How's the carnival coming?" She changed the subject.

"It's good. We've got it just about ready." Hoping to entice her with the excitement of life in Potter. "You should see how everybody's pitched in. Ervin, Penny, all the deacons. And Courtney's been great with the organizing."

"Courtney . . . Williams?"

"Yeah, you know her. She's president of the ladies' group, volunteers all the time?"

"Oh, I know her. She of the *LeFleur* cosmetics." Amanda heavily accented the French term.

"You should have her over sometime. She's really nice. I think you two could be friends."

The silence on the other end of the line told him his wife thought otherwise. He overcompensated for the awkwardness. "You know, she's divorced. Apparently had a tough time of it. Married to a real jerk. No kids. She could probably use a friend like you."

"Maybe," Amanda said. "Maybe she wants a friend like you."

"Don't be ridiculous." Mark rolled to his side, squishing the pillow. "She's committed to the church. To the kids' program. That's all." He switched to the defensive. "It's not like you to be jealous."

"It's not like you to go on and on about other women."

"Mandy, let's don't do this. When are you coming home?" Same song, same dance.

"I don't know."

In his mind he heard, *I don't want to.*

Still, he told her that he loved her.

*Me too,* she'd whispered across the miles, then left him alone in the dark, the receiver pressed tight to his ear.

The roar of the carnival broke through Mark's memory. He lifted his head from the door and rubbed his temples. He'd call again tonight. Maybe just a few more days. He left the sanctuary of the closet and let the carnival swallow him again.

Returning with the promised glow balls and erasers, Mark handed them over to a still-swamped Courtney.

"My hero!" she announced, sorting the toys into her bins.

"Do you need anything else? A Coke or something?"

"How thoughtful. But I don't think I'd even have time to drink it." She turned to the game. "No, no, sugar. You've got to put the duck back *into* the water. It's not to take home. But here, here's a brand new eraser from Pastor Mark."

The toddler looked up at him, awed. He knelt down and gestured for a high five. The child's light slap on his hand left a sticky residue.

"Oh look. You're so good with kids," Courtney gushed, gathering tickets from the next player.

"Thanks," he said, straightening. He wondered if the church's bathroom soap had antibacterial qualities.

"I know what I'm talking about." Handing out a Kit Kat, she informed Mark over her sleeve, "Teaching elementary, you get a knack for that kind of thing."

The microphone amp crackled at the cakewalk. He should get over there and check on it. "Sure about that Coke?"

"Hmmm." Courtney checked the gym clock, high above the pushed-in bleachers. "I can't right now. I still have another thirty minutes on my shift." She faced him, guileless in her Alice blue. "But how about later?"

# wrong turn

Green-gray clouds swam over the Houston moon, bloated and heavy. In her parents' house, Amanda peeled back the bed comforter, pink roses on brushed cotton. As if on cue, her Princess phone rang its warbled tune.

"Hello?" She balanced the phone on one ear, settling in for her nightly visit with Mark.

"Hello, Mrs. Reynolds. Forgive me for calling so late. This is Dale Ochs, from the Lakeview Board."

"Yes, Mr. Ochs." Surprise made her voice louder. Dale the Watchdog, calling her long distance in Houston. "Is everything all right?"

"Oh yes. And please call me Dale. Actually, I'm calling on

behalf of the board to check on you. To update our prayer logs for members. Tell me, how is your father?"

"Much better, thank you," Amanda said, relieved. "He's home now, getting stronger by the day."

"Wonderful. Can't tell you how glad we are to hear it."

An awkward pause filled the line, as if Dale expected further discussion. Or maybe an explanation for her continued absence.

Amanda wasn't about to give one. Or inform the deacon that she planned to head back to Potter Springs tomorrow morning. Mark deserved to be the first to know.

She hadn't meant to stay so long, but problems in Potter Springs seemed bigger, and harder, than simply easing into life in Houston. She slept in her childhood bedroom and played cards with her father, convincing herself that his continued care, and her companionship, provided reason enough to stay.

Going home meant facing truths she wasn't sure she could handle. The hurts on both sides, she realized after the van fiasco, ran deeper than she'd thought.

But the calendar ticked by and her father looked better by the day. Amanda sensed her usefulness as a houseguest coming to an end.

"Why don't you come with me to the fund-raiser this Saturday?" Katy had asked over eggs Benedict at the breakfast table this morning, flipping through her calendar.

"I don't think so, Mom." She'd been to enough of the things to know she'd be squished into panty hose surrounded by her mother's obsequious friends, as plastic as the Botox in their faces.

Amanda imagined bringing some of *her* new friends to such a function. Kendra Sue in her socks and Earth sandals, or Pam with her gastric problems and puffy sweatshirts. With a smile, she realized she missed them. "Besides, I should be getting back."

"What for?" Katy adjusted the tie on her cashmere robe.

"For Mark," Amanda answered easily. The truth dawning as she spoke. "He needs me."

She couldn't wait to tell him when he called. He'd ask, *When are you coming home, Mandy?* and instead of her standard, *I'm not sure,* she'd whisper, *Tomorrow.* After weeks of pleading, and persuading, he'd be so pleased.

"Isn't Fall Festival this evening?" Amanda made conversation with Dale, wondering why he lingered on the line.

"That's right," he answered. "Just finished up. Quite a turnout. Your husband is rather *effective* with the congregants."

The way Dale said it didn't sound like a compliment.

"He's gifted that way," Amanda agreed. She flipped through one of her mother's fashion magazines, noting that most of the outfits cost more than her car. Her old car anyway.

No stores back in Potter carried that kind of high-end couture. Everybody shopped at Super Wal-Mart or Target, and Amanda found a freedom in the simplicity. A lack of ferocious fashion and competitiveness she'd experienced in her mother's world. She decided she liked the Potter Springs way of things better.

"Between the Ladies' Guild and Mark," Dale went on, "it was a tremendous showing. They've worked closely together."

"Who?" She didn't like the way he slid through "closely together."

"Mark and the Ladies' Guild president, Ms. Williams. Do you know her?"

"A little." *As much as I want to.* In the magazine, an article promised to reveal "Ten Secrets to Sizzling Romance."

"They've become quite a team. A regular Frick and Frack."

"How nice." Amanda stifled a yawn and looked at the clock. When would Mark call and get her off the line with this nutcase?

"In fact," Dale added, almost as an afterthought, "they must have some follow-up work to do this evening."

"Follow up?" The glossy pages rustled.

"Oh, it's nothing. Nothing at all. They left together, after the carnival. Courtney's hard to miss in that Camaro. Perhaps he needed a ride home. The church truck, from what I understand, is in the shop for repairs. That would leave him without transportation, now wouldn't it? Thank goodness he and Courtney are such good friends."

*Left the carnival together. Red Camaro. Such good friends.*

Blood rushed to Amanda's head and the magazine fell shut. High on wooden shelves, her porcelain doll collection became jeering gargoyles in the shadows of the room.

"Yes. I guess so." Hollowness filled her. She focused on one doll, its Shirley Temple curls forever perky, the rosebud lips pursed just so. Smirking.

"Anyway, just wanted to check in about your father. We're praying for you. On behalf of the board, let me extend our best wishes for a continued speedy recovery."

"Thank you for calling." She could hardly breathe.

"And can we expect you back in Potter Springs anytime soon?"

His question slithered down her neck, reptilian and cold. "Yes," she answered, the pressure crushing her throat. "Soon." She hung up the phone and rubbed her ear.

Ugly scenarios whirled in her brain like a film reel.

Courtney, ever the saccharine saleswoman, going on about LeFleur's incredible products. *Just feel my skin!*

Courtney tossing her hair. Courtney licking her gloppy lips. Courtney crossing her Barbie-doll legs.

*Wow,* Mark would say. *That's some lotion.*

Amanda picked up the phone again. Dale Ochs must be wrong. Checking the clock on her desk, she figured it out. The carnival. Mark must be exhausted. He probably went straight home and fell asleep. That's why he hadn't called.

She dialed. No answer. The click of the machine. No one home. She imagined the brown phone by the bed, its cord twisted in knots, the ringing loud enough to wake the dead. The one he whispered *I love you* into each night, to her. *Me too,* she always said. But not tonight. Tonight, he wasn't home.

She didn't leave a message. Her heart twisted, and nausea surged. The thought of it, of Mark with Courtney, roiled inside her. She ran to the bathroom and vomited. Wiping her face, she stared in the mirror. Her eyes streamed, sorrow and fear pinched her brow.

Could Mark have done this?

No. After what his father had done to Marianne, he couldn't. He wouldn't, because he knew better. Didn't he?

A DREAM CATCHER hung behind Courtney Williams's velour couch, the long feathers dangling above Mark's head. Her oak bookshelf held a variety of titles. *When Good Men Leave. He Said, He Lied. The Delightful Divorce.*

Courtney thrust a glass in Mark's hand, carbonation fizzing at the top. The bubbles brushed his nose. He drank, then sputtered.

"I hope you don't mind. I put a little something in it." She winked, standing in front of him in her Alice costume. "Thought you might want something stronger than a Dr Pepper, after working so hard. Is it too strong?"

"No, it's fine." *Surreal,* Mark thought. That he sat on Courtney's sofa, her etched Coca-Cola glass in his hand. His Moses wig and beard lay in a scraggly pile on the floor, the Ten Commandments propped against the wall.

"Thanks for helping me with those decorations." Courtney pointed to a pile stacked in the entryway. "I had no idea how many boxes I'd have to carry up here by myself. I'll take you home whenever you're ready."

"Sure." He shrugged. Nothing to go home to.

"Listen, if you don't mind, I'm going to change." She stepped past him, her Mary Jane shoes shining in the shag carpet. "Be back in a flash!"

Just a friendly little drink, she'd said. A reward for carrying five thousand pounds of festival paraphernalia up two flights of stairs to her apartment.

Mark stared at her coffee table, glass inserts under a floral arrangement. He reached out to touch the flowers. Fake. As Courtney rummaged in her bedroom, Mark took another drink, and this time it didn't burn going down.

He remembered the apostle Paul's biblical admonition to young Timothy. *No longer drink only water, but use a little wine for your stomach's sake, and your frequent infirmities.* Mark tipped his glass skyward. A tribute to the wise theologian. Maybe next year's carnival, he'd wear a Paul costume.

"I'm back." Courtney settled beside him on the overstuffed couch, the only other seat in the small apartment. "Whoops!" The thick cushions propelled her weight toward him and she pushed against his thigh. Her nail polish twinkled against his burlap costume for the briefest of instances. "Excuse me."

She wore loose pajama bottoms and a sleeveless top.

He tried hard not to guess if she had anything on beneath the shirt.

"Like another?" She lifted the glass.

He found himself nodding, and watched her pad to the kitchen. "Thanks."

When she reached for the ice, the tank top inched up just enough for him to see the small of her back, tanned and slender.

"Good carnival." She placed the refreshed drink on a wicker coaster.

"We did a good job."

"Sorry Amanda couldn't be here to see it. I bet you miss her."
Courtney brushed her hair back, revealing a bare shoulder, round
and shining, like a caramel apple.

"I do," Mark said. He should be calling his wife now. She never
called him first.

"Amanda's been gone for quite a while," Courtney said. "You
think she'll be back soon?" Sipping her drink, she held her pinkie
aloft.

"I hope so."

"Must be tough." Concern turned her ever-present smile
downward. She placed her hand on his arm.

"Yeah." He rattled the ice.

"So difficult. I know."

" 'S not so bad."

"I know what that's like. Even though it's been over a year for
me. Still, it's hard when they leave." She sighed, the top stretching
against her curves.

"Amanda's coming back." He tore his gaze back to the table.

"Of course she is." Leaving the couch, Courtney bent in front
of the stereo. Phil Collins sang through mediocre speakers.

She returned to his side and they sat, listening to the music.
Mark sank deeper into the cushions, tilting his head back, the
velour soft on his neck. He thought of simple pleasures. Rock-
lite. A cold drink. Sitting next to someone on a couch. An attractive someone.

Courtney brightened. "It's good to have friends, though."

"Friends." He nodded. Gomer Pyle for a boss and the Wicked
Witch for a secretary. Dale the Watchdog sniffing around his
heels, ready to steal his job.

Got no wife. Got no friends.

*Maybe she wants a friend like you,* Amanda had said.

Maybe so, he agreed to himself, and polished off his cocktail.

"I'm so glad you came over," Courtney said. "This is nice."

"Nice," he repeated, his voice soft.

"Just so you know"—her eyes sparkled at him, pearl teeth caught the swell of her lip—"I'm here for you." Her breath smelled of sweet cherries and whiskey.

She went to take his glass. "You done with this?"

"Not yet." He stopped her wrist, and held it. *Maybe I want a friend like her.*

A charge pulled him, drew him in. A slow motion frame inching forward. The light caught the gold on his ring finger, wrapped around her hand, shimmering like a faded dream.

"ARE YOU *INSANE*? Back *off*!" Amanda tapped her brakes like an SOS pattern. On Houston's deadly I-45 interchange, she resorted to red-light communication with the eighteen-wheeler on her tail.

The behemoth bellowed its displeasure in a long, low moan. Amanda had long since turned the radio off to better calm her nerves in the traffic. She hated Phil Collins anyway.

She wondered if she had made a mistake. After packing in a fury, she wrote a note to her parents and left within an hour of Dale's phone call. Downstairs, she slipped out to the driveway with her bag over her shoulder. The engine started with a faithful hum and she backed into the overcast night.

Now, on the freeway, the truck behind her finally whipped around and passed on the left. It cut into her lane, not six inches between their bumpers.

Driving blind behind the gigantic box-on-wheels, she concentrated on not hitting the orange barrels on either side of the van. Her skills were rusty from puttering around Potter's lazy streets. Stop signs there outnumbered traffic lights a hundred to one, and the only freeway was on the outskirts of town, for coming or going.

Still, if she didn't ding the van, maybe Steve Boyd would take it back after all.

Entertaining that hope, she forgot to double-check the scrambled interchange, as if she could see anything beyond the silver metal of the truck.

Much later, in the darkness, she spotted her mistake. HIGHWAY 59, read the sign. *That's right. But wait.* Her worn-out eyes had played tricks on her, tired as they were. That cost her a few more miles.

South, the next marker confirmed. She wasn't headed toward Potter at all. Through a slight of the road, aided by confusion and abetted by emotion, she was speeding in the wrong direction.

She found herself driving in the middle of the night on Houston's busy southbound route.

The road to Mexico.

# the number

S tars spread high and bright over a blackened sky in downtown Potter Springs. The courthouse, a ghoulish presence with stone made green by the streetlamps, oversaw the proceedings of the square. Activities that were, at this late hour, nonexistent.

Mark paused at the northern corner, waiting absurdly for the walk sign. Next to him, a banged up Pinto crawled to a stop. The window rolled down, releasing the dead, sweet odor of marijuana and heavy metal riffs played at full volume.

Mark recognized the tune. "Welcome to the Jungle."

"Sweet, fancy Moses!" High-pitched snickers came from inside. "That you, Pastor Mark?"

"Hi, Benny." Standing alone, wearing Fall Festival attire in the starkness of the intersection, Mark saw no point in denying the charge.

"Whatcha doin' downtown in the middle of the night?" Lakeview's junior janitor asked. "Wearing . . . that?"

"Just taking a little walk." Mark's Moses wig and beard dangled from his grasp like a boneless rat, twisting in the wind.

"Wanna ride?"

"No, I'm fine."

"Come on, dude, it's getting cold," the shotgun passenger said to Benny. "Roll the window up." The youth, in a black T-shirt adorned with gigantic lips, looked at Mark through red-rimmed eyes.

"Chill," Benny said. "I can't leave him here, he's my boss." He turned to Mark. "This is Hoover."

"Nice to meet you," Mark offered.

"Whatever," said Hoover.

"Get in the back," Benny told his friend.

"Unh-unh."

"Get in the back! Dude, he's got a skirt on, okay?"

Clearly resisting the demotion, Hoover emerged and arranged himself in the backseat.

Seeing that Benny wasn't going anywhere unless Mark availed himself of this unwelcome hospitality, he slid into the car and let the smoke waft around him.

"What's on you?" Benny asked, staring at Mark's wet robes.

"Dr Pepper. I spilled it."

"Try not to get the seats wet, okay?" Benny threw the car in gear and they roared toward Mesquite Street, drowning in the angry melody of Guns N' Roses.

*The roses,* Mark thought. He'd knocked them over.

While the car drove to the rhythm of eighties metal bands, Mark pushed away questions as to how Benny knew his exact address. He didn't want to know. Instead, he relived the latest debacle of his life.

Reaching for Courtney in his lonely fog, reflexes dulled by whiskey and misuse, he had tipped his empty drink. The ice cubes scattered slippery as bugs and he chased them with slow fingers. Fingers that accidentally unsettled the fake arrangement. Dumped it to the shag carpet, where it bounced and the stems came out like emaciated legs, the heavy rose heads upside down and dusty.

In the process, he managed to upend Courtney's full soda, which splashed an ugly brown swoosh on her tank top. And then she shrieked about her couch, and don't step on the flowers, and that's Gran's vase.

The sight, the sounds, cleared the haze away. The wrongness of the moment penetrated his being. This time, he embraced it. "I better go," he told her, and slipped out the door. He remembered in the parking lot that he had no car, but he didn't glance backward.

Night air sobered him quicker than the icy liquid on his lap, and the wind whipped the folds of his costume. He walked the streets, shuffling in sandals that rubbed his ankles like tangled ropes. *The sin that so easily entangles,* as Paul would say. He waited for a message, a thunderbolt to zap him from the recesses of the sky for even thinking about what he'd almost done.

Instead, he got a couple of stoned teenagers in a Pinto and an uncomfortable yet speedy ride home.

On Mesquite Street, Mark was deposited without ceremony on his driveway. "See you t'morrow," Benny said. The strains of "Paradise City" shadowed along with the Pinto's blue smoke as it screamed down the lane.

The house condemned Mark with emptiness, dark and quiet. He went directly to the machine. No messages. On caller ID he saw a call that came through at 10:45 from Ben Thompson. Amanda.

*She actually called. I wasn't here. She called, and I wasn't here.*

He checked the clock. 12:38. Too late to wake her. Maybe just plain too late.

He stumbled to the bedroom where he lay facedown on his pillow with his arms flung wide, still in the dampened costume, too tired to change.

THE NEXT DAY, the cold sun touched the plains with the barest warmth and brushed Lakeview's sloped roof. Near the entrance, Dale Ochs ground his cigarette in the sand tower ashtray. Mark swept past him.

"Morning." Dale fell into step alongside him. "You look beat. Long night?"

"Nope." Mark strode on.

"I'm doing the receipts for the carnival today." Dale struggled to keep up, burgundy tassels dancing on the tips of his pointed loafers. "Have you got them?"

"In my office."

"Good. I'll follow you there."

They passed Benny in the hall, who ignored Dale completely and gave Mark a faint chin nod. "Hey, dude."

"Hey." A silent agreement between men. Men who had bonded in the darkest hour through one of life's most unbreakable pacts. A midnight ride, no questions asked, no stories told. It would not be discussed again.

Maybe Mark had a friend after all.

"Good morning, Ms. Hodges," he said to Letty.

"Is it?" Seated at her desk, she licked an envelope, her pale tongue long and skinny against the fold.

Mark shuddered inwardly. "I hope so."

In his office, Mark handed Dale the packet with leftover tickets and exchange logs, along with a zippered pouch full of the evening's take.

"Why didn't you make a night deposit?" Dale ran a hand over Mark's shelves, as if testing them for strength.

"Had other things to do. It was safe here."

"Other things. Oh, that's right." Dale checked his fingers for dust, then rubbed them against each other. "Helping our lovely Ms. Williams. Does the Camaro ride as fast as it looks?"

Mark's blood slowed as it pounded in his ears, full of bass and fear. "She had some boxes."

"Of course. Nice of you, all those boxes. What a friend."

*I could use a friend like you.*

"Did you need anything else?"

"This should do." Dale lifted the small pile. "When I update our prayer lists, I'll make sure to give you a copy."

"Thanks." Mark clicked on his computer, a not-so-subtle dismissal. It warmed up with various growls and clicks, the ancient beast coming to life.

"Oh, and congratulations on your father-in-law." Dale paused in the doorway.

"Sorry?"

"His improving health. I spoke to Amanda last night." Dale's smile was the stuff of nightmares. "She says he's doing much, much better." His tiny shoes tapped down the hall again, and Mark detected a pattern of joy in the rhythm.

Dale talked to Amanda. Last night. And Amanda tried to call. Didn't leave a message.

What had Dale told her? What had he seen?

Mark imagined the deacon pressed against Courtney's balcony window, beak nose squashed against the glass. Long enough to know nothing happened? Or had he been there at all?

He checked his watch, Mandy should be up by now. He'd have to face her sometime. Explain what happened. No telling what venom Dale had spewed.

No need to panic. He'd clear everything up with a simple phone call.

He posted the In Conference sign and shut the paneled door. Saying a quick prayer, he set his gut and dialed.

"Thompson residence." Katy's cool alto answered the phone.

"Hello. This is Mark." He never knew how to address her. Mother wasn't right, Mrs. Thompson too formal. Katy, maybe. Dragonlady, his favorite, clearly unacceptable.

"Hello, Mark." She sounded disappointed. "Mandy make it back all right? I was waiting to phone, hoping she would sleep in."

*Mandy . . . make it back?* The words skipped around his head like errant pinballs. He couldn't get them in the right order. *Back. Mandy. Mandy isn't back.* "She's not in Houston?"

"Of course not. She left last night."

Stale coffee from his I ♥ MY WIFE mug wafted up at him. A gift from Amanda when they got engaged, he drank from the souvenir every morning. Hand washed it before leaving so he could use it the next day.

"Say that again." As he stared at the bright red letters on the cup, his voice hoarsened.

"I said she left," Katy repeated. "I didn't get her amusing little note until this morning. Naturally, she didn't ask *my* opinion— driving off in the middle of the night . . ."

The bottom of his office chair fell into an abyss.

What had Dale *said*?

"She gets it from her father. Never mind worrying her mother to death."

"When?" His own mind whirled in circles, touching down at odd points. *Note. Driving off. Morning.*

"Last night. I already explained—what's the matter with you?" Katy's imperialism had no problem traveling long distance.

He fought for calm, for the clarity to speak. "She's not back. She hasn't come home."

"Whatever are you talking about?"

"She *isn't here.*"

"That's not funny, Mark."

"Are you sure she left?" Hope, like a fragile shield, held the whirlwind at bay.

"Quite. Her room's cleared out. The van is gone." She paused. "*Stunning* color, by the way."

He let that slide. Unable to comprehend Dragonlady's jabs while her daughter might lie dead, crashed on the side of the road in a volcano of metal.

The clicking of a lighter sounded over the line.

He took measured breaths to quell the spinning hysteria. "So, what do we do? How do we find her?"

Inhaling deeply, Katy didn't answer right away. Then, "Call her cell phone."

"Her what?"

"Cellular phone. Portable. Wireless. The kind you can take with you, in a car for instance. Or a minivan, if you're so blessed."

"She doesn't have one," he said. "She doesn't have a cell phone."

"Yes, she does. I bought it for her when she got here. I'll call her." With a click, Katy Thompson ended the conversation.

A cell phone. Still holding the extension with his shoulder, Mark pried his hands off his desk, one digit at a time. He prayed for a miracle while the empty line beeped in his ear.

He hung up, defeat washing over him like a stain.

Then the truth hit.

*My wife has a cell phone. And I don't even have her number.*

CHAPTER 24

crossing over

At the border crossing, a flashing light warned travelers to stop. Deadlocked in traffic, Amanda ignored the cell phone ringing in her bag and stared at the atlas. The open window siphoned in sounds of other road travelers, running engines and children squabbling. A faint tinge of sewage stained the air.

She looked for a good place on the map, somewhere near the water to spend the night. Or rather, the day. Having driven through the morning hours, a long nap in a warm place sounded like Christmas.

She considered Mexico's boundaries, and chewed a Snickers.

Since finding herself on the wrong road last night, the idea had tickled the edge of curiosity and kept her driving. Mile after mile passed, carrying her farther from Potter Springs. What started as a mistake evolved into whimsy, then escalated into full-fledged flight.

After so many wrong turns in her life, could this one be a piece of serendipity?

Evening clouds had lifted, revealing a star-spread midnight sky. She put the minivan on cruise control, coasting to nowhere. To anywhere.

Why make the long journey to the Panhandle, without knowing, truly, where she and Mark were headed? The perfect pastor and his wife. With hidden secrets and hidden hurts eating them both alive.

She had no desire to play childhood games anymore. In Houston with her parents or in Potter Springs with Mark. Playing house as the new bride. A raggedy doll with a perfect smile and an aching heart. Destined to twirl on that spindle, headless and trapped.

The minivan's radio stayed silent as the music of her thoughts passed the time.

Mark needed her. She knew that without question. From the yearning in his voice, his relentless pursuit of her. Yet last night, he wasn't home. Maybe he'd grown tired of the chase.

Maybe he was chasing someone else.

She wouldn't speed back to prove Dale right or wrong. The deacon and his gossip didn't matter. She had no power to stop an affair, if that's what Mark wanted. He would have to make that decision on his own.

However much she loved him, she had to find her own way. With the edge of dawn, her head cleared and purpose hummed with the promise of day. Night turned to morning, and still she drove.

Now, at the crossing, she teetered on the edge of Texas.

Another country lay ahead, beckoning with unfamiliarity and adventure. Did she dare, really, to cross the border?

On the map, a name printed on the eastern coast caught her attention. Laguna Madre. A small inlet, carved into the seaside. She trilled the alluring name aloud. *Laguna Madre.* The Mother Lagoon.

Not too far away, but far enough. Maybe there, alone with the sea, she'd find the solution.

*What do you want?* echoed the question in her heart.

*I want to get better.*

Folding the map, she eased the van into the traffic flow once again. The road straightened, narrowing like a painting on perspective. The future a mere pinpoint on the horizon. She snapped on the radio and found a station with an upbeat tempo in a language she didn't understand.

She would find her joy, she decided. Even if she had to go all the way to Mexico to do it.

THE HOT-PINK HOTEL with scraggly palm trees exuded a relaxed cheerfulness. After passing several others, cracked adobe with peeling signs, Amanda feared she'd never find her oasis. But there it was. Palacio del Grande. The lobby smelled of salt water and coconut oil, and the humidity caressed her skin.

When she checked in, a slender man behind the counter voiced a hearty welcome and gave her a tiny bottle of tequila and a magnet with a sombrero on it. MEXICO! it proclaimed in block letters. "Do you need some help with luggage?" He handed her a keycard emblazoned with the hotel's name.

"No, this is it." She held up her small bag, full of unsuitable clothing. Jeans. Long-sleeved shirts. Fall in Potter clothes. "Do you have a gift shop?"

He pointed the way to a minuscule room full of postcards,

shell jewelry, tanning lotion and swimsuits. She chose a turquoise bikini, a garish metallic she'd usually never wear. But it was either that or a grandma suit with a knee-length skirt. At least it wasn't a thong. She added sunblock, a pair of flip-flops and a *Cosmo* to her pile.

Handing over the "Katy credit card," Amanda silently thanked Jesus and her mother for the family account. Somehow, she knew deep in her heart that if anybody could see a runaway trip to Mexico as necessary emergency spending, it would be Katy Thompson.

She'd call Mother later, maybe tomorrow after a full night's rest, to let her know where she was and okay the expenses. But she had to have at least one night, even if it took months to pay it back.

Upstairs, she opened the window and let in the sounds of the gulf while she examined her new quarters. Clean, with local accents of painted pottery and art. A wrought-iron lamp by the bedside, a small but tidy bathroom. She put her suitcase and new purchases on the foot of the queen-size bed. The marble floors chilled her bare feet after nonstop socks and tennis shoes. She pulled the tags off the swimsuit and grabbed a soft towel to wrap around her waist.

A quick elevator ride and a short pathway later, Amanda arrived on the beach in all its glory. The waves winked at her under the white sun as the undulating blue danced a timeless step. The tide laved the powder shore with gentle foam, a lover's caress between land and sea.

Smoothing the wind drifts in a sunny area, she spread out her towel and lay on her stomach, snuggling into the sand. A few tourists drank beer and a brown-skinned boy splashed in the water, playing games with the breaking surf. His laughter rol-licked with the waves, musical and free.

Something nagged at the back of her mind. Something she'd forgotten to do or pack. Whatever it was, she refused to let it bother her. Instead, she closed her eyes, listening to the eternal ocean and the calls of the gulls, letting the warmth of Mexico lull her to sleep.

DUSK HAD SETTLED when Amanda woke. A puddle of spittle formed on the towel beneath her and sand crusted in her eyes. The coming night chased away the day's heat and sunset tipped the waves with orange caps.

She rolled over and a thousand tiny needles pierced her. Somehow, in her slumber, someone had shrink-wrapped her back in scalding plastic. Flipping to her stomach, she reached a hand behind her and felt the fire on her skin.

The sunblock. That's what she forgot. Still in the yellow bag upstairs. Unopened. A typical tourist mistake. With all her years at the family lake house, she should have known better.

She'd just been so tired. Tired enough to sleep for hours on an unknown beach in a horrific bathing suit with no protection on her fair skin.

Wincing, she gathered her things and slipped sandy feet into her new sandals. She gathered the towel around her, thankful for its cover as the cool lobby air hit her cooked body.

"Oh, senorita!" A dark-haired woman in a flounced skirt halted at the sight of Amanda's flaming skin. "The sunburn, ouch it must hurt!" Holding a clipboard in one hand, the woman fluttered the other, talking with heavily accented speech. "You must put on the medicine. The green . . . aloe."

"Do you know if the gift shop carries any?" Amanda pulled the towel tighter, shivering.

"Yes, they do. But the day, it is over, and the store is no longer open."

Amanda tried not to break into tears in front of the stranger. A familiar insignia decorated her bright lapel. "Do you work here?"

"Yes, I am Consuela. A hostess for the hotel." She smiled. "And the store is closed, but we have a treatment, for the skin. A massage in the spa with the aloe."

"A spa? I didn't know you had one. . . ."

"It is new and very small. We are just starting the service, but I can make a call for you?"

GENTLE CELLOS FLOWED from the small radio as cool hands lightly stroked the salve into Amanda's fiery back. Surrounded by pale marble walls on a padded white table, she faced straight down with closed eyes and let the masseuse do her work. The aloe smelled fresh and pleasant as it slid into her pores and stopped the stinging.

A sheet covered her lower half, the room a mild temperature. She relaxed in the calm atmosphere, enjoying the professional touch.

She missed Mark's touch. The way he knew her body and accepted her. What she thought were flaws, her round thighs and full bottom, he adored. Made pet names for her, whispered wild compliments in her ears while they made love. Even now, she blushed into the table's comfort, remembering.

After losing the baby, his touch hadn't been the same. Careful and fragile. Like she'd turned to ice and would shatter with too much pressure.

The weight of the masseuse's hands skimmed the tautness of her skin with the gel, gently massaging the tension from her neck and shoulders. The strokes manipulated the tightness, tendered the brittle.

Maybe she was ice, maybe she would shatter.

Maybe she *had* been cold, with the walls and the cave. Too

withdrawn into her own broken heart. Did she, drowning in her loss, somehow chill them both?

Yes, Mark must make his own choice, but had she forced his hand? Could he have turned to Courtney in desire? In desperation?

Sadness welled inside her, brought out by the cool, the smell, the firm hands. Tears fell slowly to the padding that held her face. The tip of the iceberg, revealed in the balm on her skin, melting with the burn's fiery heat.

Her husband in the arms of another woman. Her lost baby. The loss of babies never to come. Her childhood dreams of happily-ever-after tossed to the wind, landing in the pool of her sorrow.

Yet she kept quiet, and let the rhythmic hands run over her body without judgment or condemnation.

With puffy eyes, she assured the receptionist that the massage had been perfect. "Just what I needed." She signed the charge and made it back to her room in a daze.

Moonlight poured through her open windows as she lowered herself onto the wildly printed bedspread, flowers bursting from palm trees, peacocks nesting among the branches. She burrowed her head into a pillow, the sadness breaking free in shudders and sobs.

Why? Why her? Why was she chosen, out of the masses of women, to never bear a child? To never be a mother, to love and be loved in that most precious of ways?

And now, running away from home, leaving her life a million miles away, abandoned in a wake of hurt.

Pain smothered her, held her under, choked her as she gasped and heaved. A dual-handed grip clenched her throat, fingers taut with death and fear. The death of her child, and of her dreams.

Fear of trusting a God who disappointed her so deeply. And fear of moving toward a future she couldn't see.

Grief's waters covered her, drowning her, pressed beneath layers of opaque darkness. She'd been under for longer than this moment. Had spent weeks, even months, gazing up through distorted waves, unable to feel the sun's pure light.

She'd been trapped for so long, she'd forgotten how to breathe.

She gasped, even now, emptying her lungs of stored-up tears. Letting it out, where it couldn't suffocate her anymore.

She took in life-giving oxygen, her body shuddering with the effort. Marveling in the strength, of the power to simply breathe. To live. She would live. She would move forward. If only she knew which way to go.

Dried tears brought a tightness to her face. She curled around a hotel pillow, wishing it would breathe and smell like Mark, holding her, whispering that everything would be okay.

But Mark wasn't here. She must find this path for herself. Not leaning on Mark, her Goldenboy, to illuminate the way for her. Still, the ache—the sheer, raw loneliness—drew her eyes closed.

As sleep wrapped its comforting numbness around her, the promise called out to her heart.

*Weeping may last for the night, but joy comes in the morning.*

If only she knew how much longer her night would last, and if, come morning, Mark would still be waiting.

CHAPTER 25

shadow man

Little old ladies lined up in the second row, their heads looked like Easter eggs, rounded pastel tufts. One leaned over and whispered to her companion, louder than a stage yell, "Oh, that Pastor Randalls, isn't he so good?"

Onstage, Mark threw an extra big smile their direction as he finished the last of his song. No matter they couldn't get his last name right, poor birds.

Some, like Ruby Weatherby, hardly knew where they were but clapped and sang along anyway. Making joyful, if unintelligible, noises to the Lord.

Tonight's Hoot 'n' Hallow was a record breaker. Families lined up in the pews for the Sunday-evening worship service. Volunteer deacons had bused in the ladies and other shut-ins from various homes. The sanctuary reverberated with the praise of the saints, young and old.

But behind his face, Mark felt as alive as a skeleton with skin on. A shadow man. *Sing us a song, you're the shadow man.* Each day Amanda stayed gone, he faded away from himself. Without her to sharpen him, he blurred. It was a wonder others could see him at all.

Amanda had been gone, counting the stay at her parents', for over a month now. He hadn't talked to her since before the festival. His calls to her cell phone went unanswered. His only updates consisted of terse remarks from his mother-in-law, running interference.

Cahoots. They were in cahoots. With Katy's financial support, Amanda could stay gone as long as she wanted. And apparently, she wanted.

His wife—he knew now, after drilling Katy—was in Mexico. Lolling about on the beach "finding herself." Probably getting hit on by various and sundry Latin lovers with big pecs and great tans, while he was stuck singing songs and preaching by rote like a windup puppet.

Behind the eggheads, in the third row next to her gran, Courtney twinkled at him. The church's lights glinted off her hair. He refused to make eye contact since just last night he'd fielded a strange visit from the Ladies' Guild president.

"Mark?" Courtney had tapped on his screen door, peeking in. A strong wind filled the hazy November sky with dirt, hanging thick even at dusk. The sun shot pink behind her.

"Yes?" He did not motion for her to enter. His last dealing with Courtney Williams had sent serious shock waves through his marriage, and he wanted to thwart any further seismic pulses. He made sure any passerby would see her on the porch, him safely ensconced inside. Fully dressed in the entryway.

"Hi. Oh, you look nice." She managed to purr her chirpy voice, showing no signs of awkwardness from their last encounter.

On a Saturday evening, in sweats, and he hadn't showered or shaved all day. No, he did not look nice.

"Thanks. What can I do for you?" He hoped to sound as businesslike as possible, in spite of the chili stain on his T-shirt. Canned chili.

"I'm so sorry to bother you at home . . . and at such a time."

At such a time? What was that supposed to mean?

"I'm calling on you, to let you know you're in our prayers." She tilted her blonde head sideways and fiddled with some papers in her hands.

She'd slipped into the plural. Mark didn't know if she was affecting the royal *we*, or if she somehow represented a larger, more frightening group.

"Uh-huh?" Mr. Chesters slinked by. Mark grabbed him for a distraction and was rewarded with a burning scratch down his right arm. He let the cat go, and it raced across the street, nimble as a kitten.

"You might remember that I'm president of the Ladies' Guild?" As if anyone within microphone distance of Lakeview Community Church could forget. "I'm also, you probably didn't know this part, but I'm the organizer for the prayer chain."

Confirmation. Larger, more frightening group.

"We were just so happy with the news of Amanda's father getting better. That she'd be back soon." Courtney actually said this with a straight face. With sincerity.

Had he imagined the whole lust fog? Of her subtle seduction of him on her couch? Or had she simply been herself, and he, deluded by his misery?

"But now"—she coughed gently, pearly pink nails fanned out

over glossy lips—"we're wondering if there's anything we could do for you since Amanda . . ."

Mark stilled as his insides cranked on hyperdrive.

"You see"—Courtney tried again, blinking rapidly—"Dale called the Thompsons for another prayer update and he's let us know that Amanda has—"

*Left*, Mark filled in. *Amanda left. Left me. Left the country. Gone.*

Molasses took over his voice box. He couldn't even clear his throat, let alone change the course of conversation.

"Anyway," Courtney interrupted her own pause, "we've organized some meals." She revealed a color-coded chart full of names and phone numbers. "I've got several women who'll bring by casseroles for you to pop in the freezer and heat up at your convenience. I think we have enough volunteers to cook hot meals at least this week."

A sinking sensation tugged Mark's gut. *They know she's gone, that she's not coming back, and I'm a total loser who can't even make a casserole.*

Across the street, Mr. Chesters hung tenaciously in a neighbor's tree. The dog next door barked, frenzied and high. Mr. Chesters regained his footing and seemed to enjoy taunting the other animal. The dog's yelps escalated to a fever pitch.

"That's awfully nice of you," Mark heard himself say. "But I'm not sure it's necessary."

"Oh, not at all," she assured him. "Everything's planned out. In fact, I've passed around a sign-up sheet for laundry and ironing." She produced another list. "And right now, we're working out a schedule for housework, grocery shopping and lunches for you to take to work if you're interested." She dug in her purse for a pen and flipped her paper stack to a blank sheet. "Is there anything you're allergic to or just plain don't like?"

His mind reeled. What to do now? They don't teach you in seminary how to handle the Ladies' Guild Meals on Wheels. Or, for that matter, what to do when your wife runs away to Mexico.

In spite of his projected outer calm, Mark's body—primitive, instinctive—knew the course of action. A burning, like reflux but deeper, dropped from his chest, twisted the walls of his stomach and bubbled through his lower digestive track. Scorching cramps alerted his rational mind, in case it wasn't "in the loop" that he now faced *Great Emotional Stress,* signaling the onset of explosive diarrhea.

Obviously, he needed to get rid of Courtney. Fast.

"No, there's nothing. No allergies."

Rushing through pleasant inanities without any idea what he'd agreed to, he concluded with a hearty, "Fine, that's great." A little strangled sound escaped him. "Thanks a lot."

The screen door shut with a comforting click as Courtney revved up her Camaro. Racing down the hallway, Mark had executed a beautiful side-leap to the bathroom, a move his college football coach would have appreciated.

Tonight, at the evening service, he intended to steer clear of the Ladies' Guild president at all costs. He sang his songs and played his part and fulfilled the associate-pastor role to the best of his abilities. Even the eggheads loved him.

Afterward, Ervin announced the monthly board meeting, which Mark internally translated as *bored* meeting. Dale Ochs usually helmed the proceedings. Even now, the chairman lurked in the foyer, ready to whip the wayward servants of Lakeview Community into shape.

As the church members filed out, emptying the sanctuary of their chatter, Mark packed the Martin guitar and music away. A small scratch marred the sheen on the wood. He'd buff it out later. As he clicked the locks closed, Ervin put a hand on his shoulder.

"Great singing tonight."

"Thanks. I'm glad you liked it."

"Heck, that kinda music makes me happier than a hog in sunshine." Ervin rubbed his beard. "How's Amanda doing?"

Ervin, much in the way of the mentally challenged or small children, had a habit of mentioning the unmentionable.

"Oh, fine. She's doing just great." As far as he knew anyway. No falsehood there. Mark stood, the guitar balanced at his side.

"Listen." Ervin fiddled with his belt buckle, a large truck adorned the silver-and-gold rectangle. His Sunday night buckle. This morning's had a bronco on it. "You don't need to come to the meeting tonight."

"No arguments here. But why not?"

"Don't worry about it." Ervin shoved his hands in his denim pockets and rocked back on his boot heels. "Just some old goats bleating about a bunch of nothing."

"Like what?"

"The usual. Building maintenance. Whether or not to print a weekly newsletter. Who's the best high-school running back. Important stuff."

"So why shouldn't I be there?"

Ervin stared at the back row of pews a few moments before speaking. "There's been some grumbling," he admitted. "About Amanda's being gone. Some of the members want to discuss it."

"Members like Dale Ochs?" Mark couldn't keep the anger from his voice.

"Mark, I hate to say this, but there're questions that need answering." Ervin looked at his boots. "Your future on staff, for one. They're saying, what with a missing wife—"

"She's not missing. She's on vacation." *An extended vacation that may result in the end of our marriage.*

"I know," Ervin agreed. "But trust me. You don't want to be at tonight's meeting." He slapped Mark's back. "I'm going to bat for you, son. You can count on that."

"Thanks." Mark decided to heed Ervin's advice and skip the meeting, choosing to hide in his office and arrange bookshelves instead. Thus postponing the trip home to an empty house, for an empty evening. Again.

A LONE LAMP in the corner cast a mild glow on the worn desk and gray utility carpet. Mark sat on the floor and alphabetized his seminary books. Just above his shoulder, the window shade knocked in the wind, the fall breeze cleansing the stuffy room. Every once in a while, the wind shifted, hitting the garbage bin and sent the drift inside.

Still, he kept the window open, not knowing the worst evil— the odors from musty carpet or the rotting smell from prayer dinner leftovers.

He arranged book titles in groups. Angling his picture frames just so, he picked up a photo of his wedding day in a square silver frame, tarnished at the edges. He rubbed at the discoloration, tilting it away from the shadows to better illuminate the faces.

Surrounded by family, he towered over most of them. Amanda, pale and sweet, stood beside him, the whiteness of the gown stark against her freckles. Happiness and anxiety on both their brows. He more stoic, she holding a rainbow of squashed flowers.

He heard a rumble of steps outside, the church's side door slammed. The board meeting must be adjourned. Cigarette smoke filtered through his shade, along with the murmur of male voices.

"Now, I'm not so sure I'm ready to just up and *fire* him," one man said at full volume, obviously unaware of the open window or Mark's presence inside. "Took us long enough to get an associate. I hate the thought of starting over."

This was not a conversation Mark wanted to overhear. Yet part of him, like a rubbernecker at a car wreck, was drawn to the impending carnage. He stayed motionless.

"No one said anything about firing him. I'm saying we need to be in prayer over it." The sanctimonious voice of Dale Ochs blew in with a fresh exhalation of smoke. Noxious. "Consider what the Lord thinks is best and whether or not this man deserves the time and the freedom to work on his marriage."

"Freedom without a paycheck?" the other man tossed back.

"The Lord will provide for him," Dale argued. "It's not our job to worry about such things."

"But who would take his place? He does a heck of a lot around here—"

"Again, God is greater than our fears. Who knows, he might have in mind someone right here from Potter to take his place," reasoned Dale. "Someone local, already living a godly lifestyle, of unquestionable character. Somebody who really knows this congregation's needs."

"Someone like you, Dale?"

"Well"—a humble chuckle—"I wouldn't be opposed to answering that call. Of course I'd have to pray about it."

"Tell you what." A new voice joined the mix. Deeper, with more twang. Unmistakably Ervin's. "I'll think on it, Dale. You're right, we do need to consider what's been said tonight. Your leadership here and your loyalty to this church, well, let me just say I appreciate you."

"Why, you're quite welcome." The conversation drifted away as boots ground out burning stubs. Pickups sparked to life and rolled into the night.

Mark sat alone, the lamp's yellow light weak around him. He remembered Ervin's promise. *I'm going to bat for you, son. You can count on that.*

"Some at bat," he said in the silence, looking down on a smiling bride long since gone, her face captured under glass. "I'm not sure what I can count on anymore."

He grabbed his keys and turned off the lamp. "Or who."

CHAPTER 26

tether

The phone rang in the curtain-drawn hotel room. Swathed in blankets in the blast of the air conditioner, Amanda struggled to wake. A cold room in hot temperatures worked like a drug on her. She'd never slept so hard. Or so late.

"Yes?" Reading the digital clock on the nightstand, she tried to sound lucid. She'd missed the breakfast buffet by a good two hours. Luckily, lunch was right around the corner.

"Still having a good time, dear?" As usual, Katy bypassed hellos.

Of course, Amanda knew it would be her mother. No one else had the hotel number. Katy remained her only link to the outside world.

"I don't know that I'd call it a good time, but I'm working on it." Disappointment had tasted so bitter, for such a long time, she yearned for something fresh. Spending hours each night with her journal and her memories. Reading the Psalms, looking for answers. For her joy.

Instead, as the onion-thin pages rustled like silk, she had found less of an arrow to point the way than snapshots of realization.

Scrawls in her diary had stained her fingers as she relived the moments, wondering where, and how, they'd gone so wrong.

Mark's distance when she lost the baby. His refusal to acknowledge her grief.

Her inability to reach out to him, an unwillingness to scream out for help.

The countless hours of church work, Mark ministering to others while her heart withered and died.

But she'd never asked him to please stay home.

Victim versus victor, no longer so clear, smeared into muted blue. The color of regret.

They'd missed each other all along. And now, she missed him so much she ached, but she still had work to do. More pages to fill, truths to uncover.

She cradled the phone to her chin, twisting the cord around her finger. "I can't thank you enough, Mom. I plan to pay you back someday."

"Nonsense. My payment is knowing you're thinking things through." Katy never mentioned Mark directly. Just casual remarks about happiness and choices.

"How's Daddy?" Amanda walked to the window, dragging out the long beige cord. She winced in the sunlight and took in the view below.

Endless water waving at her. Same as yesterday. Time ceased to

exist in Mexico. Days floated by, surreal. The past whispered away
in each morning's fresh-drawn beach, white and pure.

"He's fine. In fact, we're going to the lake house again this
weekend."

"You're spending lots of time there."

"The sun does him good, I think. He's like you. Sun wor-
shiper." Katy audibly shuddered. "Plus, getting away helps."

"Away. With you." Amanda pulled the tropical curtains aside
and tugged the drifty sheers into place for privacy. As if the sky
stretching from horizon to horizon would spy on her and judge
her in its length.

"Yes," Katy replied, exhaling smoke. "With me."

She heard her mother's smile. "I'm glad for you, Mom.
Really." Standing in front of the mirror, Amanda's face didn't
match her words. Sad around her mouth. Full blue eyes, blinking
slowly. Older. She looked older. Older and alone. She turned
away.

"Well, it only took about twenty-five years and a heart attack,
but we may get the hang of this marriage thing yet."

Amanda smiled, bittersweet. "Is that all?"

A deep inhale. "You know Mark is nothing like your father."
Katy sounded the first shot. The unspoken ban on the *M*-word
lifted.

"And is that supposed to be good or bad?" Amanda thought of
her father, forever working in his garage, now laid up and taking
getaways with his wife. Daddy. Her childhood hero. Her measure
of a man, in spite of his shortcomings. Those bad habits landed
him in the hospital, almost through death's door.

Amanda remembered, as a girl, helping her father build a picture frame for one of her mother's blurry watercolors. It was her
first time to direct the saw on her own, and she carefully followed
her father's pencil traces in the wood. Steady and slow.

Even so, the blade knew her inexperience and bit her, cutting into soft flesh and stealing her breath away. Her father cleaned and bandaged it himself, assuring her, "Why, I've had worse spots on my eyeball."

Her tender daddy. Always taking care of her. But no more. She must learn to stand on her own.

"That's not for me to say," said Katy. "Have you talked to him? Your *husband*?"

Amanda ignored the extra inflection. "No. He tried the cell. I turned it off."

"I still haven't given him the hotel number, but he's making me crazy with the calls. Isn't it a little ridiculous you won't even *talk* to the man? What exactly did he do?"

"It's not so much what he did or didn't do. I'm in this too. Not talking to him may seem ridiculous to you, but it's crucial to me."

Mark's persuasive ways had convinced her more than once. His gifts for speaking, for influencing, crossed over into his personal life, and she couldn't risk her heart on emotion for the moment.

"Well, I'm a little tired of playing go-between for the two of you. Have you thought about contacting a lawyer?"

"Mother, I've told you—"

"Experience tells me if you wanted to make a go of this marriage you wouldn't still be in Mexico."

"If it's the money, I'll check out today." Not that she knew where to go. But she wouldn't be indebted, or play games out of guilt. She'd sleep in the van if she had to. Lord knew there was plenty of room in there. "I don't have to stay here." She picked up keys from atop a pile of well-worn paperbacks. They jingled, sharp in her hand.

The stupid van, a fumbling gift that revealed the truth. Though joined by marriage, they traveled completely different paths. In spite of their connection when they dated, maybe he didn't understand her at all. Didn't know her.

Whatever happened with Courtney merely unveiled one more aspect of the tangle. Like a mirror in the morning, harsh and unwelcome.

Maybe Amanda didn't know him either.

"Don't be silly. Of course you can stay, as long as you like. You know, whatever it takes, I'll help you. I never wanted you to go through the same things I did. And I'm not one to say *I told you so.*"

"Mother, I'm not silly." She tossed the keys on the desk and shuffled through the books. Favorites and disposables. "I'm not ridiculous. And no, I don't want a lawyer." She thumped the last book down, and it smacked in the quiet room.

"Well, you don't have to get in a huff about it. I'm just trying to help you sort out your priorities."

"It's not a huff. It's the truth." She was tired of the facades, of the pretty jabs and parries. "You've given me the resources, the freedom, to work on what's wrong. So I can figure out if there's a future for us or not. But I can't do that when all I see, when all I hear in my head, is you."

"That's nonsense. I—"

"Mother, you're wonderful, and I adore you." She took a deep breath. "And know that I love you. But—I'm sorry for this— please don't call me. I'll call you."

And with that, she gently eased the phone back to the cradle, disconnecting with her last tether to the outside world.

CHAPTER 27

take backs

A ball-peen hammer drove its way into Mark's skull about the same time he realized Mr. Chesters must have bypassed the litter box and used his mouth instead.

On the couch, Mark braced himself, waiting for the painful thuds to quit. For a blessed second, they did. He steadily, painfully, rose to a seated position. What happened?

In front of him on the antique trunk stood a saucy stack of beer cans. Mocking him. One lay at his feet, dribbling sour brew onto the carpet.

Aha. The *bored* meeting. Dale Ochs and the boys discussing his "qualifications to pastor." Ervin Plumley caving like Styrofoam under Dale's pressure.

Mark had slinked away into the night like a kicked dog, looking for some carbonated comfort.

He had found it in the Beer Barn, an awkward red building with a flashing neon sign. Adult beverages to go. He pulled the church pickup in, edging close to the drive-in window so the kid behind the counter couldn't see the Lakeview insignia on the side.

"Whatcha need?" The clerk had severe acne and a pleasant expression. His name tag read ROBERT.

"Coors. Cold, please." Mark pulled down the rim of his ball cap and pretended to adjust the radio.

"Sure. We've got a special tonight on twelve-pack cans—"

"Whatever, that's fine." He scratched his forehead, shielding his face.

"Or, did you want bottles? Because the longnecks are buy three, get . . . Hey, you look familiar. Aren't you—"

"Cans are fine. I'm in a hurry."

Robert handed the heavy paper sack over, and Mark had to reach out of the pickup to grab it. "Thanks."

"Wait a minute. You're that church guy." Robert poked a finger, grinning at having solved the puzzle. "Lakeview, right?"

Mark shrugged and put the truck in gear.

"My grandma goes there," Robert chatted on, oblivious to Mark's discomfort. "Letty Hodges. You know her?"

Mark gunned the gas and drove home, dashing into the house with the chilly cans tucked under his arm. Ready for a *fuhgeddaboutit* party of one.

Vaguely, he remembered singing Willie Nelson tunes along with the stereo. Slurring about lost jobs and missing women. Between the beer and Amanda's record collection, he'd almost fooled himself into painless delirium. *Happy without her,* he'd informed Mr. Chesters. Don't need her, don't want her. Just us boys, doin' fine on our own.

He hadn't had this much to drink since his glory days in college. Now the alcohol sucked the water right out of his body. Even his eyeballs felt dry.

He'd cut off his right arm for a cold glass of water, but the kitchen seemed too far away. Instead, he flopped back on the couch, shut his eyes and prayed for a miracle. A water miracle. Preferably of the mountain spring variety, bottled and chilled, to appear majestically before him. On the trunk, where he wouldn't have to move. Hadn't God done it for Elijah in the desert?

But this was a desert of his own making. And he was no Elijah.

*Wham! Wham, wham, wham!*

There went the hammer. He whimpered and covered his ears. What on earth? The sound, on second reflection, came from *outside* his head. Nearer to the front door.

Someone knocking?

Although his subconscious mind whispered, *Amanda's home*, rational self argued that she certainly had a key.

Still, he jumped up too fast and slammed his knee into the trunk with all his strength. Profanities rolled with the cans as they clattered to the floor.

"Just a minute!" he called out, his tongue a terry cloth slab. "Be right there!"

He hustled the cans to the garbage, smelling stale alcohol throughout his living area. *Please, God, don't let it be someone from church.*

With his luck, it would be Dale Ochs, with a pink slip and a box of Mark's office belongings. And a big grin.

Smoothing his hair, Mark made for the entryway and hoped his eyes weren't too red. Maybe he could plead sickness. Get rid of whoever had the audacity to knock his door down on a Monday morning. His day off.

The squeak of the hinges nearly leveled him, but he clenched his teeth and stood strong. Morning sun streamed behind a gaggle of ladies, all smiling at him. Truly, a gaggle.

Peggy Plumley led the charge. "Good morning, Mark!" she sang in an impossibly cheery voice. "We're here for the house-cleaning shift." She pushed past him, nearly knocking him over with a gigantic yellow pail full of cleaning supplies.

Behind her stood Missy Underwood, Shelinda James and Pam Hart, each dressed in work clothes and carrying bundles. Shelinda and Pam chattered as they swept in. "I've brought some King Ranch for your dinner." Shelinda's mittened hands held a steaming casserole.

His stomach flipped. "Thanks." Flattening himself against the wall, he counted the troops. Invaders. Four, counting Missy who ran back to the car.

Pam Hart sniffed deeply as she entered. "Why, it smells like a fraternity house in here!" she announced to the room at large. "I know, because my daughter from Chitapee . . ."

At this familiar phrase, Peggy made a face and disappeared down the hallway.

". . . once dated a boy in a fraternity out at OSU." Pam breathed excitedly, adjusting the waistband on her stretchy pants with a vigorous snap. "And I visited, and it smelled just like this!"

Shelinda jammed an elbow in Pam's rib cage.

"Ouch!" Pam cast an injured look at her younger friend.

"We've got plenty to do without standing around here gabbing." Shelinda looked pointedly at the broom and dustpan in Pam's hands. "Get moving."

Pam balanced the equipment against the wall and gripped her ample hips. "I *know* what I smell and that smells like *beer*—"

"Pam!" Peggy's authoritative voice called from the back of the house. "I need your help here in the bathroom. You can scrub the potty."

Shuffling away, Pam grumbled, "Well, I never."

"Probably not," Shelinda agreed under her breath. She nodded at Mark and turned to the kitchen.

Wincing at the idea of strange women scrubbing his toilet, Mark held open the door for a trailing Missy. She maneuvered down the sidewalk, holding her prize with both hands.

A glass pitcher, full to the rim. Sweat beads from the cold trickled down the sides. Ice bobbed, fruit slices twirled in the heavenly liquid. Lemonade.

"I made it fresh this morning," Missy told him. "At the last minute, I just thought . . . that maybe you'd like some."

Mark lifted silent hallelujahs and ran for a glass.

Seated on the couch, he finished the last of the pitcher, sucking it down like a 10K runner in the Sahara. Greedy and grateful.

When his stomach quit the churn cycle, he realized women inhabited every room—scrubbing, washing, poking through his belongings. He tried to intervene. "I can get this, really." He pulled at Peggy's laundry basket.

"Now, Mark, let us do this for you." Peggy insisted. "You just step aside and we can get to work. We'll be done in a jiffy." Brooking no argument, she squished down the hall in her nurse's shoes, carrying a folded load of his underwear.

Mark wondered if escape might be his best option. Maybe a quick jog through the neighborhood. Clear his head and get out of the house.

He went to the master bedroom to grab his running shoes. As he shut the door for some privacy, he heard a fumbling in his closet. "Ooof!"

Thank God he hadn't started changing into his workout clothes, or else he'd be giving new meaning to "Just As I Am."

"Who's there?"

"It's me." Peggy came out, her handkerchief askew, rubbing a red mark on her head. "I was putting some things away, and knocked this over."

She handed him a boot box, cracked open with papers spilling over. "Looks like it could be important." What appeared to be a doctor's bill poked out the side.

"I'm afraid they got a little mixed up. Sorry about that." She handed him the mess, her eyes soft. "I'll go get the girls. We should be about finished."

The door clicked behind her.

The edge of the bed squeaked under Mark's weight. He wondered what Amanda would store inside an old box. He handled all the financial bookkeeping and didn't know of anything missing.

Cautiously, he opened the cardboard container. The pink paper slipped out, the edges wrinkled, scrawls at the bottom barely discernible. A hospital charge. From when Mandy lost the . . .

He tossed the receipt on the mattress, digging deeper into the box. That terrible day. He saw no need to revisit it by poring over old medical charges. Katy had paid them in full without batting an eye.

Old Dragonlady did have her strong suit.

Next, a string of blurry photos, long and narrow on a shiny roll. Each focused on what looked like a see-through peanut, floating in a tornado. Ghost white lines in cloudy black ink.

The baby. His mind voiced it before he could catch himself. The sonogram photos of the baby.

His throat squeezed shut, and he coughed into a fist. Must be the hangover. Maybe he'd go out and get a big glass of water. Put these relics away and go for his run.

He cocked his head to the side, listening. No hens clucking. No vacuum roar. They must have gone home.

The urge to run slid away.

He turned his attention to the photos, trying to remember.

Wishing he could forget.

As he traced the images in the pictures, he named each place he could identify. The top of the head, the face. Perfect. He recalled that much.

He'd been so worried that his and Amanda's heated scramblings, illicit exchanges, had resulted in a mistake. A physical punishment for physical transgressions.

He'd prayed for mercy each night, for forgiveness, expecting none.

When he saw the screen that day in the tech's room, he'd almost wept with relief. He held himself in check, though, frozen by the image swirling on the screen. Transfixed by the technician's voice, pointing out all the parts.

Femur and fingers, tiny toes and great big eyes. Or at least, dark pockets where the eyes were. Little sage, floating. Protected. A perfect gift for imperfect people.

The baby's heartbeat thudded in time with his own. Love personified. Powerful pulses that thrilled and scared him.

And Amanda in some awful robe-thing, gray-blue cotton in a cold room. Her eyes darted to his. Biting her lip, she laughed and cried all at once, pushing her hair out of her eyes. Happy.

One of the last days he saw her that way.

The perfect gift he hadn't wanted, taken back. Passed in a pool of blood around his lover's feet, her face wild with the pain. He'd gathered her close, held her to his chest and carried her to the car. He caught a scent of pennies. Copper pennies, spent and gone.

The whole time his heart pounded, louder than the day at the tech's room. Calling in silence to their baby, his baby, as he drove, frantic in Houston traffic. *Hold on. I do want you. Can you hear me? I want you. Hang in there. Daddy's heart is here for you.*

But it hadn't worked. His blessing, his punishment, had slipped away, quiet as it came. Leaving broken people behind, one of whom refused to crack.

He set the sonograms carefully on the bed and returned to the box. The baby book. On the very bottom, still in the bag from the card shop where she had bought it. The plastic wrap crinkled as he pulled it out. On the front, little mice danced among ribbons and flowers. Raised, scroll lettering for the title, bumpy under his fingers. *The Story of Baby.*

He opened the cover and flipped through thick pages, preprinted with areas for lists and photos. Spaces for the sonogram. Baby's first picture. Room for remarks from Mommy. From Daddy.

All empty.

Not one line filled.

No evidence that a baby ever existed. Because that's the way he'd wanted it.

A white rectangle, no bigger than a playing card, floated out and landed on the carpet by his feet. He picked it up. Betty's Hallmark. The receipt, for $21.95.

She'd kept it in the book. Why?

Then he remembered. How he'd scolded her when she bought the album. Her middle barely rounded from the pregnancy, showing him her purchase. Blushing and excited.

He'd told her it cost too much. That they'd need to save their pennies because his severance was running out. There'd be time for books later, he'd said. Keep the receipt so you can take it back.

Take backs. He hung his head in his hands. He wished he could. To start over, from the beginning. But not all the way.

Just to the part where he had quit being human.

He'd been right about one thing. It had—all of it—cost way too much.

CHAPTER 28

for the roses

M otor scooters zoomed by little pastel houses as Amanda walked along the cobbled streets of Laguna Madre. Washed-out patterns on clothesline sheets fluttered as they baked in the sun. Waving her along, even as her feet wearied.

Heavy with books, her straw bag cut into her shoulder. She'd found, under Consuela's guidance, a fabulous used book store chock full of American paperbacks. Excited as a child at a candy shop, Amanda loaded her peso bargains high on the dusty counter.

Now she wanted to find the right spot to indulge. A cold Zapata soda, a good read and shade sounded like sweet heaven. The beach, her hotel, seemed too far to wait. Besides, she'd grown tired of her corner of paradise on the beach, sun dappling in between the fronds of a palm. The view never changed.

Amanda stopped in a small rose garden on a side street, just down the block from her hotel. She'd admired it on her walks, the bushes blooming full in the middle of November.

Everything would be dead back home in Potter. Dry and brittle. Brown and dull, skeleton branches whipping in the wind. Lifeless.

But here, hot and humid, it smelled like flowers.

A stone bench nestled under a tree, the shade inviting after the white-hot street. An ideal roosting location, she decided. To rest her shoulder and slip her flip-flops off, to wiggle her toes in the grass.

She loved the beach, but she did miss grass.

She flipped through her satchel and picked out a mystery. Setting the soda on the bench, she tucked her feet underneath her and enjoyed the sounds of birds flitting in the trees. They sang as she turned the pages, losing herself in another world of intrigue and suspense.

A rusty squeak broke through the story. An aged gardener, sweating in the midday sun, pushed a wheelbarrow filled with tools and mulch. His feet looked like leather, bronzed in thick sandals. He tugged a straw hat off his head and wiped his brow with a kerchief.

"*Hola.*" He nodded.

"Hi." She smiled back.

He creaked down a pathway, stopping in front of a gathering of roses. Pinks and whites spilled together, red ones topped yellow, some loosened blooms withered on the ground. Abundant glory with a heady fragrance.

"It's beautiful," she observed, hoping he'd understand her compliment. The locals grasped her English better than she did their Spanish.

*"Gracias."* He tipped his hat. Polite, but intent on his task. He picked spent petals from the ground and put them in a bucket. Broken twigs, bits of windblown trash, all went into the can on the wheelbarrow.

She wondered how long he'd tended this garden. The healthy plants and vigorous growth spoke of dedication.

The gardener clipped the greenery, shaping each plant, cutting dead wood away. He whistled, a low happy sound, as he knelt in the dirt, heedless of Amanda and her book.

She watched, strangely enthralled as he continued pruning, gently parting the sharp limbs with his bare hands. A thorn caught him, cut deep through thickened skin and brought blood. The song stopped.

Bringing a rag to his finger, he rubbed the wound. Several spots stained the cloth and he tossed it without further examination into the catchall wheelbarrow.

*Maybe now, he'll get some gloves,* she thought.

But he returned to his work and the song began again.

"Doesn't that hurt your hands?"

He shifted on one knee to face her. "Senorita?"

"Your hands." She lifted hers to show him. "The roses," she pointed. "The thorns. Don't they hurt?"

*"Sí."* He laughed and held his palms up, turning them to reveal whisper-thin white lines on both sides. Spiderwebs engraved in the flesh.

"Then why do you—"

"It is worth it," he interrupted. A king in his kingdom, sweeping grandly with one arm, sweat stained underneath. "Is worth it—for the roses." Not asking if she agreed. He began his whistle song, turning back to his clipping.

Amanda nodded to herself. For the roses.

Ignored again, she gathered her books and stuffed them in her tote. The small stone church stood in the back of the grounds, just around the gardener's path. She followed the walkway, drawn by the fragrance of the flowers, compelled to the dark mahogany doors. She pushed one open and entered the sanctuary.

Dark and cool, with a slight odor of old velvet. Ancient reverence and quiet. Hymnals lined in rows along the pews, long red cushions flattened from ages of use.

Hushing the flap of her shoe against her heel, Amanda slid inside. The wood pew backs felt cool to her palm, her fingertips skimmed along the rounded curves. Halfway down the aisle, she sat under an intricate stained-glass window.

Sunlight shone through ruby and sapphire, royal and serene. Amanda bowed her head to its grace, watched the shadow play on her fingers as the sun dipped behind the clouds outside. A kaleidoscope. Her mind twirled, brilliant images past and present.

She needed to be still, to find her center.

*What do you want?*

Almost audible, the question echoed in the hollows of her heart. She shifted in the pew. She had focused for so long on what had gone wrong. But the time for bitterness and loss had passed.

What do I want? she asked herself.

What she'd always wanted. Home. Family. Love. To know and be known by the ones she cherished.

Daddy at the workbench, holding her hurt finger. Daddy, squeezing her arm as they walked down the aisle. Daddy, pale and wasted, a ghost in hospital greens.

Then Mother, waiting alone in mismatched clothing. Minutes on the hour. Cigarettes and phone calls. Signing the hotel charges, no questions asked.

*Don't call me, I'll call you,* Amanda had said. Cutting the tether.

A change in light and color. Surprisingly, the women of Potter. Missy. Shelinda. Peggy. Peggy called her honeygirl and held her as she cried. Shelinda's laugh, Pam's string of plastic pictures, Missy's little hands holding Amanda's.

Her friends. Waiting in Potter. Accepting her and loving her. *That's how I started up with God again,* Missy had said. *He sent those women, girlfriends, to walk me through it.*

And Amanda had walked away.

The wheel turned again, floating. Her blood thumped in rhythm, and she recognized it. That sound, the only voice she'd heard from baby Grace. Precious one, loved and lost, never to be known, never to laugh. Her chest tightened.

*I want a family. I want babies.*

*Close to impossible,* the doctor had said.

And the grief had swallowed her whole.

Then, Mark. Clearest of all. His soft eyes above her, his strength around her. Tender and human. Saying and doing the wrong things, but adoring her all the while.

*Welcome home,* the card had read. Dark roses and a minivan. Unlit candles and sorrow in his spine.

Did he hurt the way she hurt? Had she expected too much of him? To fill spaces in her that no mere man could ever breach? Had she made him her God, her savior, following blindly and demanding perfection?

She blinked tears away and turned the kaleidoscope, looking for the next picture.

Amanda Thompson, afraid of a marriage like her parents'. Amanda Reynolds, nauseous and happy in a wedding dress. Amanda, the new wife, balled up in a hospital. Mrs. Mark Reynolds, starched in a luncheon. Mandy, angry over a car.

Amanda. Standing with old eyes in front of the mirror. Alone.

*What do you want?*

Shining and bright, the answer cut clean through her soul the way the gardener had cut the dead wood away. Sharp as the prism in the sanctuary around her. Whispering, guiding her.

*I want the roses.*

Like the gardener, she counted the cost. Weighed the vines of heartache, the thorns of change and the high price of forgiveness. Though the suffering had angered her, she had never been promised it would be easy.

It would hurt, she knew, to tend what she'd neglected. It would take the surrender of pride and the dedication of time. And faith. Trusting when she could not see the way.

She would face her fears, and walk her path. Not out of circumstance, a mere twist in the wind. No, she would choose to embrace the life she'd been given with all the strength and love she had. And then some.

It was time. Time to return and work in her garden.

Time to go home.

Outside the church, the weight of her decision hit her with the blinding sun. For the first time in her life, when she'd thought of home, she meant Potter Springs.

*Weeping may last for the night, but joy comes in the morning.* The promise followed her like a Sunday benediction. Now she would be ready to face the thorns. Any more hardships coming her way would be worth it.

For the roses.

AT THE HOTEL, she stepped into the cool marble interior. A young employee vacuumed the thick lobby carpet with an industrial machine. She hardly heard its roar for the swell of plans in her mind, the excitement singing through her.

Amanda waved to Consuela, busy on the phone. An irate customer, judging from the hostess's drawn brows and animated speech. Consuela covered the receiver and motioned Amanda to come over.

"Later," mouthed Amanda. What she wanted was a shower, and to begin packing. She would leave in the morning.

Her friend waved again, more frantic, still on the phone. She tried to speak over the vacuum, moving her magenta lips in an exaggerated fashion.

*"Mother,"* Consuela seemed to say.

*What?* Amanda shook her head. Her mother was in Houston, or probably the lake house in Conroe by now. She splayed her fingers at her friend. *Ten minutes. I'll be back in ten minutes.*

Amanda turned in her flip-flops, only to be caught by the snake cord of the vacuum cleaner. She lost her footing, tripped over and dropped her bag. Paperbacks tumbled out like movie popcorn, littering the hotel's immaculate floor.

Blushing, she gathered them quickly and shoved them into her bag. Scooted on her knees to retrieve the last one.

A pair of navy pumps stopped her midshuffle. Amanda's gaze met crisp cuffs, traveled up the length of pleated khakis and rested on a peach sweater set and the inevitable strand of pearls.

"Well, hello, Amanda." Round brown eyes blinked under cropped, perky curls. "Need some help?" A small hand held out a worn copy of *Pride and Prejudice.*

"Thank you," Amanda murmured.

"You're welcome," answered Marianne Reynolds. Her mother-in-law, the Queen of the Baptists.

Thorn number one.

# eyeballs

"Erv, I need to talk to you." Mark stood at the entry to his boss's office. The space duplicated Mark's work area—dark paneling, teetering shelves, musty odor—with about ten more square feet. Minus, of course, the enticing view of the Dumpster. "There's something we need to discuss."

Ervin looked up from his computer, where he was no doubt e-mailing Peggy. Since he'd gotten computer savvy in a church staff's development seminar, he and his wife were known to send each other flirtatious zingers via electronics.

Once, Mark intercepted a love letter by accident. *Hey there, hellcat,* read the note. *What say we chase each other round the room tonight? You let me catch you too quick last time, you little devil!*

After that, he opened e-mails from Ervin with a finger ready on the delete key.

"So, you have time today?" Mark said.

"Sure, son." Ervin rolled across the laminate floor, skidding cowboy boots to a halt in front of his desk. He flipped through a calendar. "Got a meeting in about five minutes. How's this afternoon for you?"

"Fine. When?"

"Later. After lunch. Say, three?"

Mark didn't ask what Ervin planned on doing for that long of a lunch break. He didn't want to know. "I'll be here."

Returning to his office, Mark worked awhile, then opened his sack lunch. Less than exciting, but edible. Bread with lukewarm salami and a Coke from the machine. He'd run out of casseroles and had taken to packing his own meals. Better that than reinvoking the interference of the Ladies' Guild.

At 2:55, he headed back to Ervin's office. Empty. He asked Letty, "I'm supposed to have a meeting with Ervin?"

Heaving a sigh, she rewrapped waxed paper over her sandwich. Letty snacked on homemade takeout throughout the day. Pickled eggs. Blue cheese on toast. Sardines.

Mark smelled the tuna from his comfortable distance of about four feet. Not pleasant.

Letty handed him a yellow sticky note. "He said to meet you down the hall. Room 125." She went back to her lunch, picking at it like a feline.

In front of 125, Mark stopped cold. The counseling room. Outside the shut door stood a metal-inscribed sign on a pedestal. QUIET PLEASE. IN SESSION.

*Good God, I'm in counseling.* He rapped softly on the door, waiting for the punch line. Surely this was a joke. A mistake.

Ervin ushered him in, shaking his hand like a long lost friend.

A white-noise machine whirred in one corner and a box of tissues and a Bible rested on a table between two worn leather chairs. An amateur oil painting of a wooded lake dominated one wall. Lakeview.

Ervin sat down and gestured for Mark to do the same. "Thought we'd be more comfortable in here. No phones, no secretaries, no pesky congregants." Ervin smiled. "It's one of my favorite hiding places."

"Good idea." Tension released from Mark's shoulders when he realized Ervin hadn't planned a secret sabotage on his psyche.

"What did you want to talk about?" Ervin rested his palms on his knees, relaxed. Just two guys talking, his posture seemed to say. Not, I'm-about-to-fire-your-sorry-self-because-Dale-Ochs-told-me-to.

Still, looks could be deceiving. Mark knew that from looking in the mirror.

"You know about Mandy. That she's gone. You've probably figured out it's more than her father being sick. More than a vacation."

Ervin nodded, quiet.

"I know the board wants me to leave. And maybe I should. But first I need to tell you why," Mark said. "Why she left in the first place. Why we've been having trouble." The catch in his voice surprised him. He coughed and rubbed his hand on his pants. "It's not an excuse and I'm not here to beg. But the air needs clearing, like you said."

"Go ahead." Ervin leaned back in the chair. "You can trust me."

*Is that so?* Mark didn't voice the doubt aloud. At this point, he had no choice. He just started the telling. Pulled forth what he'd buried deep inside, had hidden away in the darkness in himself.

Maybe in doing so, he prepared his own coffin, paving the way for Dale to replace him. But if Mark was going out, he'd go out honest, with the truth etched on his grave. For the entire world to see.

He raised the chisel and started at the beginning. "We were together before we were married. Do you know what I mean by *together*? I know we should have waited, and I wanted to, but not enough, and it's my fault. . . ."

The scent of confession smelled sour and dead. Mark wrinkled his face against it. Each word hurting as he spoke, tugging the truth, bone by bone. "I didn't leave Houston because of God's calling at all. I was fired. My best friend looked me in the eye and said, *You can't stay here. . . .*"

He pressed on, digging deeper, bringing the darkest parts to light. Unearthing his need to hide, his desire to be perfect. To appear perfect, no matter the cost.

Copper pennies. Take backs.

Little sage, heartbeats floating over him. Gone, without ceremony. No name, unclaimed by a father. Sorrow painted the memory in shades of blue.

Shame forced Mark's vision to his knees. "And she lost it, the baby. I found her and she was bleeding and she had to go to the hospital. . . ."

He looked at Ervin, expecting condemnation. Some sort of a judgment at all Mark's deception. The disappointment he'd seen from James Montclair.

Yet, Ervin's face held the same open expression, like a blank page. Not childlike or gullible at all. Just accepting.

A countenance of grace.

It helped Mark finish what he'd started. To reveal the fault lines that had finally broken him down. "I kept trying to break through, to fix her somehow, but I couldn't. We didn't connect anymore, and she left in the van. I don't think she's coming back. . . ."

Given air, the past breathed anew. Less scary and not so dark. What had seemed grievous secrets revealed to be . . . ordinary. The sins of an imperfect soul.

Now emptiness took the place of secrecy. Mark sat back, exhausted. "Well?"

"Well, what?"

"Aren't you going to say something? Fire me? Call me a hypocrite? *Something?*"

"Is that what you think you deserve?"

"I don't know what I deserve. I just want to know what you think."

"I think you're an idiot." Ervin's eyes sparkled.

"Thanks." Mark tugged a tissue from the box. For some reason, his nose wouldn't quit running.

"What matters more than what I think is what *you* think," Ervin said. "You're thinking wrong."

"You've lost me."

"Well, son, being lost is a good way to start getting found. You asked me to tell you something, I will. Ervin Plumley didn't fall off the turnip truck yesterday."

"That's beautiful, Erv. What are you talking about?"

"I'm talking about the two eyeballs the good Lord gave me sitting smack in the middle of my head. The ones resting in front of my mighty-working brain."

"And . . ."

"I've been using them, Mark. Don't you think I knew something was wrong when you two pulled into town? That a guy like you coming to a place like this had to have a history? Your pretty little wife with more pain in her face than anybody has a right to?"

"I didn't realize."

"I know. That's the problem with the invisible elephant. Pretty soon, it's all you can see. I've just been waiting for you to be ready. Willing to admit a giant Dumbo's stomping around your life."

"So"—Mark took a shaky breath—"it's all been for nothing. I'm a fool."

"Yes, but now you're a broken fool. I'll tell you another little secret, Mark." Ervin leaned forward in a stage whisper. *"We're all fools."* The preacher sat back. "Everybody falls short. Lord says so himself." He tipped his head toward the Bible on the table. "Likes working with us, I guess. 'Cause the only place to go is up."

"I can take a leave. Put in my resignation. Maybe I—"

"Maybe *now*," Ervin interrupted, "you're ready to be a minister."

"But when the board finds out . . . Dale Ochs is ready to see me swing."

"You let me take care of the board," Ervin said. "God love 'em, but those goats got more skeletons than the Smithsonian. Yours looks downright puny in comparison."

"There's something else." Mark might as well get it all out now. On the table. Away from his soul, where it tangled him, choking and dark. The last of it. "About Courtney Williams. And me."

Ervin looked less excited. "Go on."

"It's nothing, really. Nothing happened. But it could have, I think. Maybe. More on my part than hers."

"Be clear. Speak English, boy, and tell me what you're saying."

"That I came close to making a really stupid mistake with Courtney Williams. It was my fault. But I didn't. We didn't." *By the grace of God and a glass of cold Coke.*

Ervin crossed his arms. His brows lowered. No more buffoonery, no trace of a simpleton. "You think it might happen again? The almost stupid mistake?"

Mark looked Ervin dead on and spoke the truth. He found its rhythms easier now. "No."

"Then watch yourself. You know what they say, 'Take heed, lest you fall.'"

"I will. But there's a problem. Dale Ochs knows."

"Dale Ochs couldn't find his butt with both hands." Ervin snorted.

"What? I thought you and he—"

"Mark, have you ever thought that part of my job is keeping the peace around here? Making sure everyone has a place and feels valued?"

"Dale Ochs wants my job," Mark stated the obvious.

"I know, and people in hell want ice water. Don't get me wrong." Ervin shook a finger. "Dale Ochs is a fine deacon and we're glad to have him. But his . . . *talents* . . . are best suited to the board, and that's it. You get me?"

"I get you."

"Then that's all we need to say about that. What's been said between us, as far as I'm concerned, stays between us."

"Fine with me." He accepted Ervin's handshake. The shadow of James Montclair fell away as new respect and trust dawned in Mark for this West Texas pastor. Not worship, but respect.

"Besides, it's not about the past, Mark." Ervin stood.

The head pastor of Lakeview Community Church, a full foot shorter than his associate, strode out of the counseling room with all the authority and vigor of Tom Landry. Leaving Mark no choice but to follow.

"Not what's gone on before, but what lies ahead." Ervin increased in volume as he quoted Scripture, walking down the church's hallway. "We . . . you, me, the board, all us fools!" He bellowed, tossing a hand in the air to great effect.

Mark could see how the former high-school football coach had taken a Division 3A team to the play-offs eight years running. Precalling, as Ervin liked to say. Mark wondered how much

Ervin's vocation had actually changed. Different uniforms, different playing field, but the work—encouraging the team to the goal line—stayed the same.

"Our job is to press on. It's about the future." Ervin punctuated this with a hearty punch to Mark's upper arm.

"The future," Mark echoed, slightly overwhelmed at the idea. *Our job.* He had a job. Still.

He hadn't thought much past this point. The meeting, the getting through the truth part. What would face him on the other side? *What,* he wondered, *lies ahead for me? For Mandy?*

Ervin actually slapped Mark on the rear as he hustled him through the exterior doors into the church's chilly parking lot. "Yes, son. The future." Ervin grasped him on the shoulder.

*Son.* The nickname, though familiar, took on new meaning. An invisible mantle of approval slipped over his shoulders. An honor he thought lost forever, when the El Camino pulled away.

"Your future," Ervin continued. "And I believe it's high time you went out to get it." The glass door clanged behind Ervin, leaving Mark alone underneath the overcast sky.

He couldn't be sure. Had Ervin said to go out and get *it*?

Or *her*?

CHAPTER 30

shall we dance?

"Is Mark all right? My father?" Frantic questions fired faster than Amanda could stop them. Why in the world was her mother-in-law standing in the lobby of Palacio del Grande? She knew Marianne's job as a secretary at Lubbock Community College didn't pay enough to send her to Mexico on a flight of fancy. "How did you get here?"

"Slow down, dear." Marianne patted Amanda's shoulder in a movement both condescending and irritating. "Not to worry. We've got plenty of time. Why don't you go get changed out of your beach clothes, and then we can visit in that darling little restaurant back there?"

Amanda fingered the edge of her floral dress, purchased at a shop downtown. Not beach clothes. She nodded and escaped to

234

her room. In the steaming shower, the scalding water soothed her fears, for the moment. She made up her face and pretended Marianne's appearance at the hotel was a welcome event and not an impending sign of disaster.

In Antiqua Grill they sat across from each other, old enemies with bright smiles. Marianne in her traveling outfit, still starched in spite of the humidity. A suitcase at her feet.

Checking in?

After ordering a cup of hot tea, Marianne shooed the waiter away. She glanced at Amanda as if she didn't know where to start and fiddled with the sugar packets. Flicked the edges, then shook it in the tea.

Ninety-eight degrees outside and the woman's drinking Earl Grey. Amanda sat quiet, waiting for the Queen to pounce on the pawn.

Marianne obliged. "As for your first question, Mark is fine. He's held up beautifully."

Amanda winced at the knife in her stomach.

Marianne must have noticed her expression. "No, let me rephrase that. I don't want to get started off on the wrong foot."

They'd danced on the wrong feet since day one. Why change the steps now?

"You asked how I got here. Your mother and I have been in contact." At Amanda's raised eyebrows, Marianne nodded. "I know that surprises you, but we mother hens tend to cluster when our chickens wander. And since you hadn't called her . . ."

Amanda thought of her mother as less a hen, and more a drill sergeant, ordering her troops in line. Apparently, the woman had gotten strategic and enlisted Mark's mother behind Amanda's back.

"Katy has kindly provided the, ahem, *means* for me to come

visit you. She's been busy"—Marianne colored prettily—"with your father at the lake house."

"Yes, I know. Since Dad's heart attack, they've been second-honeymooning." Strangely, Amanda didn't feel angry at her mother's interference. After all, Katy Thompson carried control as comfortably as a Chanel tote. More than that, she loved her daughter. Somehow, sending Marianne to the rescue seemed a sweet gesture, however bizarre.

Family. Maybe it looked different than her childhood dreams of happily-ever-after, but she'd been blessed with a family after all. Twisted and strange perhaps, but they were hers.

"Well, I wouldn't know anything about second honeymoons." Bitterness pinched Marianne's features, then passed away.

Amanda remembered. Mark had told her about Doyle, left and gone with the busty blonde. "I'm sorry."

"Not your fault. Not mine either, of course. Just bad luck, I suppose. Bad luck and poor choices."

Amanda wasn't sure whether to agree or try to defend Marianne's marital history. She decided on a vague "Hmm."

"I thought," Marianne went on, "maybe I could help with that. The voice of experience and all."

Bracing herself, Amanda prepared for a tongue lashing of the in-law kind. She wondered if she had time to order a stiff drink from the bar before the onslaught.

"From Doyle . . . the divorce . . . Mark has this—how should I phrase it—tremendous sense of *duty*," Marianne began.

Ah. Mark as perfect son, Amanda as lousy-ruiner-of-Golden-boy's-entire-life. A well-worn theme.

"I suppose you'd call it duty. Honor, perhaps. Toward me, the church. You." Marianne turned the teacup in her hand, sunlight reflected off the silver rim. "I think his *honor* didn't know what to do when . . . when he didn't cope with things quite as perfectly as he'd hoped."

The surprise, the second major one of the day, nearly knocked Amanda from her chair. "What do you mean?" *That, for once, something is not all my fault?*

"With the baby." The cup clicked against the saucer, the delicate china ringing high and clear.

Amanda's ears rang with it. The baby.

"Having it too soon," Marianne continued, "and then, not at all." Her hands fluttered, drawing Amanda's gaze. "He reacted poorly."

An understatement, but Amanda would take what she could get. After all, none of them had known what to do. Yet somehow, everyone had turned to Mark, including Amanda. They'd all expected perfection, not understanding he had a grief of his own to work through.

No wonder he fell short. With the pedestal they placed him on, he'd had so far to fall.

She nodded, staring at a tiny chip in Marianne's pale pink manicure.

"I did as well. Amanda, I'm sorry for not being there for you. And for Mark." Her gaze, round brown eyes, rested on Amanda. Like a bird, still and unwavering.

"Thank you," she managed. And meant it.

A slender bridge stretched between them.

"Actually, Mark has been a mess." At flight once again, Marianne lit on the silk flowers in the table arrangement, twisting the stems to her liking. "I've talked to him more now than ever before. He misses you, terribly."

Amanda's heart leaped, bringing quick tears to her eyes. Mark was a mess. Over her. Not Courtney. And he missed her. Terribly. She liked that part the best.

"I miss him too," she admitted. "In fact, I'm heading back to Potter. Tomorrow." She'd take her joy and face the morning. No matter what.

Intent on the bouquet, Marianne shook her head. "No."

"Excuse me?"

"It's not the right time, dear." Marianne frowned as she sought perfect placement for a peony.

"I think it is. I'm ready. I know what I've done wrong and how we can work on things." Well, maybe she hadn't gotten the *how's* all figured out, but at least she wanted to try.

"Mark's not."

"Not what?" Amanda bristled, tempted to yank the daisies from her mother-in-law's hands and shake her.

"Ready."

"But you said he missed me, and that means he still loves me so he *has* to be ready." As she rose from the table, Amanda's knees shook. So did her voice. "I'm going to call him—"

"Oh, you don't want to do that. I've spoken with him myself, frequently." Marianne pursed her mouth. "Give him more time. As much as your little . . . home away from home has done you good, I think the solitude has helped Mark too. Leave him be, a few more days."

"What do you mean it's helped him?" Amanda sank back down, hoping she wouldn't start crying.

"You know, spreading his wings."

"In what way?" Familiar jealousy hummed in her throat. In a flying-into-the-arms-of-another-woman way? But she'd sooner shrivel up and die than ask Marianne if Mark the perfect son was sleeping with the president of the Ladies' Guild. She wouldn't surrender that kind of ammunition. Especially not to her mother-in-law.

"Nothing to worry about. I'm sure he'll tell you all about it when it's time. But for now, allow him his space. Trust me."

*Trust you? I'm not sure I even* like *you.* "But what am I supposed to do? Wait in limbo? No, don't answer that." Amanda thought about Mark, and the waiting she'd forced upon him.

"That's why I'm here." Marianne tilted her head to the side, tiny pearls shining at her lobes. "The entertainment committee has arrived!" She reached across the table, careful of the cooling tea, and squeezed Amanda's arm. Girlfriendish. "What shall we do first?"

"I don't exactly feel like—"

"Nonsense." The comrade tone disappeared in an instant. Instructive Marianne back in full force. "I've traveled all this way and I want to see Laguna Madre. Everything, the shops, the sights—"

"There's really not much—"

"Well, let's start with that ocean out there. You've got a nice color to you."

Unbelievable. Instead of the usual zinger, an actual compliment from Queen Bee.

"Courting cancer, no doubt, but when in Rome . . . ," her mother-in-law remarked in a sing-song. Finished mangling the flowers, she stood from the table and tugged a polka-dot bathing suit, complete with granny skirt, from the nearby bag. "Shall we?"

# CHAPTER 31

eating crow

A brass sculpture on the desk displayed a wiry man dangling high above a three-dimensional cube. THINKING . . . OUTSIDE THE BOX, read the inscribed stand.

"Let me get this straight. You want the car back?" The swivel chair groaned under Steve Boyd's weight.

"Yes." Thankful to be in the warm office, Mark rubbed the red from his fingertips.

They'd gone over this several times in the Hemp's Used Motorway parking lot, frost glistening on the car hoods, before Mark suggested to the manager they step inside.

Mark hoped for a cup of coffee, but judging from Steve's irritated half-twists in the chair, he didn't expect any to materialize.

"The same car you traded in over a month ago. For the beaut.

Green Tourister. Full size, right?" Steve Boyd shook his head. "Great price on that van. I remember."

"Yes, it was. Thank you."

"Nearly *gave* it to y'all." The used-car manager spoke with resentment. "For the Lord's work, you said."

Mark steered him back to the topic. "About the Toyota—"

"God doing a little downsizing?" Steve snickered at his own joke. "Jesus in a hatchback!"

"Where is it?" Mark bit down on his irritation.

"Gone."

"I realize that, but can you tell me—"

"Nope."

"Why not?"

"Got the signature from your wife in the mail. Not your car anymore. Not your business."

Mark concentrated on a mustard stain on Steve's tie. He exhaled slowly and smoothed the tension in his forehead. "You don't understand. It wasn't really my car in the first place."

Steve Boyd's fleshy neck turned red. "Are you meanin' to tell me you traded in a hot one, 'cause preacher or not I'll—"

"No, no. It belonged to my wife. Her car." Mark still remembered her panicked look when he gave her the van. The pain in her voice when she'd asked, *But where is* my car?

He hadn't realized at the time how his trading the Toyota hit her personally. By disregarding another of her treasures, he'd wounded her deeper than the loss of metal and steel.

He couldn't make up for the other loss. The real one. The baby. There was no replacing a life, however much he wished he could.

This, he could do. He'd make restitution. Even if it cost him his last dollar, and he had to deal with every redneck between here and Chitapee.

"Oh yeah. *Mrs.* Reynolds," Steve grunted. "Red hair, mad as a burnt rat. Tried to renege on the deal."

"That's her. Except the rat part. Anyway, it was *my* deal, not hers. I made a mistake, and I'm trying to fix it." Mark wondered if a bribe would help. He had emptied their meager savings this morning.

Then he'd driven the church truck to EZ Pawn, finding the dilapidated shop in an aging strip center. He hefted the guitar case from behind the upholstered seat for the last time. Inside, dusty electronics and a tattooed clerk waited. He handed the Martin over, its panels gleaming like gold, and signed it away.

He remembered the party at Pleasant Valley when they gave him the guitar. The blessings with the gift. *Wherever he takes you . . . the Lord will use it to his glory. . . .*

The bills in his hand seemed so light after the heft of the instrument, but he counted each dollar as a step toward Amanda. Real glory. He hadn't looked back as he left the shop and drove toward Hemp's, praying for a miracle.

Steve uncrossed his sausage arms and pointed a finger across the desk. "I'm not taking the van back. You got that? A deal's a deal."

"So I hear."

"But if you're dead set on the import"—Steve huffed in disgust—"I may be able to point you in the right direction."

"Anything. Whatever you can do."

"It'd have to be a cash transaction . . . and bring it with you."

"Where's the car?"

"Out at my cousin's place. Bought it for his daughter. She's got three tickets for speeding in that tin can, he's threatening to sell. You might get him to talk if you show up with the money in hand. Tell him I sent you."

\*　　　\*　　　\*

BENNY ARRIVED RIGHT on time, tires squealing black marks in his driveway. This time, the passenger seat was empty.

"Thanks for the lift." Mark climbed in. Small seeds rolled in a groove on the dash when he slammed the Pinto's door.

"Sure, dude." Benny's hair appeared freshly combed, and his Quiet Riot T-shirt held no trace of Chee•tos.

"You look nice."

Benny grinned and cranked up the stereo.

"You know where it is?"

"Yeah." Benny left Mesquite Street shaking in his wake. The cool wind blasted through the open windows, picking up the music and tossing it in Mark's ears.

He felt about sixteen again, and liked it.

Twenty minutes later, by great fortune or divine intervention, they happened to drive up to the cousin's place right in the middle of a domestic disturbance.

The teenager, a skinny girl with buckteeth, shouted at her father in the dusty front yard just as they arrived. "You *cain't* ground me from it, it's *my* car and you *gave* it to me!"

"That's Jessie." Benny smoothed his eyebrows.

"You know her?"

"Dude, why do you think I gave you a ride?" Benny looked incredulous at Mark's stupidity.

Mark felt almost thirty, and liked it.

"I'll sell it, I swear I will!" the potbellied father shouted. "I cain't afford no more gol-durned tickets!"

Happily, Steve Boyd's cousin, the irate father, *did* want to sell. He took Mark's offer without dickering, while Jessie and Benny circled each other like roosters in the yard.

Jessie swore vengeance and bad behavior when her father announced the transaction, but Mark thought the tirade might be more for Benny's benefit.

"Let's go," Mark said to the young janitor, who sat beside Jessie on an abandoned tractor tire, pulling at weeds in the dirt.

"Later," Benny said to the girl.

"Later," she echoed, jutting her hip.

The cousin promised to deliver the vehicle himself within the hour, straight to Mark's driveway.

A funny clanking sound in the Toyota's engine announced the prompt arrival later that afternoon. Signing the papers, Mark guessed Jessie must have driven like she talked—loud, fast and irreverent. He took the car to AutoZone, cringing at every ominous clunk. There, he had just enough money to purchase an extensive car manual, with the rest of the savings allocated for trip funds.

It would be impossible to bring the car to a real mechanic, because of his self-imposed schedule and severely flattened wallet.

He'd just have to read the book and see if he could make sense of it himself. His gut sank as he pulled in the driveway, wondering if his plans had enough holes to drive that minivan through.

If only Amanda were here. He flipped through the intricate drawings and instructions. After all her tutelage in Ben Thompson's garage, she'd have this thing running clean in no time.

Of course, if Amanda were here, he wouldn't be trying to squeeze a lifetime's worth of mechanical knowledge into one afternoon.

If Amanda were here, the fire under him would be less hot. The crazy idea of driving across Texas to go get her, to give her the Toyota and his heart, would never have entered his mind.

He popped the hood, book in hand, and tried to make sense of Greek. Actually, he knew some Greek, thanks to seminary. This looked much harder.

*    *    *

TWO HOURS LATER, Mark sat on the porch, his head in his hands. He'd just have to get a plane ticket. Rent a car near the border. Beg his mother-in-law for money and show up empty-handed.

He'd wanted to wow Amanda. What he'd managed was worse than a whimper. He sat alone in his defeat.

Mrs. Zimmerman had already been over three times, once with soup and twice to walk Princess. Checking things out, nearly dying from curiosity. She'd run out of excuses, he guessed.

Down the street, a diesel engine rumbled around the corner. Mark lifted his head, watching as a white dually truck, big as a Greyhound bus, barreled down the road. It stopped in front of his house.

Men eased out, broad chested and deep bellied, boots thumping on the curb.

Joe Don Wexley, Jimmy Underwood and Ervin Plumley.

Ervin shuffled up the driveway, carrying two Thermoses. "Coffee," he announced, handing one over. "Been a long day?"

"You have no idea." Mark unscrewed the cap, the pungent aroma rising like incense. "What's up?"

"Aw, a little bit of nothing." Ervin leaned against the porch rail. "Heard you got the car."

"Yep."

"No, I mean I *heard* it. Drivin' by the Dairy Queen earlier." Ervin paused to swig and smacked his lips against the heat. "She running good?" He asked, polite.

*Good as a garbage can on wheels.* "Nope," Mark said.

"That a fact?"

"That, Erv, is a fact."

"Too bad."

Joe Don and Jimmy rambled forward, identical in thick corduroy jackets, Wranglers, and with silver Thermoses. After shaking hands, Mark repeated the same conversation with them, almost verbatim.

They murmured their condolences and sipped the steaming brew, quiet for a few minutes.

"Hey, Mark." Ervin broke the silence.

"Hey, yourself."

"I ever tell you how handy Joe Don is, what-all he did on your house?"

"Yessir. Never could thank you enough, Joe Don. Sure appreciate it."

"Aw." Joe Don scuffed a boot.

"And Jimmy here . . . you know he carries the mail."

"Sure do. Does a good job." Mark nodded at Jimmy, who tipped his John Deere cap in response.

"Yeah, but you know what he did before that?"

"No, sir."

Ervin grinned from ear to ear as Jimmy rocked back on his heels. "Auto mechanic."

"That so?" An internal click sounded for Mark. A sense of rightness. An alignment with the world. He smiled.

"Whaddya say we have a looksee?" Jimmy suggested, nonchalant.

Mark thought he could have kissed Jimmy on the spot. Wisely, he kept such thoughts to himself. "Sounds good."

Joe Don went to the truck and removed tools from the metal chest.

Jimmy revved the Toyota, poking his head out the open window to listen. Engine heat made puffy clouds in the chill.

Ervin stood guard, hovering over the motor, tweaking gadgets here and there. He shouted something to Jimmy, who gunned the gas again.

Angels in work boots.

Saving Mark without ceremony or grandeur, or even much conversation. It was their way.

At that moment, the sight in his driveway moved him more than any sermon he'd ever heard. No PowerPoint, no expensive orchestra, no high rise cathedral.

Just the simple service of men, the smell of gas and oil, and the taste of hot, potent coffee. Real and tangible, it pressed Mark's throat and filled his eyes.

He blinked it away, brushing his hands on his jeans, and joined them in their task.

Once strangers, and then friends. Now, these men, they were his brothers.

CHAPTER 32

the craziest notion

On the beach, mariachi music tapped Amanda's nerves, threatening to explode her tension headache into a full-blown migraine. She flipped to her back and considered her mother-in-law beside her. "Another drink, Marianne?"

"Why, yes, that sounds lovely." Marianne turned in her gigantic straw hat, face barely visible beneath the orange rim. She smiled. "Thank you, dear. A larger slice of lime this time, if you don't mind."

"Sure." Dusting sand off her legs, Amanda wrapped a towel around her waist and grabbed the tumblers.

At least she'd gotten Marianne to switch to *iced* tea.

She made her way to the tiki hut for the refills. The bar-

248

tender sliced the limes to perfection, and her flip-flops sprayed sand as she returned the length of the beach, holding the chilly glasses.

Pressure burgeoned within her, ready to burst. She'd broken free of her cave and into the light. It was time to chase down her love, whether he wanted her or not. Whether Marianne approved or not.

Time to deliver the "I'm going home and you have to leave too" talk.

But when Amanda reached their sunning spot, Marianne set her book aside and chirped, "Let's go for another dip!"

She removed her hat and skipped to the water, polka dots flapping in the breeze. "This salt water is downright invigorating," Marianne called as she bobbed in the surf. "Afterward, we can play another game of gin. I'm so glad I thought to pack the cards!"

Amanda entered the water and let the warm wall splash against her, thinking if she had to play another round, she might start screaming. "Sounds super!" she exclaimed with false enthusiasm, and sank under the waves. The tide rocked her body for a blissful moment.

Underwater, heedless of the salt, she opened her eyes. Sand swirled in the clear motion. A little crab scuffled around her toes, then dug a hole, hiding itself completely. Her lungs cried out for air as her eyes started stinging. She had to breathe again.

Returning to the beach, Amanda dried the sticky water off her legs and settled into her lounger and watched as Marianne made similar preparations.

The woman adjusted her towel to ironing-board smoothness. She whisked away every granule of sand, then rubbed in a thick layer of sunscreen with vigorous, circular movements. She rolled the towel edge to prop her ankles, wriggled her hips and shrugged her shoulders. Finally she picked up her paperback, tilted her hat for maximum sun blockage, then sighed.

"Marianne." Amanda made a conscious effort to put firmness in her voice. "I understand if you want a vacation, but it's time for me to go back to Potter Springs. Back to Mark."

Not bothering to look up from her novel, Marianne said, "No, dear. It's *not* time. I told you . . . Mark's not ready yet."

"But why? Whatever it is, we can work it out—" Amanda forced images of Courtney's long limbs, tangled in bedsheets, out of her mind.

"Hush, dear." Marianne turned the warped page with a faint crackle, running her fingertip along the rough edges. "Not now. Trust me."

It was the second instance the woman had made such a demand. And Amanda didn't feel any closer to believing that she should trust someone who elevated the in-law relationship into a passive-aggressive art form.

Trust. Surrendering pride and making her way. Thorns and vines, tangling the path.

She'd clip away what she could, regardless of the hurt. She must step forward, out of deception, and into faith. "Marianne, I have to tell you something. About why I need to go home."

Marianne set the book aside and gave her full attention, the round hat a ridiculous orange halo. "Yes?"

"When we lost the baby. It wasn't just that. We haven't told anyone. But the doctor said . . ." She felt her face contort, uncontrollable. "We can't have any. Something's wrong with me." She voiced the shame out loud, unable to name why she surrendered the secret now. It seemed important, a foothold for understanding. She handed her enemy the greatest weapon she had, hoping for mercy. Expecting none.

"I can't have a baby." Looking up, she found Marianne's perky features swathed in compassion.

"Oh, Mandy." She breathed it out, three syllables of sadness.

Marianne had never used her daughter-in-law's nickname. Before now. "Surely there are doctors?" She leaned forward and the book fell to the sand. "A specialist?"

"Maybe. I don't know. But that's why things were so hard. Between me and Mark." She wiped a tear away. "But I'm getting better."

"Of course you are, dear. It's amazing you've held up this well. If there's anything I can do . . . ," Marianne offered, her voice hollow and helpless.

"Thank you. But I'm not sure there's anything to do. It may be too late. For everything."

She would not share her fears about Courtney. To share suspicions without fact seemed wrong. A breach of promise somehow. Mark deserved more than her groundless fears, and Dale's tattletales. He deserved her honesty.

"I pulled away, I think." Amanda stared at the rainbow pattern in the towel, the stripes warbling through her tears.

"Of course you pulled away. That would be natural." Marianne patted her arm in a movement both comforting and protective. "You were hurting, you poor thing. Anybody would understand that."

In one swift move, her mother-in-law had switched from adversary to advocate.

Emboldened, Amanda shifted her gaze from the terry cloth. Letting Marianne read the naked pain on her face. "That's why I need to go back. To make it right."

"I love my Mark, and you do too," Marianne said. "But he's not always . . . *adept* . . . when it comes to handling emotions. He tends to block things off and pretend for the best."

"I know." Amanda couldn't believe the woman admitted Mark had a fault. It made it easier to keep going. To open her heart a bit more. "I haven't made it easy on him."

"It's a tremendous loss." Marianne blinked wetness from her eyes. "And one I can't pretend to understand. But I'm so sorry. For you and Mark. And me. My grandbabies. . . ." A flutter of a cry escaped her.

"I know. I'm so sorry too. I wish I could—"

"No, don't you apologize. Not for this. Not ever." She adjusted her hat. "You know Mark loves you—and I love you—just the way you are."

"No. I didn't know." Amanda pushed her toes in the sand.

"Well, I do." Marianne sat back in her chair, contemplating. "Perhaps the answer is to focus on what you already have. On what you have to give."

"I'm not sure I know what you mean."

"You have Mark's love. You have a family."

"Yes."

"Isn't that something?" Marianne raised her brows. Hopeful. "Maybe not enough, but isn't it something wonderful?"

This, coming from a woman who'd lost her love. And never quite recovered.

"It is. That's why I want to go home. I need—"

"Honey"—Marianne placed a gentle hand on Amanda's knee—"I hope you take this the right way. But maybe for now, in just this instance, it's not so much what you want. Or what you lack. What our Mark needs from you right now is time. For you to be the one to give."

The temptation to deny was overwhelming. But Amanda saw the truth in Marianne's words. She would lay down her pride, again. "Are you sure?"

"I wouldn't lie to you. Besides, it won't be long now. Trust me . . . it's closer than it seems."

Hours later, after their fourth game of tournament two, Marianne paused midshuffle. "You know, Amanda . . ." She tucked a stray curl behind her daughter-in-law's ear. A soft breeze rippled the folds of their striped umbrella. "Mandy. It's been so nice being here with you. I've enjoyed the . . . companionship."

Squinting in the sunset, Amanda didn't know how to respond. She hadn't considered what life in Lubbock might be like for her mother-in-law. That Marianne's almost rabid devotion to Mark, to the self-imposed rigors of church circles, could be indicative of loneliness.

On impulse, Amanda grasped Marianne's hand. "I've had fun too." It was almost the truth.

*I can do this,* she thought. She had something to offer. Not to take away, but to give. Perhaps there was blessing through the pain. Like Missy in the van. Listening and caring. Her loss, her Grace, a gift to others.

She watched Marianne resume her shuffle. The cards rattled, flipped apart, splayed out and fell together again.

Fanning her cards, Amanda placed the queen next to the king. *I can be patient for you, Mark, since you were patient for me. I'll wait until you're ready, even if it kills me.*

Intensity wrinkled Marianne's brow as she studied her hand. She stopped arranging for a moment. "Mandy, I've had the craziest notion. We've had quite a day." She paused, biting her lip. "What do you say we get an . . . adult beverage?"

Amanda looked up in surprise. "Like a margarita or something?"

"Ooh, yes. That sounds like just the ticket." The spirit of naughtiness flushed Marianne's cheeks.

"Fine with me. In fact"—Amanda stood and gently popped Marianne with the tip of her towel, eliciting a giddy squeal—"I'm buying."

# racket

Mark stood in the kitchen, updating his things-to-pack list and barked at his mother-in-law on the telephone. "Listen, Katy." Desperation pushed him past what to call Dragonlady at this point. "You can tell me where she is or I take an eight-by-ten glossy of her to every hotel in Mexico."

"Really?"

Katy's sarcasm drew the word out, as if he were a third grader planning a trip to the moon.

"Yes, really. With or without your help, I'm doing this. I'm going after Mandy and, frankly, anything you have to say against it is a waste of time."

"*Excellent.*" She stamped her approval with a quick exhalation.

Apparently, Ben's brush with death hadn't curbed her nicotine habit.

"What?"

"I couldn't be more pleased. She's staying at the Palacio del Grande in a little town called Laguna Madre."

Mark's hand shook as he wrote the address and phone number on his little yellow pad. An address. A real live location for his wife.

"You should be able to find it rather easily," Katy said. "I'm glad to see you're taking some initiative. There may be hope for you yet."

It was the nicest thing she'd said to him since he'd married her daughter.

"Oh," Katy added. "Say hello to your mother for me." She hung up, without good-byes or further comment.

Odd. Mark hadn't thought Katy and his mother were on the "say hello" level of friendship. He chalked it up to progress and crossed *Call Katy* off his list. Next up, packing.

He selected jeans, T-shirts, running shoes and shorts for the warmer weather. He added another bag with a few surprise essentials. Some things Amanda had left behind.

Saving the most dreaded duty for last, Mark swept up an unsuspecting Mr. Chesters and stuffed him in the traveling box. Mr. Chesters' claws, sharp as his reflexes, drew instant red lines on Mark's forearm. Trapped in the cage, the cat moaned, demonic and low. Not a pleasant sound. Mark washed his hands in the kitchen sink, the welts already rising in allergic reaction.

In the driveway, he loaded his luggage in the back of the Toyota, saying a prayer as he clicked the latch closed. *Please make it to Mandy. Get me to Mexico.* He opened the back door for Mr. Chesters' cage when he heard a caravan making its way down Mesquite Street.

The send-off committee, no doubt rustled up by Joe Don, Ervin and Jimmy. They pulled to a stop, a bunched-up caterpillar of trucks and cars.

Mrs. Zimmerman, at her weekly seniors' meeting, would be absolutely sick she missed all the action.

The women—Peggy, Missy and Courtney—emerged with a basket of boxes and little floral things, tied with a large bow.

Courtney retied the ribbon to a plumper formation. "For Amanda," she said. "Just some beauty supplies and such. It's the best we could do on last-minute notice."

Peggy hefted a container into Mark's hands. "This is for my honeygirl."

Inside were homemade treats, a candle and a stuffed bear.

"Tell her we love her," Peggy said. "Tell her to come on home."

"There's trail mix in here, in case you get hungry." Missy Underwood handed him a grocery bag. "And things for the road. Wipies, a phone card, bottled water. You let me and Jimmy know—"

Jimmy put his arm around his wife, affirming her sentiment with the gesture.

"I will." Mark placed the supplies and gifts in the backseat, careful not to squish the bow.

Dale Ochs hopped down from his gigantic truck and landed on stacked ostrich boots. He shook hands with Joe Don and Ervin. Sauntering up to the Toyota, he kicked the tires with a pointed toe. "She roadworthy?"

"I think so." Mark crossed his arms.

"She's dropping some transmission fluid," Jimmy reminded Mark. "Should make it okay, but keep an eye on your levels. Make sure you cap 'em off."

"I'll do that."

"Good." Dale nodded, as if satisfied. Like he'd done the work himself, or at least commissioned the others. "Listen." Tugging Mark's elbow, the deacon led him closer to the house. "Ervin and I had a little talk. I've got something for you, on behalf of the board."

"Yes?" Mark hated Dale tugging him anywhere.

Dale handed over an envelope, then stuck his thumbs in his jeans pockets.

For an instant, Mark feared the worst, opening it in front of others. A crazy thought that Ervin had changed his mind. Humiliation to go. *You're fired. Have fun in Mexico. God bless and Godspeed.*

Instead, it was a neat stack of cash. God bless, indeed.

"Traveling money." Dale bowed his chest out, his strong nose shining in the afternoon sun. "It's from the special-needs fund. And we figured if ever there was a special need, well, you might just qualify."

The board chairman grinned, and for the first time, Mark saw his humanity.

"Thanks." Mark shook Dale's hand. On instinct, he added, "Hey, Dale, let me ask you something. You know how swamped Ervin is. While I'm gone, we'll need your help to hold down the fort. What do you say?"

"Absolutely." Dale nodded vigorously before Mark finished talking. "You have my full support."

The man seemed to grow two inches, stacked boots or not. "Great. When I get back, we can talk about putting you over some of my responsibilities, if you'd like."

A glint in Dale's eye told Mark he'd struck gold.

"Things like next year's carnival. Organizing committees. Building our finances." *Busywork,* Mark thought to himself. *My headaches, Dale's specialty.*

The man was nearly aquiver with excitement. Dale the Watchdog, sniffing out injustice and ineptitude, on behalf of Mark Reynolds. "You can count on me."

Joe Don rambled up, his legs bowed out like a wishbone. "Seen the Weather Channel anytime today?"

"Nope," Mark said. "Don't have cable."

"Looks like a storm's rolling in down south. One of those tropical depressions, set to hit the Mexican coast in a coupla days. Might be nothing, but it could get ugly."

"I'll be careful," Mark promised.

"That cat don't look too happy," Ervin noted. He scratched behind Mr. Chesters's ears, flattened through the square grid of the cage. The animal quit moaning for the briefest of seconds.

"It never does," Mark agreed, sliding behind the wheel.

"Got everything you need?"

"Yep." Mark met Ervin's gaze. "Thanks for the money."

"What money?" Ervin grinned and slapped the Toyota's hood. "You best get going. Daylights a-burnin'!"

Mark honked the horn, an absurd chirpy sound, and left them waving in his yard.

HE DID NOT, it turned out, have everything he needed. When he pulled into the motel parking lot, he realized by Mr. Chesters's increasing screams that he'd left the cat food next to the dryer in the garage. The special diet food for heinously cranky cats on their last feline lives.

The motel sign blinked a neon vacancy, and Mark stepped into the lobby.

A gum-smacking girl worked the counter, her eyes blackened under layers of eyeliner. She didn't look up from her magazine.

"The sign says you have a vacancy?"

No answer.

"Could I get a room, please?"

"How many?" She stood, boredom battling irritation for control of her facial muscles.

"Just one room."

She looked at him as if he were the stupidest person walking the planet. "How many *people*?" Her tongue piercing, a miniature dumbbell, dulled her speech.

"Oh. One. Plus a cat."

She sat down again, propping a combat boot on a footstool. "No animals."

"He's in a carrier. I won't let him out."

"*No animals,*" she repeated, snapping her gum.

"What if I leave him in the car?"

She arched a penciled brow at him, still reading.

"Thanks for all your help." The bell jingled overhead. He heard Mr. Chesters before he opened the car door, and then the yowls and the piercing stench of urine hit him all at once. The cat had sprayed the inside of his cage. Again.

"Fifty more miles, buddy," he informed Mr. Chesters after checking the map. "And you better pray they have a motel, a Wal-Mart and a hose."

An hour later, Mark crouched in the gas station parking lot, hosing out the plastic carrier. One thin strip of neon illuminated Gary's Gas station and a CLOSED sign hung on the glass door. Silence reigned in the residential area around the station. Little houses, with rickety porches like loosened teeth, slept in the midnight hour.

When Mark finished, he released the cat from the backseat, where he'd curled into a baseball shape on top of Mark's bag. "Let's go, buddy." He scooted the furry mass out the door.

"*Mraaawl!*" Mr. Chesters took a deep bite from the fleshy part of Mark's left hand and pranced off to a nearby plot of grass.

"You ungrateful, godforsaken pile of . . ." Mark dug for Missy's wipies. Wrapping one around his hand, he shouted at the cat, still picking its way among the green blades. "Now's the time," Mark ordered. "Not in the cage, not in the motel."

Mr. Chesters mewled again. His yellow eyes reflected the neon sign.

"It's fine, see." Mark got down on his hands and knees, tapping the grass like the hair of a good child. "It's a great place to go."

Mr. Chesters squared his hind legs and lowered himself.

"Good boy," Mark whispered, afraid of interrupting nature, yet sensing a gentle encouragement couldn't hurt. "That's a good boy."

At the last second, the cat, instead of eliminating, leaped forward with all the force of his hind legs. Away from Mark's reach and toward the back of the garage, where piles of tires had been stacked to the station's roof. The cat's tail snaked through black rubber, then waved a saucy good-bye and disappeared.

"Mr. Chesters?" Mark whispered, unbelieving. Abandoned by a cat. Alone in a town with no Wal-Mart and a closed gas station—and miles and miles away from Amanda.

He was tempted to leave the animal, to fend for himself at Gary's Gas.

*Take care of Mr. Chesters for me,* Amanda had said. One of the last things she'd asked of him.

So, by all that was holy, he would. All the way to Mexico. "Mr. Chesters?" he called again, this time louder. He glanced at the houses, weighing safety against anger. He let his frustration rip.

"Mr. Chesters!" He shouted at the maze of tires, creeping toward the pile. "Heeeere, kitty, kitty."

His voice sounded less like a loving pet owner and more like Jack Nicholson in *The Shining.*

The tires shifted. The tower nearest Mark leaned to the left and he shoved it back. Too hard, unsettling a high-rise of hubcaps.

The stacked wheels danced like a tin man, scraping and wiggling, then, in a shower of metal, clattered to the ground. But not before one particularly mobile piece bounced off rubber and hit him in the forehead.

The ensuing noise made a rebel symphony, with metallic pitches high and low and Mark's furious shouts added to the mix.

"Mr. Chesters!" he bellowed, bracing the head wound with his palm.

The cat raced from the tires into a field behind Gary's Gas. He darted past a clump of shrubs and out of sight.

"Mr. Chesters, *come here!*"

At a house nearest the station, a porch light blared on. The front door flew open, and Mark heard the unmistakable sound of a shotgun, cocked and ready.

The gun's bearer could have been an extra from *Deliverance*. "I don't know no Mr. Chesters, but you best quit that racket or I'll quit it for you."

CHAPTER 34

buns

Marianne giggled as she tripped on the edge of the thick carpet. "Watch out, Mandy, that one's tricky!"

"Got it." Still in the doorway, Amanda brushed sand from her legs and tightened her sarong.

"Ohhh, there's a bar!" Marianne whipped around, her grasp on a melted margarita tenuous at best. She pointed, as if Amanda couldn't spot the crowded area for herself.

The lobby looked like a carnival, full of spandex, sounds and languages. People danced and talked and laughed. Some dressed for the evening, others simply wore cover-ups and shiny tans. The spirit of the beach had blown indoors for the evening.

"You know what I wanna do? One of those drinks in a little glass!" Marianne pointed to a low table next to the door, where a

263

group of sunburned Europeans stacked their empties and roared at one another over the din of the cover band onstage.

"Tequila? You want a tequila shot?" Amazement raised Amanda's voice. What had started with a few innocent margaritas had taken a decided turn for the worse. "I'm not sure you should have any more to drink."

"Nonsense"—Marianne huffed—"I'm a grown woman, and I'd like to have a shot of tequila!" She shuffled to the bar, skirting the dancers on the edge of the parquet floor, leaving Amanda no choice but to follow.

Marianne straddled a high stool and plopped the orange hat next to her. "Yoo-hoo! Bartender! Tequila, *por favor!*" She flapped a hand in the air.

He nodded and turned to pour the shot.

"Look at the buns on that bartender," she whispered.

"*Shhh.*" Amanda retied her mother-in-law's cover-up, where it threatened to slip away. "It's getting late, let's go."

"Oh, pooh. Don't be a spoilsport." Flashing a wicked grin, Marianne launched into a singsong, *"Bartender buns, bartender buns, bartender buns."*

Expressionless, the man handed the drink over and waited for the signature. Amanda mouthed, "Sorry," and sank into the nearest chair.

On the other side of them perched a woman with leathery skin, stuffed in a sequined catsuit. The bartender placed a shot in front of her.

Marianne tapped the lady. "How do you do this?"

"You lick the salt, take the shot, then suck on the lime." The woman showed her, with the panache of a seasoned professional.

"Oh, how nice! You did that just beautifully," Marianne complimented. "Let's see." It took her twice as long, movements awkward and slow. Her eyes widened as each taste set in. She slammed the glass down and grinned. "I did it!"

Catsuit woman lifted her refilled glass in salute.

Marianne spun on the bar stool and clapped to the music. The bunny hop. "You'll watch these for us, won't you?" She pushed their beach bags closer to their bar companion.

"I ain't going nowhere."

"Thanks!" Cramming her hat on with a flourish, she grabbed Amanda's hand, with a grip suddenly like steel. "Come with me, o daughter of mine."

"Oh no. No way. I am not doing the bunny hop."

"Oh yes, you are. . . ."

The chain wriggled through the lobby like a reeling Tilt-A-Whirl. Amanda found herself shoved in line and mercilessly pushed forward with a stranger's heavy mitts on her shoulders. She lost her mother-in-law in the mix and looked for her in the crowd at the song's end.

"How about the Cotton-Eyed Joe!" A perky voice yelled at the band. On the other side of the room, Marianne hopped up and down, waving. "We're from Texas! Play the Cotton-Eyed Joe!"

The band obliged and Amanda slipped back to the bar, hiding as she watched the proceedings unfold.

Marianne taught other dancers the simple steps, her hat flopped over her eyes. It fell off in the shuffle and got stepped on. When the song's stomps and yells subsided, someone sailed the hat like a distorted Frisbee and it landed in a nearby palm.

"This one's for our friends from Texas!" The dulcet tune of "Blue Bayou" poured out as the revelers crept to their seats or found partners. Not exactly a Texas song, but close enough.

A tall, dark man asked Marianne to dance and she clung to his shoulders as they swayed across the floor.

*"I'm going back someday, come what may . . ."*

Amanda thought of Doyle, who never came back again. And of Mark. When would he be ready? She didn't think she could last much longer. She ached with the longing, her heart rose and fell with the music. Mourning for what was lost, hoping for the future.

*I'm coming home, Mark. Come what may.*

When the couple turned, silver streaks wet her mother-in-law's cheeks.

Amanda retrieved the crumpled hat from the palm tree, and approached when the song finished. "I'm a little tired. What do you say we head back to our rooms?"

"Tired." She nodded, her face slack as a sleeping child's. "Back to the rooms."

"Thanks for the dance." The man smiled kindly.

They made it to the elevators, where Marianne leaned against the wall with her eyes closed.

Digging through the fuchsia carryall, Amanda found the room key. Inside, the dark room smelled of fresh sheets and the ocean. She clicked on the bathroom light. Toiletries lined up in precise circles. Illumination hit the open closet, where shoes sat in rows with aligned heels. Clothes hung on equidistant hangers.

Amanda gently guided her mother-in-law to the bed, where she flopped back, legs dangling off the side. She poured a glass of water and set it on the nightstand. "Need anything else?"

One brown eye pinched open. "Do you think something was wrong with those limes? I feel a little . . . odd."

"The limes?" Amanda shook her head. "We're in a nice hotel. If anything, it might be the—"

Marianne sat upright with panicked eyes and raced to the bathroom. A polka-dot whirlwind.

"Tequila." Amanda finished.

Horrible gurgling sounds came from the bathroom. Amanda slumped on the bed and stared out at the darkness, preparing for the long night ahead. She reached for a water glass and the phone caught her attention.

*Trust me,* Marianne had said.

*Can't go home, he's not ready.*

But they never said anything about calling.

One eye on the closed bathroom door, Amanda picked up the phone and dialed.

MARK'S EARS RANG from the warning shot fired just over his right shoulder, landing harmlessly in the field behind him. Tasting the burnt gunpowder, he threw his hands in the air à la every bad Western he'd seen. "Don't want to cause any trouble. Just looking for my cat."

The man with the gun lowered his bushy brows like hairy shades. He thrust his chin toward the gas station. "More like you're looking to break into Gary's."

"No, really. I'm traveling through and my cat ran off." Mark put his hands down. "I'm a minister. From Potter Springs. Honest."

"A minister?"

Suspicion marched across the man's face, wrinkling it further. "Prove it."

"Well, I've got a business card." He edged his wallet out, slowly, and held out the piece of paper.

The man edged closer, trying to read from thirty paces.

"Listen, I'll go." Mark started to put the card away, but the man snatched it up. "If you can point me toward a motel, I'll get out of your way and come back for my cat in the morning."

"No motels round here." The man propped the gun on the floor and drew a sleeve over his nose, reading. "If you're who you say you are, don't guess it's right for me to turn you out. Name's Clark Myers. You need a bed"—he gestured to the screened-in porch with the card—"there's a cot out here."

"I couldn't possibly—"

The man's brows shot up, nearly reaching the creases of his bald head. "Why, if it's not good enough for a fancy man like yourself from the big city—"

*Potter Springs, a big city?*

"No, no." Mark eyed the shadows. At least it was free. "I'll take it. Thanks."

Mark spent a sleepless night tossing in the crusty folds of Clark Myers' cot, clutching a moth ridden blanket to his shoulders. He used his shirt as a pillow, wiping the soft cotton above his eye, where the cut from the hubcap throbbed. Twice he killed spiders inching their way up his arms.

Clanging sounds from Clark's kitchen woke him at dawn. With his back in a vise, he lay still, turning only his head. Sunless light showed the mess he'd made at Gary's next door, tires and hubcaps lay about like the aftermath of a tornado. Still no sign of Mr. Chesters.

Mark sat up, groaning, and smoothed out his shirt. Blood stained the front and dirt streaked in the cotton weave. He slipped it over his head, his back cracking like fireworks.

Careful of his throbbing hand, he picked through the strewn tires, balancing tires against his chest. The oil left tracks like he'd been run over. He stacked them, one by one, as the sun rose higher. The heat and humidity soaked him and his clothes clung to his skin.

From inside the house, Clark hollered, "Found him!"

Mr. Chesters hunched in a corner of the screened porch, wolfing down eggs and bacon in great lurching gulps.

Clark took a deep drink of coffee from a heavy ceramic mug.

"Never did know a cat to refuse a little breakfast grease." He tipped his head toward the frying pan. "Want some?"

"No thanks, Mr. Myers. I'll just get changed, and we'll be out of your hair."

Outside, Mark reached in the Toyota's open window and found Peggy's goody bag torn apart. Next to the bear and candle, the remains of the brownies looked decidedly chewed. He forgot to shut the window, and Mr. Chesters apparently had enjoyed a midnight feeding frenzy.

Mark stared at the destruction in silence, noting the candle had melted in the heat and was stuck to the bear's fur.

"The cat's been in here." Clark stepped behind him.

"You think?" Four-toed chocolate footprints smashed into the Toyota's upholstery.

"No. I mean, the cat's been *in* here." Hands on his waist, Clark shook his head.

Mark looked at his unzipped duffel bag, where he'd pulled the wipies out last night to stop his bleeding hand. He leaned closer, and the unmistakable odor of Mr. Chesters' spray hit him. Gingerly he touched the clothes. Damp.

"Looks like he's marking his territory. Either that or a grudge of some sort," Clark observed from over Mark's shoulder.

Hoping to find something worth putting on, Mark tugged the bag out. Even his shaving kit had been fouled. His clothing reeked, beyond salvation. He zipped the bag to contain the odor and shoved it in the farthest corner of the trunk. Thankful that the second bag, the one with special things for Amanda, remained unharmed, still dry.

"Guess I'll just have to stay in what I'm in." He turned and nearly bumped into Clark, the man stood so close. "I need to get on the road."

Clark looked him up and down. "You know, I might have

something you could wear. My son's bigger than me, about your size. He left some old things here at the house."

The older man disappeared and an instant later returned with a strange smile and a neon yellow T-shirt. He held it up, displaying the front with four women in thong bathing suits. Across the gleaming buttocks, a cheery airbrush read SUN YOUR BUNS!

Clark bit his lip, a hint of mischief on his face. "How's this?"

The short sleeves waved at him. Clean. Cool. Dirt and blood and sweat-stain free. For the second time in less than twelve hours, Mark heard himself say, "I'll take it."

Hours later, stuck in San Antonio's swampy traffic with a greasy cat, a nifty new T-shirt, and the wound on his forehead turning into a third eye, he wondered if Amanda would even recognize him when he found her.

If he found her.

# ill advised

"I brought you some orange juice. And crackers." Amanda peeked into the hotel bathroom. "Since you missed breakfast . . . and lunch."

Head resting on the side of the toilet bowl, Marianne slumped against the marble tiles. Dark rings formed semicircles under her eyes.

"Leave them by the bed," she whispered, her pallor a distinctive green. "I'll be there in a minute."

"No hurry. I've got some Imodium too, if you want it." Amanda softly closed the door.

"No, I"—a choking cough, then a splash. A flush, water running—"need to let this run its course."

Amanda clicked on the television to muffle Marianne's misery and afford her some privacy. Maps of the coast splayed over the screen. The weatherman circled the Gulf Coast with a pointer and swooped toward the south.

He chattered on in Spanish, but Amanda watched where he pointed the arrow. Looked like a storm blowing in, a considerable distance from Laguna Madre. Clips of old hurricanes cut back and forth, images of ravaging winds and floods. The weatherman looked serious, unsmiling.

Marianne emerged, her hair wild, walking with the gait of an old woman. She peeled back the comforter and lowered herself by degrees onto the bed.

Amanda pressed the remote. "Looks like a storm's coming." She stood by the balcony, the afternoon clear as cut glass. Prisms danced on the waves as they calmed from the day's activity. The white beach looked like a bride's smooth satin, wrinkled here and there in tiny waves. No signs of a storm.

"From what I could make out, it looks like it'll hit south of here. Still, could be bad. Do you think we should leave? I've got a long drive ahead of me." In the van, her albatross.

Amanda glanced at the pad of paper next to the phone, where she'd doodled through countless calls to Mark, last night and this morning. Sitting at the desk, she'd written, *please, please, please,* over and over, blue scrawls on the square white page. Super-scripted, outlined, underlined. Surrounded with frantic flowers. Anxious daisies.

He hadn't answered. Not even in the darkest hours of night when she cared for his vomiting mother, when he should be home asleep. Not in the morning, long before his workday began.

The breathtaking view stretched beyond the window. The same view as her own room.

Paradise.

Prison. Held in a cell of her own choosing, longing to break free. She wanted to go home, but home apparently didn't want her.

"I couldn't possibly travel today." Marianne covered her eyes with the back of her hands, as if daylight hurt. "You can go if you want."

"No." Amanda drew the curtains. "We'll stay."

THE TOYOTA GAVE out in Berna Lista, Texas. After pulling away from Officer Martinez and the near ticket, Mark pressed ahead, staying under the speed limit, searching for the next town. The heat mesmerized him, the road lulling him to a half-aware state, so he hardly noticed the change. No warning light flashed. The engine didn't bang or smoke. It simply lost power, coasting to the feeder, until it rattled to a stop.

*Watch that fluid,* Jimmy had warned.

Mark sat in the car, narrowing his eyes against the sunset. A front of clouds rolled in, riding, floating, moving faster than clouds should. Perhaps it took minutes, perhaps an hour. The gray-black eclipsed the brightness.

*Could get ugly,* Joe Don had said.

Mark knew only the purrs of Mr. Chesters asleep in the back, the throb of a headache in his forehead and the bitter taste of yet another failure.

It had all been so clear before.

His bladder pressed in discomfort. He creaked the door open and stood on the side of the road, oblivious to the occasional car as it zoomed by. There was, literally, no place to hide anyway.

Zipping his fly, he turned to the familiar sight of flashing lights slowing to a halt behind the hatchback. No siren.

Officer Martinez heaved himself out of the vehicle and crunched toward Mark, shaking his head. "I thought I told you not to break any more laws today. Could cite you for indecent exposure, you know." Martinez stared at the Toyota. "Run out of gas?"

"I don't think so." Mark stared with him. "I think it's worse than that."

Martinez lifted the radio from his belt. "I'll call you a wrecker, see what we can do."

Two hours later, in a shop that smelled of gasoline and cigarettes, the mechanic wiped a rag over his sweating forehead and pronounced the verdict. "Transmission's out. Had a leak. Good-size one if your friend topped it off two days ago. Need to replace it."

"The transmission? The whole thing?" Mark set the three-year-old *Readers' Digest* back on the wobbly table.

"We can get the parts, start work in the morning."

Mark checked the clock and the full dark outside. He knew the shop should have closed, but the owner, Tony, stayed late as a favor to Martinez. So many favors.

He felt his luck running out, slipping away as he spent his favors one by one. "But I can't. I don't have the money . . . the time. There's a storm coming and I need to get to Mexico."

"I'm not sure this vehicle will get you there." Tony rubbed his stubbled chin. "Course you could just load up on the fluid, keep her full. Still, it's ill advised."

"No offense, mister, but right now my whole life is ill advised." Mark opened his wallet, counting his remaining cash. "I'll take the transmission fluid, to go. As much as you've got."

# disturbance

Amanda woke to the sound of crying outside her window. At first it sounded like a baby, then like her name, rolling on the tongue of an old woman. Calling out to her. She fought to find it, dragging out of exhausted sleep. She clung to whispers of alertness, crawling out of her slumber.

Danger neared, she felt it in the moaning.

Lifting her heavy head from the pillow, she tried to make out what had scared her. Her eyes adjusted, the grains of black and white taking shape. The clock blinked 3:25 A.M.

She'd finally gotten Marianne to sleep around ten, then made her way to her own bed, thankful for the quiet. Her own space. A room without the odor of bodily functions.

Now it had an odd scent. An earthy smell. The air thickened.

Fully alert, she lay still, heart pounding. Hair on her arms prickled, yet she sensed no physical presence. The chair, the desk, all appeared normal, as far as she could see. Something outside?

Pushing the comforter aside, she went to the window, the marble floor cool on her bare feet. The curtains, soft in her hand, squeaked on the rod as she drew them wide.

Silver light poured in, carrying with it the high-pitched keen. Not imagined, but real. She tugged the heavy patio door open. The screaming escalated. The wind slashed her nightshirt up around her thighs.

The ocean, no longer calm and tranquil, churned in its depths like a single, unified creature. The unfriendly moon cast green. And like the underbelly of a reptile, the clouds slid across the sky.

Rain stabbed the water, dotting its skin in spikes as it crawled, advancing toward the shore. The roiling surface bubbled in anger while the wind whipped it taller.

Amanda stood, transfixed, and watched the beast approach.

A knock sounded from far away, a frantic rapping nearly drowned by the tempest outside. Even before opening the door, Amanda knew who it would be.

Marianne, in the hallway, her white face lit with fear. "We're to go downstairs. The storm turned. It's headed straight for us."

RAIN SLID IN sheets down the Toyota's windshield, blurring the opaque view. Wind slapped against the car, sometimes rocking it violently to either side.

Mr. Chesters, free from his carrier, clung with sharp talons to the top of Mark's head. He mauled a painful dance and made a whimpering sound.

"It's okay, buddy. Mandy's just fine. Don't worry." Ignoring the claws needling his scalp, Mark peeled one hand from the steering wheel and reached back to tickle the cat's ears.

This time, Mr. Chesters didn't bite him.

Howling wind had a strange effect on the animal. The cat's eyes widened in the rearview mirror. His fur shot bolt upright, and he sat frozen. His mouth, pale tongue just visible, hung open as he panted.

The radio, at full volume, competed with the tempest outside. The weatherman broke in with a drawl.

"Doppler Dan here to update you on the disturbance down south. For those of you just in from outer space, Hurricane Megan has wreaked havoc on our Mexican neighbors for the past several hours. With winds up to 115 miles an hour before losing strength, this storm's tearing through the coastline, leaving mass destruction in its wake."

Fear tensed Mark's arms. They ached from holding the car to the road. Ached from emptiness.

"We've received reports of roofs ripped off buildings, trees shorn away at the roots and homes reduced to rubble. There's no estimate at this time on the level of damage, or of fatalities, which are expected to be great."

*No fatalities. No fatalities,* Mark repeated in a soundless whisper.

"Needless to say, roads are dangerous, blocked off in places. Safe travel remains impossible."

*Impossible. Blocked off in places.* He would not turn back. Everything that meant anything lay ahead. *Not what's gone on before, but what lies ahead.*

He would keep going. He had to get to her.

"Stay put and stay tuned to KNZT. I'm Doppler Dan."

Mark snapped off the radio and pressed harder on the gas. Willing the Toyota to make it, praying the tires would stick to the slippery concrete, he sped forward into complete blackness.

CHAPTER 37

the garden

Broken glass sparkled like crushed diamonds in the lobby. Morning smelled fresh, as if carnage's stink clung to the darkest hours and swept straight through Laguna Madre. The beach no longer resembled a bride's white satin. Soiled, with the ocean's treasures laid out to dry, along with man-made wreckage displayed in chunks along the way.

Still shaking, Amanda stepped past clusters of hotel guests and found a quiet corner with a phone. Angling the prepaid card to read the numbers, she made the call. Her second of the morning, because the first had gone unanswered.

"Mom, we made it."

The crackly reception couldn't mask her mother's tears. "I

tried to call, and couldn't get through. . . . Oh, baby, we were so worried. . . ."

"I know. Me too." Amanda's eyes burned at the memory, the terror of crouching with strangers in the dark, hiding behind kitchen counters in the hotel's one windowless room. The screaming. The mindless force of the water as it crashed through the hotel glass.

The murmur of prayers in different languages, gripping the hands of people she'd never seen before.

Even now her knees quivered. She'd tensed them through the hours, as if by clenching her body still, the earth would hold firm underneath them and they wouldn't be washed away in a great black flood.

"Is Marianne . . . ?" Katy's voice sounded small.

"She's fine. A little banged up. She bumped her head in all the chaos. But she'll be okay." Marianne stood in line at the concierge desk, jostling for information about a flight back to Lubbock.

"Let me put your father on the phone—"

"Mom, I'll try back later, but I really can't talk long. We've got to figure out what we're going to do."

"Just promise you'll call."

"I will. Listen, I know this is a crazy question, but have you heard from Mark?"

She tried, in the dead of night, with only the light from her emotionless cell phone, to reach him. *No service. No service.* She'd get a tenuous line, then sob through the cutoffs, frantic fingers dialed again and again. All she wanted was a chance to say good-bye. *No service.*

Minutes on the hour. She never got through, even when dawn broke and the storm whispered away.

"It was meant to be a surprise." Katy paused, as if searching for a way to explain. "He's coming down to get you."

"What? He's coming here?" Thrill raced through her. Sheer adrenaline pumped her heart and heat rose to her face. "But when—"

"Days ago." Katy's words came out flat, deflated. "If he left when he should have, that would put him—"

The heat chilled as horror froze her hope. Amanda finished the thought her mother couldn't voice. "Right in the middle of the storm."

The lobby closed in on her, with its bright colors and animated faces. The vacuums sucked up window chips. She couldn't breathe. Couldn't talk. Somehow she managed to say her good-bye to Katy and hung up. Walking to the concierge desk, she spotted her mother-in-law waiting in the irritated line of guests.

Marianne hugged her. "Did you get through?"

"Yes. Everything's fine." *Your son is lost. He's swept away in the middle of a hurricane and it's all my fault.* "I'm going for a walk."

She left, a liar and a coward.

THE TOYOTA BURNED to a grinding halt. Mark rested his head against the steering wheel. So weary. He'd driven through the night by sheer will. His body felt like he'd played a Super Bowl against God. Run over, defeated. Unable to go any farther.

Miraculously, he had found Laguna Madre.

In the midst of the storm, he had stopped to pick up highway road signs flattened by the wind. His headlights gleamed on glints of metal, twisted clues for him to follow. Rain battered him as he crouched, pouring transmission fluid into the great gaping hole, praying for enough to keep going.

When he made it to the outskirts of Laguna Madre, it looked like scattered puzzle pieces. Houses leaned at crazy angles, clothes dangled from trees, debris floated in rushing streams on either side.

He'd come all this way. Fought through a storm to be stopped by a failed transmission.

He was so tired. Tired of fighting. Not knowing where he was going, not knowing what awaited him around each turn. Keeping fear at bay through determination and drive.

*No fatalities.* His mantra and his prayer. He clung to it—else he'd dissolve in his fear.

*You've come on a fool's errand. You're a fool. A lost fool.*

"All us lost fools," Ervin had said. "Being lost is a good way to start getting found."

*As long as she's alive, I haven't lost her.*

He'd lost one already. The baby, gone without knowing a father's love. Slipped away before he shared his heart.

He wouldn't risk another by listening to pride's whisper again. Even if she didn't want him, she would know he loved her. That he'd entered hell and come out broken. A fool. Her fool.

Mark released his seat belt and scooped up Mr. Chesters. He retrieved the one bag that meant anything and slung it over his shoulder.

*She's alive,* he convinced himself. *And as long as she's alive, there's a chance.*

Tucking the cat under his arm, he started walking.


AMANDA PICKED HER way down the cobbled roads. She stepped past garbage, leaped over streams of rushing water. The morning sun brushed the carnage with absurd cheer.

Mud sucked her tennis shoes and splattered against her favorite floral dress, thrown on in last night's panic.

She rounded the corner, to the street with the old church. Its appearance was so altered, she might have missed it. The huge tree was upended, roots like arteries torn from the earth's heart.

The leaves withered. It had fallen on her stone bench and broken it in two.

An oversize branch blocked the entrance to the courtyard. Amanda stepped around it, bracing herself against a limb. Pointed wood scratched at her arms, but she wiggled through.

Inside the courtyard, she paused in surprise. The gardener. He had with him a woman and several children. Together they cleared the smaller brush away, loaded it in his wheelbarrow. The children chattered while they worked.

Once beautiful petals lay like tired confetti all around, not one bush had a bloom left on it. The plants were knotted, with huge bunches broken and ripped away. The gardener's clippers flashed in the light, his whistle like that of a warrior. No longer sweet and mellow, but a fight song to battle.

She passed them, silent as a specter, and entered the sanctuary. Water puddles formed in the aisle, bare bits of sky peeked through holes in the roof. Amanda stepped inside, nearly overcome by the damp smell and the rot. The destruction.

Still, her kaleidoscope windows shimmered in the sun.

This time, she didn't ask questions or search for answers. This time, she knelt on the sodden floor and bowed her head.

So many blessings. Why hadn't she seen them before? With Mark, she had all the family, all the love she ever needed. She only needed to open her eyes and see the glory all around her.

She would journey the chosen path, she would celebrate her joy, but she wanted her favorite person by her side. And for that, she had no power to make it right. So she poured out her heart like water. Knowing only hands bigger than her own could grasp the power of life and death.

The storm had proven that much.

"Please keep him safe. Give us another chance. Please . . ." She lost the rest in her tears, but after a while, she lifted her head with a sense that she'd been heard. Even when she didn't have the strength, or the words, to speak.

She left the sanctuary and, for the need to help instead of hurt, to work instead of wait, she joined the gardener and his family at their task.

MR. CHESTERS HUNG limp under Mark's arm. Perhaps calmed by the trauma of days on the road, the fury of last night's storm or the physical aftereffects of greasy eggs and bacon working through his system.

They walked miles, passing trashed storefronts and waterlogged ditches. Mark spotted a steeple in the distance. He thought people might be gathered there after a storm. For comfort, for community, clinging to the fact they survived.

He picked up the pace, hoping to find someone there to help him. To take time for a stranger and point the way to Palacio del Grande. The bag slapped his side as he hurried and his shoes squished blisters into his heels.

A man and his family crossed the muddy road on the other side, the children carrying rusted tools.

"*Hola.*" The man smiled in a flash of white teeth.

A good sign. "*Hola.*" Mark waved a free hand and they disappeared around the corner.

He neared the church. Casing the perimeter, he found a wrought-iron entrance to the church's courtyard, partially hidden by a felled tree. Roots dangled overhead. Not hearing the hoped-for murmur of conversation within, disappointment sank in his chest.

Still, maybe a priest lingered inside the building, at prayer. An English-speaking priest. There had to be someone.

He bent low under the branches, the bag slung over his shoulder, clasping Mr. Chesters. He braced his shoulders and pushed his way inside.

On the other side, he saw her.

Amanda.

She sat on the ground against a crumbled bench in the shambles of the garden. Tears streaked her face and her nose flamed. She didn't hold a journal in her lap, but broken stems of roses. She stroked at the petals, petting them as she cried.

Her dress, a bright floral print splattered with mud. Tennis shoes clumped with filth covered her precious feet, else he would fall to the ground and kiss them.

Her hair was pulled back from her face, a small twig stuck in it. Her face, whiter than he'd ever seen it.

*I am looped in the loops of her hair.*

For a minute, he stood frozen. Then he inched forward as if in a dream. The old game, the one from a thousand years ago in a park in Houston, unfolded. How close could he get without her noticing?

Would she accept him when he got there?

His life, swinging in the balance, waiting for her to catch his heart and make him whole.

A stick snapped under his step, announcing his presence. He spoke. "Mandy."

# grace

*andy.* The sound. The precious sound of him saying her name poured out like fine oil. She lifted her face to it, unbelieving.

He stood before her, holding her cat. A scruff on his cheeks, his hair matted. Swollen blackness claimed one eye, and the other blinked at her. A horrible T-shirt that would normally have made her smile.

Not Mark. This was not her Mark but an insane dream. An illusion brought on by hurricanes and heartache.

His image bent in slow motion, lowering Mr. Chesters to the ground. The cat pounced forward, purring violently.

She reached forward to pet the animal on foolish instinct. Knowing the orange fur couldn't be real, even as she kept her vision locked with the ghost who looked like her husband. But Mr. Chesters brushed solid beneath her hand, his whiskers pricking her like gentle needles.

Real.

She pushed herself to stand. She wished for breath, for speech. "Mark." It came out as a sob. She half ran, half stumbled to him, fell into his chest with all her strength. He smelled like sweat and sorrow, of road and rain.

Arms wrapped around her, muscle and bone. His face pressed to hers.

He shuddered, and she realized he was crying.

Crying, crying for her, arched over her, clinging to her as she clung to him. Saying her name over and over as his body shook, holding her so tight she couldn't breathe.

She didn't care. Oxygen meant nothing as her pores opened wide, faint hairs like tiny nerves, sensing every touch. Soaking him in. Drinking his scent. Breathing through his presence.

Together they sank to their knees, mouths mingled with tears. No words spoken. No room for words with all they had to say.

In a different country, a strange city, but together, they were home.

She couldn't stand to leave his lips. Yet, she had to see him. She pulled away.

Red rimmed his eyes as his gaze touched her. Knowing her. Staring, as if memorizing her features, her form.

"How did you . . . the storm . . . ?" Wonder brought her fingers to his face. Real.

"For you." Hoarseness thickened his voice. "I'm here for you." He traced the shell of her ear, her brows, her cheekbones. "Is that okay?"

"Okay . . . is it okay?" She swallowed, took in clarifying air. "What took you so long?"

He smiled, then winced, bringing a hand to his beaten forehead.

"What happened?"

"Later. I'll explain everything later." He shifted and pulled a small bag to his lap. "This is more important." Clearing his throat, he smoothed the wrinkled canvas. "I've brought something for you." He stared at it, as if pondering whether or not to hand it over.

She scooted closer, touching her knees to his. Wondering what he had brought with him, this far. She opened the handles, and she saw the baby book inside. Her baby's book. *The Story of Baby.*

The one that never got told.

Her fingers trembled as she ran her hand along the familiar spine. The edges of the sonogram photos, slick white paper, slipped out the top. She pulled the strip out, frame by frame, careful of the dirt on her hands.

Her eyes blurred as she stared at the familiar shape. Little one. Captured for a moment, then gone.

Why? Why all this way? Why now?

His fingers enclosed hers. "I want to fill in the empty spaces." He looked scared, unsure of her reaction. But he didn't let go. "With you. Where we can. I want to talk about the baby."

"Her name," Amanda whispered. "I call her Grace." Would he think she was crazy? Naming a baby she'd never seen, never met?

"Grace," he echoed. "Beautiful." He cupped her cheek, catching her tears on his thumb. "She would have been beautiful, you know. Like her mother."

"And tender," she replied. "Like her father."

He held her to him, and she pressed her face into the hollow of his neck. A favorite spot. She thought she could stay there the rest of her life.

A bird called high and clear. Rose petals danced as the wind shifted, the wet earth smelled like spring. New beginnings, delivered on the wind.

He turned his face, scratching her with his scruff.

She embraced the roughness. Real.

Bringing firm lips to hers, he gathered her closer as tears dried on her cheeks. Souls and hearts connected through the hunger of their mouths. Gentle, yet insistent.

A verse, wood and ancient, older than the broken building behind them, took a breath and moved in her heart. Echoes from their wedding gathered tendrils of her soul, weaving strength and truth within her.

*And a man shall leave his father and his mother . . .*

This man is mine.

*And take a wife . . .*

I am his.

He tilted her head farther, kissing deeper, the sun shining and her eyes closed, red-hot through the lids, the moment blossomed in her soul.

The past, fault and faltering, slipped away. Sharp lines of regret blurred to memory. Forgiven.

*The two shall become one.*

# epilogue

**M**oonlight filtered through the filmy sheers as Mark played with her red curls, lost in the blue eyes twinkling up at him.

*I am looped in the loops of her hair.*

"I have to go now," he whispered.

Her brow furrowed and tears clouded the brightness.

Oh no. The tears undid him every time. *"Shhh."* He ran a fingertip over the shell of her ear. "Don't cry. It'll only be a while, up at the church. I promise I'll be back soon."

He pulled the blanket up and kissed her soft cheek.

The door cracked open and light streamed in. "Is she still awake?"

Amanda tiptoed over to the crib and peered down, her long locks falling over the side. "Rosie, you naughty girl."

The baby grinned at the game, grabbing at her mama.

"No, no." Amanda gently loosened the chubby grip. "Gramma Mar-Mar's coming to watch you. Mommy and Daddy have a date." She twisted the mobile and a tinkling tune filled the nursery.

Rosie settled, intent on the dancing stars and moons.

"Night, sweet girl." Mark couldn't resist one last peek. "Daddy loves you."

His gaze followed Amanda as they stepped into the hall. "You look fantastic." He spanned her waist, catching her. "You *are* fantastic."

"Why, thank you." Slipping from his grasp, she tapped ruby slippers together and led the way to the kitchen. She pushed a low stool his way. "Sit here, where I can reach you."

She slipped the cone hat on his head and rubbed silver paint on his nose. "You look great too."

"No." He sat still under her ministrations. "I look ridiculous."

"Maybe a little." Her dimple flashed at him.

Speaking without moving his lips, he said, "A letter came for you today. On the table."

She turned and wiped the paint from her hands. As she picked up the envelope, a strange look crossed her face.

"Funny," he said. "It looks like your handwriting."

"It is."

"You wrote a letter to yourself?"

She nodded and set it down unopened. "A long time ago."

"Why?"

"Just to remind me, there's no place like home." Flaring her gingham Dorothy skirt, she curtsied.

"Glad to hear it." He sat, a blessed man to be gifted with such a woman as his wife. Blessed with not one miracle, but two. Baby Rosie.

*Impossible,* the doctor had said.

Mark liked to grin over that part and dream of more possibilities.

"Wait, you've forgotten something." She pulled a scarlet piece of felt, cut in the shape of a heart, from her pocket. Leaning close, she pinned it to his chest, working through the aluminum-foil vest. "There you go, my Tin Man."

He drew her in his arms. "You ready for this?"

"The infamous Lakeview Fall Festival?" She laughed. "I wouldn't miss it."

He kissed her, leaving behind a trace of silver. She dazzled him, with or without the paint. And he planned to tell her so, and little Rosie too, every day for the rest of their lives. They were his miracle, his highest calling. He would not overlook them again.

He'd been given a second chance, and he vowed to make the most of every moment. With his family by his side.

A knock sounded at the front door, announcing the arrival of Gramma Mar-Mar.

Mark grabbed Amanda's hand. "Then let's go."

# acknowledgments

I give my deepest thanks to my friends and family who labored alongside me in the creation of this book. I could not have done it without you.

I am grateful to the ministers in my life, past and present, for their leadership, honesty and humanity. My thanks to Clarice Cassada for teaching me about grace, Jennifer Auvermann who first encouraged me to put words on a page and dream big, and Leann Gabel who said, Why don't you just shut up and write it?

My Thursday Night Divas—Jodi Thomas, Marcy McKay, Dee Burks, April Redmon, Jenny Archer, Rob Brammer, and DeWanna Pace—taught me the craft and gave me my start. Many generous authors, including Marsha Moyer, Lisa Wingate, Kimberly Willis Holt, David Marion Wilkinson, Kim Campbell, Sharon Baldacci and Laurie Moore, took time from their busy schedules to read my work and guide me along the path. Thank you all.

Thanks to my friends at the Amarillo Police Department, the saints at AUMC, my Wednesday morning "peeps," David Blackstock and his magic foil, photographer extraordinaire Kern Coleman and the following fantastic writers' organizations: Texas Writers' League, Panhandle Professional Writers, North Texas Romance Writers, and the DFW Writers' Workshop.

Many thanks also to the talented Candy Havens for reading countless drafts, and for emoting with me each step of the way.

I owe much gratitude to my agent, the incomparable Marcy Posner, for championing this book and finding us the right home. Every writer should be so blessed to have an editor like Steve Wilburn. Thanks also to the amazing team at Warner.

And for my family, words fail. I owe you so much more than thanks. Mom, the world's greatest cheerleader and patron of the arts. Dad, who said he always knew I could do it. My precious sisters (all four of you), and the rest of our family who asked—how's the book coming?—with genuine care and enthusiasm.

To the rest of the Coleman Four, you are my very heart. My sweetest Kern, thank you for believing when I didn't, and for making me laugh in spite of myself. You'll always be the best part of me. I love you.

For Dan and Megan, the most wonderful children on earth. Your patience and excitement, and your tender prayers, carried me along on this journey. See, Mommy really did write a book!

# about the author

BRITTA COLEMAN'S career in fiction began with a simple question, prompted by two toddlers wriggling their fingers under the door as she attempted a private bath. What if, she asked herself amidst the bubbles, I ran away from my life and did something else? The momentary fantasy evolved into her first novel, *Potter Springs*.

Britta's passion for books and writing started at a young age, with fairy tales, diaries, and midnight reading sessions via flashlight. While her school years revealed no particular skills in sports or science fair projects (who knew salt would kill a houseplant?), Britta showed an aptitude for words and storytelling.

At Texas A&M University, Britta majored in English and was awarded an undergraduate fellowship. Many library fines later, she presented her senior thesis, graduated, and landed a job as a communications consultant in Houston.

After marrying her own fairy tale prince, Britta produced two children and, by virtue of motherhood, was forced to awake at unholy hours and acquire an addiction to coffee. She began chronicling her family adventures with a newspaper column called "Practically Parenting," which she still writes.

While pursuing her writing dreams, Britta met *USA Today* and *New York Times* bestselling author Jodi Thomas. In true fairy godmother style, Jodi took the aspiring author under her wing and into her critique group, and the rest, as they say, is history.

Britta enjoys speaking to groups about the craft of writing and daring to live out one's dreams without running away from home. An almost native Texan (she arrived at age six), she lives in Fort Worth with her husband, two children, and a fussy Chihuahua named Rosie.

Visit Britta's Web site: www.brittacoleman.com